Books by Ann McMan

Hoosier Daddy
Backcast
Festival Nurse
Beowulf for Cretins
The Big Tow
Dead Letters from Paradise
The Black Bird of Chernobyl
Switch

The Jericho Series
Jericho
Aftermath
Goldenrod
Covenant

The Evan Reed Series
Dust
Galileo

Short Story Collections
Sidecar
Three Plus One

Anthologies
Soul Food

SWITCH

ANN MCMAN

2025

Print ISBN: 978-1-61294-321-3

Bywater Books First Edition: July 2025

Printed in the United States of America on acid-free paper.

Cover design by TreeHouse Studio

Bywater Books
PO Box 3671
Ann Arbor MI 48106-3671

www.bywaterbooks.com

*For JoAnn and Adam—the real life conductors
who graciously answered (and tolerated) all my ridiculous
questions during numerous research jaunts,
riding the rails with them on Amtrak's Vermonter.*

*And for Sandy, who was instrumental
in bringing this project to fruition.*

There isn't a train I would not take,
no matter where it's going.

–Edna St. Vincent Millay

CHAPTER ONE

Catfishing for Amateurs

Believe me when I say that the last thing I wanted to deal with after grinding my way through two back-to-back twelve hour shifts on a shopworn train hacking its way through the remnants of a good old fashioned Nor'easter—followed by a sleepless eight hour overnight spent tossing on the sagging mattress of a nondescript Hampton Inn in downtown Rensselaer—was finally returning home, only to be smacked in the face by the noxious odor of something profoundly . . . *dead?*

Rotted? Fetid?

Putrid?

That was it!

It smelled *putrid*. Freshly putrid, too—if that were even possible.

The smell was so overwhelming it caused me to stagger backward as soon as the elevator doors opened.

"What fresh hell is this?" I clapped a hand over my mouth and immediately apologized for stomping on the foot of the woman standing behind me, who'd also been waiting on the building's only working elevator. "Sorry," I blurted, waving a hand toward the elevator. "But that's . . ."

"Lutefisk?" she offered.

"What?" I asked.

"I think it's lutefisk." She shrugged. "'Tis the season for it."

"'Tis the season for what?"

"Lutefisk. If memory serves, it's a Norwegian dish traditionally served at Christmastime."

Who was *this person? Some walking compendium of epicurean delights?*

"And you know this . . . because?" I asked.

"It's sort of my job," she explained. "I write restaurant reviews. Well. That's not entirely accurate. I mostly edit them."

Okay . . . so that was kind of cool.

"You do?" I asked. The woman nodded. "Who for?"

"*Philadelphia Magazine.*"

"Interesting." The elevator doors started to close. I lunged forward and blocked them with my body. *Dear god . . . the stench was even worse inside.* "I honestly don't know if I can ride on this thing."

"What's your floor?"

"Twenty-six."

The woman eyed my rumpled uniform and small roller bag. It was 9:30 p.m. on a Friday night, so it didn't take a MENSA baby to figure out that I was returning from a trip.

"Your choice," she said. "A mildly unpleasant three-minute elevator ride, or fifty-two flights of stairs."

"You call this odor *mildly* unpleasant?"

"It's an acquired taste, I'll grant you." The curious woman boarded the elevator. She was carrying a leather backpack and an armload of manila folders. "But to hordes of Scandinavians, it's like manna from heaven."

Against my better judgment, I decided to ride with her. The woman punched in the numbers for our floors—*floor*—since she was on twenty-six, too—and we were on our way.

I was used to checking people out when they weren't watching, so I stole a look at her. I'd seen her a few times before—in the lobby, in the mailroom, in the basement laundry, hauling sheets out of one of the massive Speed Queen dryers. She was nice looking in one of those expeditious, understated, don't-blow-smoke-up-my-ass ways. Probably in her mid-forties. Short, dark hair and horn-rimmed glasses—nerdy enough to be considered stylish. It wasn't easy to tell which look she'd been going for.

"So, this . . . lute-thing," I began.

"Lutefisk."

"Right. What exactly *is* it?"

She looked amused. "It's dried fish. Usually, cod or some other whitefish. It's brined in lye then soaked in fresh water for days to remove the acid of the brine. It's then steamed for eating and is traditionally served with boiled potatoes and a cream sauce. It's also very popular in Minnesota."

How perfectly disgusting. "Yet another reason not to binge-watch *Fargo*."

She smiled. It brightened up what I guessed was a normally impassive expression.

"Where the hell would anyone get that around here," I mused, "at this time of night?"

"Oh, you'd be surprised. There are at least a dozen good Norwegian restaurants in Philadelphia—Tria Café West is only about a ten-minute walk from here."

The elevator slowed to a stop on the sixth floor, and two people carrying beat-up ladders and tool bags got on. I recognized them immediately as members of the building maintenance crew. It wasn't uncommon for me to have to maneuver my bag around their ladders as they replaced lightbulbs in fixtures along the hallways or swapped out smoke alarm batteries. One time, they'd even shown up at my place at o'dark-thirty when the bathtub drain backed up and began belching out . . . something

3

murky and mysterious. It only took them about thirty minutes to dispatch the clog. The male and female duo worked so seamlessly as a team, it led me to wonder if they really were two halves of the same person.

"Oh, Jeez Louise," one of them, a youngish man wearing a blaze-orange, fleece hoodie, fanned a hand in front of his face. "Mrs. Dahlby must be preggers again."

"No way!" His female colleague punched the button for the rooftop. "Didn't she just drop one in August?"

"No. That was her cousin up in 2808—Ludmilla."

"*Whatever.* I wish they'd get cravings for normal shit—like pizza rolls."

"Is that what you two think this is?" I spoke up. "Some kind of weird pregnancy craving?"

"Oh, hell to the yes. Last time it was—" she looked at her companion. "What *was* that shit?"

"Beats the hell outta me. Some kind of reindeer casserole."

"Finnbiff."

All three of us looked at the woman with the armload of folders.

"Reindeer stew," she explained. "It's a medley of meat, bacon, herbs, and brown cheese—surprisingly unctuous."

"No shit?" Orange hoodie asked. "They eat Blitzkrieg?"

"That's *Blitzen,* doofus." His companion looked at the magazine editor apologetically. "He doesn't get out much."

"Well, at least one of us does." Orange hoodie elbowed his partner and waved a hand at my outfit. "Pilot?" He asked me.

I shook my head.

"Ferry boat captain?"

"No."

"Limo driver?"

"Nope."

"Cab—"

The woman with him cut him off. "Jeez, Aldo . . . quit with

the third degree, already." She pointed at my cap. "See the damn logo?"

"Shut up, Luz." Aldo squinted at me. "USRail?"

"Bingo." I smiled at him. "Please take care exiting the train. Be mindful of the gap between the steps and the platform."

"No shit." Aldo sounded impressed. "You drive a damn train?"

"No, idiot." The tough-looking woman named Luz elbowed him. "She's a *conductor*." She looked at me. "Right?"

"Right."

"That's pretty badass." Luz sounded genuinely impressed. "You on the SEPTA?"

"Sadly, no. I'm on ... a lot of trains. Always jumping around."

"Like a temp?"

"No. Like an assistant conductor who doesn't yet have the seniority to hold a line."

"So, you're on the extra board?" It was the woman with the folders.

I was surprised by her use of railroad jargon. "I am. How'd you know about that?"

"It's a long story."

The elevator dinged. It was our floor. We both exited and waved goodbye to the maintenance duo.

Sadly, the smell was no better in the hallway. I wondered if Mrs. Dahlby and her cravings lived on twenty-six, too.

"I'm Izzy, by the way," I said. "Thanks for the tutorial on Scandinavian cuisine."

"My pleasure. I'm Harper. I suppose I'll see you around the place."

"Probably." We stood there another few seconds. "Well, I'm this way." She turned and headed down the hallway in the direction opposite from my place. "Later," she said, before turning a corner.

"Skoal." I replied. I didn't see her reaction, but I heard her laugh.

I watched her disappear before yawning and dragging my beat-up bag along the faded carpet toward the one-bedroom condo my parents had owned for decades. *At least it overlooked the park.*

A hot shower and sleep couldn't come soon enough.

The nagging sound of my cell phone blaring jolted me awake at 8:15 a.m. I would've turned the damn thing off and left it in the kitchen overnight, but I was still on call for the rest of the weekend, and I fully expected to get tagged for at least one more trip before getting three days off. Finally.

Life on the extra board sucked out loud. You were fodder to take the place of any asshole who decided not to show up at the last minute. The lower your seniority number, the likelier you were to get tagged to take up their slack. I'd been with USRail for twelve years, but only five of them on the trains. Prior to that, I'd worked in the yard, then in the Baltimore office. Each of those postings felt like signposts pointing toward a slow and painful death. Walking the narrow corridors of those tin rattletraps was monotonous, but I rationalized that at least I was always going someplace.

I fumbled for the phone. "Hello?"

"*Bonjour, Izzy! Tu me rejoins pour le petit-déjeuner?*"

It was Sofie Martin—my best friend—inviting me to breakfast. We'd been college roommates at McGill, but Sofie now worked in Philadelphia as an actuary at Marsh McLennan.

I considered her chosen profession to be the eighth wonder of the world. It was tantamount to appointing a Kardashian to serve as U.N. ambassador.

"Sofie? *Tu sais quelle heure il est?*"

"*Oui.* Late enough for you to roll your ass out of bed and come meet me at Morning Glory for pancakes."

"It's Friday. Why aren't you working?"

"*C'est samedi.*"

It was Saturday? Already?

"It is?" I asked.

"*Oui. Je suis arrivée il y a une heure pour obtenir cette table.* So, move your ass—I can't hold the spot forever."

I wanted nothing more than to roll over and go back to sleep. But I knew it was useless to argue with her. She'd just browbeat me into submission. Sofie always got her way. *Always.* That was the secret behind our success as roommates: I'd dare to express a divergent opinion, then Sofie would do whateverinthehell she wanted. Which was how we had ended up with a life-size ode to Nickelback painted on our dorm room wall, along with a sagging shelf containing fifty-seven different sizes of piña colada-scented candles—which accounted for why our room always smelled like a car wash.

"*D'accord, d'accord.* I can be there in," I looked at my watch, "twenty minutes." I sat up and rubbed my eyes.

"Make it fifteen," she barked. "I'll order for you." She hung up.

Pancakes? I asked myself, as I trudged toward the bathroom. *Why the hell not? I could eat . . .*

Exactly nineteen minutes later, I entered Sam's Morning Glory—after elbowing my way through a line of about thirty-five cranky-looking people, all standing in puddles of melting slush. It had snowed overnight, and the sidewalks were passable, but the wet snow was no match for the downright balmy temperature inside the popular breakfast destination. I saw Sofie seated at a cozy two-top near the counter. Two mugs of steaming coffee sat on the table in front of her. She'd been reading but looked up as I approached.

"*She lives!*"

"Very funny." I pulled out the other chair and sat down across from her.

Sofie was giving me a good once-over. "You look like

shit." She batted her eyes at me. "Dare I hope that means you had a long night?"

I added a packet of Splenda to my coffee and stirred it until the sweet foam dissipated. "No. I had two twelve-hour days separated by a short sleepless night."

Sofie shook her red head. "I don't know why you're still doing this gig. That job is beneath you."

"*Beneath* me? That opinion is too bourgeois, even for you."

"Your mother agrees with me."

"My mother also agrees with the wackos who believe climate change is caused by the underwater eruption of the Hunga Tonga volcano."

Sofie stared at me with a blank expression. "Whatever."

"Besides," I continued. "You know I'm only doing this job until I finish my degree."

"Izzy? I say this with love: that ship has sailed."

"What do you mean? I haven't been working on it *that* long."

"You're forty-two. Define 'long.'" Sofie laid her book down on the tabletop. I couldn't help but notice its lurid cover. It showed an impressive tangle of naked arms and legs, artfully splayed across a sea of rumpled sheets. I read the title: *Many Hands: An Anthology of Polyamorous Erotica.*

"Where the hell do you find books like that?"

"Like what?" Sofie asked in her most affected imitation of innocence. Except for the flame red hair that looked like it had been cut by a Vidal Sassoon laureate with a pair of Swiss-made hedge clippers, she could've been a dead ringer for Frances Ethel Gumm—*before* she became Judy Garland.

"*That.*" I pointed at it. "It looks like a how-to manual for risk averse floozies."

"Floozies?" Sofie feigned offense. "*Femme facile? Moi?*"

"You know what I meant."

Sofie snapped up the book and shoved it into her massive handbag. "Instead of criticizing me, you should be thanking me for taking up some of your slack."

"My slack?"

"*Oui. Ta vie amoureuse est pathétique.*"

"My love life is *not* pathetic." My response was delivered with a tad more energy than I intended—and, of course, I said it just as our server arrived bearing two heaping plates of pancakes, bacon, and home fries. He appeared amused as he deposited our breakfasts. "Sorry," I apologized to him. "TMI."

"Honey," he said, "there ain't nothin' I haven't heard before. Hell. This place on a Saturday morning is like a fresh installment of *Days of Our Sorry-Ass Lives.*"

Sofie laughed merrily before pouring about a pint of maple syrup on her stack of pancakes.

"Thanks," I said. "That makes me feel so much better."

"Girl—*normal* beats the hell outta the alternative." He waved a hand dismissively before sailing off. He had a point. And his flag-striped, wide-legged pants showed he lived his values.

I looked at Sofie. "I'm not sure I agree with his assessment of the human condition."

"Why?"

"There cannot be only *two* modes of being: misery or benign normalcy. I refuse to accept that."

Sofie was busy carving her stack of pancakes into perfect, rhombus-shaped bites. She'd always been that way. Her food, like her relationships, had to be equilateral—right-sized to accommodate her unique world view.

"In your case," Sofie explained over the *tempo giusto* clacking of her knife against the plate, "it's not even a question. There is only *one* mode of being in your life."

I wasn't sure I wanted her to elaborate. I looked around the noisy restaurant. It was packed to the gills with people hunched over small tables with their eggs and mugs of coffee or huddling in an untidy mass just inside the street door—glaring at diners to will them to hurry the fuck up and surrender their spots.

Sofie was still studying me with a textbook look of inquisition.

"Okay," I said. "Do I want to hear what that is?"

"*Oui. Pathétique.*"

"Come on. That's not fair."

"Izzy? You haven't been laid since you broke up with Vampyra."

"That's not true and you know it."

"You're right," Sofie agreed. "You haven't been laid since two years *before* you broke up with Vampyra."

"*Vas te faire foutre.*"

"You can tell me to fuck off all you want, but that doesn't make me wrong—does it?"

I didn't reply. It was true. My relationship with Tonya *had* gone on too long. But in self-defense, we'd had a *cat*—and I didn't want to break up with *it*.

Of course, when Tonya finally left me, she took the damn cat, anyway. So . . .

I met Sofie's raised eyebrow. "*Non.* You're not wrong."

"So," she speared a perfect square of pancake, "there's only one way to remedy your desperate situation."

"And that is?"

She reached into the recesses of her monster bag and withdrew her phone. "We're getting you a SheDate account and then we're going shopping."

I was confused. "What the hell is 'SheDate?'"

"It's a dating app for lesbo nerds."

"No fucking way."

"Don't be so pious. *Philadelphia Magazine* just did an in-depth profile on it. That alone should make it dull enough for you." Sofie was already busily engaged with her phone. "It's widely accepted that these apps are good for more than just getting laid, so stow the wide-eyed, Catholic schoolgirl bullshit."

"Really? So, I can use it to find good investment tips?"

"*Non.* But you *can* use it to find the best bars in all the offbeat towns where you seem to spend an inordinate amount of time. So, if, while you're investigating some remote watering hole, you happen to meet someone you can fuck, marry, or just kill three hours with—it's a win-win proposition. *N'est-ce pas?*"

I dejectedly took a bite of my pancakes. They were fluffy and delicious—sprinkled with just the right amount of icing sugar and cinnamon. I thought about adding some maple syrup, but Sofie had already dispatched all but a trace element of it from the bottle on our table, and I didn't want to have a reprise of my earlier conversation with our server.

"Okay. What do you want to use as an email address?" she asked. "It's wise not to use your normal one. You want to keep these communications separate from other forms of commerce."

Commerce?

"I don't suppose it matters to you that I really don't want to do this at all . . . does it?"

"Not much. No." Her fingers were flying across the tiny screen. "How about we use Anonyme440+@gmail.com?"

It took me a minute to decipher the implied insult. "Anonymous for forty *plus? Seriously?* I thought the goal was to make me *not* sound pathetic."

"Oh, so now you're on board with the plan?"

"*Fine.* That email address works. What's next?"

"We need a profile photo."

"I have the one I used when I applied for the USRail job. It's pretty good."

"Allow me to clarify. We need a photo that *doesn't* make you look like a bed-wetting serial killer."

"Thanks a lot." I didn't attempt to hide my wounded feelings. "I thought that was a good picture of me . . ."

"Sure. If your goal is to date an Uber driver." Sofie was rapidly scrolling through her own photo archive. "*Et voilà.* This one is ideal." Sofie handed me her phone. The photo of me had been taken about a hundred years ago at a birthday party in Montréal for Sofie's cousin, Giselle. I was sitting beside the Martins' Olympic-sized pool wearing a sports bikini and mirrored aviators.

"Oh, come on." I handed the phone back to her. "We can't use this one."

"Why not? It's exactly the correct tone. Just the right balance of vacuous and come hither."

"It's dishonest as fuck. I look like a fifteen-year-old refugee from Epstein's island."

"I know, right? Isn't it perfect?"

"It's clear I have no aptitude for this stuff."

"*Oui.* Now sit back and answer a few questions so I can finish filling this out. Then you'll be ready to begin swiping your way to happiness . . . or at least, satiation."

When I walked back into the lobby of Hopkinson House, Aldo and the somewhat butch woman named Luz were hunched over the front desk in hushed and earnest conversation with Dewey, our doorman. Dewey saw me enter and immediately waved me over. He hadn't been on duty when I got back the night before, so he was probably surprised to see me in the daylight. Usually, my trips dumped me off back at the 30th Street Station well after dark.

That was another of the non-perks of being a hostage to the damn "extra board"—USRail's quaint euphemism for "bottom feeders who don't have enough seniority to hold a line, so they get the sloppy seconds." Until I gained enough seniority to actually get off the board, I'd continue to get saddled with all the shit runs on the worst routes. My ultimate goal—at least for as long as my tenure with USRail continued—was to land and hold a spot working the Green Mountain Zephyr, which provided daily service between Philadelphia and St. Albans, Vermont. The occasional overnights in St. Albans would put me within spitting distance of my parents' place in Frelighsburg, Québec. They'd moved there after my mother retired from her management position with the Canadian National Railway. She'd been with the CN for decades and had been instrumental in the restoration of passenger services to the railway after its nationalization in 1995. The small village of Frelighsburg had been my father's hometown, and they'd always vacationed there in the summers.

When I reached the desk, Aldo was complaining about recent sightings of something—or someone—called "Cujo" near the trash room on the 18th floor.

"I'm telling you," Aldo was complaining, "the descriptions of this thing keep getting weirder. Either some asshole is adding PCP to the water supply and half the residents are tripping out—or we got some kind of fucked-up science experiment running loose in the HVAC ducts. Ain't no way this thing is real, is all I'm saying."

"Yeah," Luz chimed in. "That fat *puta* on fourteen swears she saw it dragging a goddamn golf shoe down the hallway. She said she screamed at it, and it hauled ass around the corner. By the time she followed it, it had disappeared without a trace—and no damn shoe left behind, either. This is getting seriously fucked up."

"What I've been wondering is what the hell is it gonna do with *one* golf shoe? I'm thinking maybe we set a trap with another shoe and try to lure it out."

"Good thinking, Einstein." Luz rolled her eyes at Aldo. "How're we supposed to know which shoe it already has?"

Dewey had heard enough. He held up a hand to cut the discussion short. "Stop," he said in a placating tone. "We ain't setting any traps with men's footwear. You hear me? I already notified the city about some kinda oversized varmint terrorizing the good people in this building. They're gonna send out a crew to look for rodents, okay?"

Aldo and Luz exchanged glances.

"Cujo ain't no rodent," Aldo offered.

"No, it ain't." Luz agreed.

"Rodents leave *droppings*," Aldo continued. "Cujo don't shit *no* place that we been able to find."

"And," Luz continued, "it left claw marks across the elevator doors on 19. *Deep* ones—about three feet off the ground. Ain't no 'rodents' tall enough to do that."

"Now, I don't know about that part," Aldo. said. It could be if it's one of them south Jersey types like the ones in my cousin Luca's neighborhood in Camden. Them fuckers could have their own zip codes."

"They *ain't* rodents, Aldo. What the fuck is a rat gonna do with a damn golf shoe?"

I was having a hard time not laughing. It was clear that Dewey had reached the point of diminishing returns in this conversation.

"Okay. Enough about this for today," he said with finality. "The city is gonna come and do its damn inspection—and we'll go from there. Okay? After that, we can decide on next steps. But until then, I don't need you two spreading rumors or freaking people the fuck out. So, keep this shit under your hats until we have more information. There's another homeowner's meeting on Tuesday night, and the board wants to keep this crap on the DL until we have a POA. Is that clear?"

Aldo just gaped at Dewey, plainly confused about the acronyms.

"The *down low*," Luz explained. "Until we have a *plan of attack*." She looked at Dewey for confirmation. "Ain't that right?"

Dewey nodded. "You two need to get on with the rest of your work and don't be fussing about this damn mysterious intruder any more today. If folks want to talk about it, tell them to call me. Now," he gestured toward me, "I need to tend to the needs of this resident."

Both of the workers seemed to notice me for the first time.

"Hey, Ms. Lebrun," Luz said.

"That elevator don't stink no more," Aldo added. "We fogged it good with Febreze."

"Heavy duty lemon fresh," Luz added.

"Thanks, you two." I smiled at them. "I noticed it smelled better this morning when I came down to head out for breakfast."

Dewey shooed them along. We watched them walk toward the elevators. Dewey shook his head. "Those two idiots are gonna put my ass in an early grave."

"They mean well," I offered.

"So did my crazy Aunt Vern, when she set fire to the nursing home thinking it would be a good way to get piss stains out of the Bingo room carpet. That didn't make her a candidate for damn sainthood."

"True."

"So, how'd you luck out and get a Saturday off?"

"Don't jinx me. I'm on call until four." I looked at my watch. "Only five and a half hours to go."

"I'm due for a break. Come on back and visit. I haven't seen you in a couple of weeks."

"Why the hell not? The only thing waiting for me upstairs is an unfinished chapter detailing engineering perspectives on ocean-based carbon dioxide removal."

"Yeah. That shit makes my ass drag." Dewey retrieved his canvas messenger bag from a drawer. "Come on outside with me."

I followed him toward one of the building's several outdoor smoking areas.

"You said you were going to quit before Christmas," I reminded him.

"So?" Dewey pulled a Zippo lighter and a pack of Camels from his bag and fired up a smoke. "I still got six weeks. Quit your yammering."

"Hey, I'm on *your* side. You said you wanted to watch those grandbabies grow up."

Dewey had six daughters—all of whom were scattered across the sexual identity spectrum like a broken strand of pearls. Two were straight. One was what Dewey described as a no-fucks-to-give, man-hating, non-flesh-eating, Zionist lesbian (she had converted to Judaism on her fourteenth birthday). One was nonbinary. One was bisexual. And another identified as something nebulous that Dewey called "aromatic"—until he realized his daughter wasn't talking about essential oils or scented soaps. She meant *a*-romantic . . . meaning *not* into romance or loving relationships.

"I think she gets that mess from her mama's side of the family," he explained. "Those women all *like* living in Southwest Philly and they mostly grow up to be Teamsters."

"I had breakfast with Sofie," I shared. "She set me up with a SheDate account. She thinks I'm desperate enough to start using a dating app." Dewey knew me better than almost anybody in Philadelphia. I was too chicken to look directly at him when I said it, but I snuck a covert peek to see his reaction. He hadn't been looking at me at all. He'd been staring at something plainly out of place on the side of the building. I could tell by his expression that Luz and Aldo were going to be hearing from him when he went back inside. "What do you think about the idea?" I asked. I really wanted to know what he thought. I was ninety percent sure he'd agree with me that Sofie's idea was a lame-ass waste of time.

He expelled a lungful of smoke. "I think it's about goddamn time."

That got my attention. "You do?"

He nodded. "It hurts my tired heart to see you dragging in here, night after night, pulling that damn suitcase behind you like a ship's anchor. You need somebody to come home

16

to. We all do."

"I don't think that's the point of dating apps." I was pretty sure he noticed that I didn't argue with his assessment of my life.

Dewey chuckled. "No. The point would be to get your knob waxed—and there ain't nothing wrong with that, either. But if you luck out and meet somebody nice in the process, why not give it a shot? It's better than waiting around for Miss Right to tie her damn ass to the train tracks so you can swoop in and set her free before she gets flattened."

"I guess that's true."

"Damn straight. So, when you gonna start fishing?"

I shrugged. "I dunno. Maybe tonight, if I don't get called up for a trip."

"I been thinking about something else that might help you out." He reached into his bag and withdrew a dog-eared paperback book.

"What's that?"

He handed the book to me. "I reckon you could call it an instruction manual."

I looked it over. The cover showed an illustration of two overly stylized women eyeing each other warily across an expanse of medical paraphernalia. If El Greco had ever branched out into cartooning, these might have been two of his subjects. Their figures were ridiculously elongated. One of them wore a white doctor's coat and had a stethoscope looped around her crane-like neck. The other looked more like some kind of uptight administrator or angry claims adjuster. *A Prognosis for Love* was labeled as Book Four in the "Mass General Sapphic Romance Series." It didn't creep me out that Dewey was reading a lesbian novel—and one that was probably full of sex, as many of the romance variety were. He admitted that he'd started doing this as a way to relate to his daughters and gain a better understanding of their relationships with other women. Now that his girls were mostly grown, he was

17

so used to reading the books that he'd developed an affinity for the genre stories and was always quick to snap up new titles by his favorite authors.

"My book club is meeting at seven tonight in the solarium," he explained. "If you don't get called up, I think you should come on with me."

"Is this the one you just read?" I asked.

"Uh huh. It wasn't too bad, either—if you overlook the lame-ass dialogue. They should've called this one Book Four in the Mass *Casualty* series."

I handed the book back to him. "I can't go with you. I haven't read this."

Dewey laughed. "Honey, half the women in this book club don't read the damn books. They just flip through them to find the sex scenes."

"Seriously?"

He nodded. "It used to be a rule that the women in these stories started getting busy on about page eighty-six. Then it moved up to page fifty-three. For a while it stayed around page thirty-six. Now? Shit. They're usually all up in something sticky right after the title page."

I was incredulous. "And reading these books is supposed to help me out . . . how?"

"Girl, I learned a long time ago that if you want to understand what makes another person tick, the first thing you gotta do is care enough to learn their damn language. All that bio, hokeypokey mess you've always got your head buried in? That ain't gonna teach you how to talk to women." He handed me the copy of the book again. "Trust me. You wanna catch a fish? Learn to think like a fish. Figure out what those slimy fuckers want. Learn what kind of bait they like and what part of the river they like to hang out in. See what kind of shiny shit makes their fannies wag. And if that ain't enough to get your ass up to that solarium today," he bent closer, "they serve the best goddamn cheese cubes you'll ever eat."

Dewey knew me pretty well. I did love a good hunk of cheese.

"You're a hard man to say no to, Dewey Pepper."

"Hell." He ground out his cigarette and stuffed the butt into the pocket of his jacket. "How else do you think I ended up with six damn kids?"

CHAPTER TWO

Swipe Right

I must've checked my phone messages a dozen times. In my exhaustive and unhappy experience, there was no way the railroad would *not* call me in. Not on a Saturday six weeks out from Christmas. But I got no calls. And every time I gave in and obsessively checked—just to be on the safe side—my voicemail box was empty. No text messages. No emails. Nothing. So, I did the things normal people did at home on Saturday. I changed my bed sheets. I sorted dirty clothes for the laundry. I paid some bills. And I cleaned my oven . . . again.

It was round three with the remnants of the six-cheese lasagna I'd made for dinner two weeks ago. While it had been true that the recipe given to me by a passenger in Springfield only called for *four* cheeses, in my humble estimation, if four were good, six were better. In fact, six had plainly *not* been better since at least two of them chose to flee the confines of the cramped baking dish and migrate to greener pastures on the bottom of the oven.

I'd been lucky the cheese magma hadn't caught fire. My impulsive foray into culinary disaster had taken place after midnight, and I was confident the other residents of the building wouldn't have appreciated being evacuated in the middle of the night. As it was, I'd had to open every window and stand on a stepstool with a hair dryer to blow the acrid smoke away from the ceiling alarm. I fantasized about just disabling the damn thing by taking out its battery, but mine was an older model that was fastened into its base with some kind of makeshift hex head screw, and who the fuck had one of *those* drivers?

Aldo and Luz at work, again.

That lasagna had *been pretty damn good, though.*

I figured I'd thank the Springfield lady for the recipe if I ever got to see her again. That encounter had taken place the last time I'd crewed the Zephyr—the time my sister, Zoé, had driven down from Montréal and spent the night with me at the less-than-deluxe station hotel in St. Albans. She'd had a business meeting in Hartford and decided it would be fun to connect with me and take the Zephyr south instead of flying. The train had been packed that day, so I'd been lucky to score Zoé the last available seat in business class. In typical fashion, Zoé'd struck up a fast friendship with the woman in the seat beside her. Typically, the Zephyr had only one business class car, and it was always the last one on the train—right behind the café car. I stopped by to check in on Zoé every time I made a circuit through the cars to alert travelers about approaching stations. After my first two passes, I could tell the two women were becoming fast friends. By about my fourth pass, they'd left their seats and taken up residence at a table in the café car—and it was clear the Tito's was flowing. The two had become thick as thieves and Zoé had been regaling her travel companion with apocryphal stories about me—her baby sister.

"I guessed right away that you two were related," the woman gushed. "You look enough alike to be twins."

"*Mais non, pas du tout!*" Zoé drained her plastic cup. "I look like our beloved mama. *Isabelle ressemble à notre jardinier.*"

"English, Zoé," I insisted. "*Ne sois pas impolie.* And I do *not* look like the gardener. We've discussed this." I made eye contact with her companion. "I look like the milk man."

The older woman laughed merrily. "You two are a hoot. And you're both pretty enough to be in shampoo commercials."

That was a new one. Usually, people told us we looked like opposite ends of a live wire.

"That's very generous of you," I said. "But Zoé is much prettier than me."

"Well, Zoé *is* lovely with those green eyes and chestnut hair. But you could be her twin."

"Except for the awful uniform and that ridiculous hat," Zoé muttered under her breath.

I glowered at Zoé before facing her companion. "Did you get any of that?"

She nodded. "But I think your hat looks cute."

Zoé picked up her plastic cup and shook it at me so the ice cubes would rattle "Refill, please?"

"Do I look like your server?" I asked.

"*Oui*. You are *my* public servant, appointed to minister to my needs."

"In that case," I quipped, "let me go find a psychiatrist."

I'd heard them both laughing as I made my way toward the vestibule that led to the coach cars.

Yeah, I thought, as I scraped away at the charred mass spread across the bottom of my oven, *that was a good damn lasagna recipe, but this cheese is going to be here for eternity.*

I finally gave up on the oven. It was a lost cause.

Four o'clock came and went. Still no call up. It looked like I was home free, at least for the rest of the night. Tomorrow it was anyone's guess where I might end up.

I decided to take advantage of the gift of free time by getting caught up on my laundry. My parents had purchased the apartment I lived in more than thirty years ago when my father, an architectural engineer, had been hired by Amtrak to work with a local design firm to undertake a massive restoration and renovation of the iconic 30th Street Station. That project kept Papa in the city for nearly ten years, so he commuted to our home in Montréal on most weekends and holidays. Some of my fondest memories were during school breaks, when papa would take me back with him to Philadelphia. Most days, I would accompany him to work, and I would spend hours sitting with my schoolbooks beneath the ninety-foot coffered ceiling of the grand concourse. More often than not, I spent those hours completely distracted from my homework assignments because I was so mesmerized by the massive Angel of the Resurrection statue that, for me, held more mystery and magic than any of the likenesses of the saints that flanked the altar in The Church of Le Gesù de Montréal, where my family worshiped. Back at the apartment while Papa prepared our dinner, I would pepper him with questions about the lives of the brave men and women who had worked for the railroad and died during the Second World War. I'd spent so many hours staring at the statue, I began to memorize the names of the 1,307 soldiers—or at least the ones whose last names began with letters A through F. Those were the names inscribed on the side of the granite base that faced my marble bench.

Papa would only let me hang out near where he was working so he could keep an eye on me.

Even though my apartment was one of the older units in the building that still allowed residents to have their own washers and dryers, I wasn't lucky enough to own a set, so I loaded up my basket and headed downstairs to the shared laundry facility in the basement. On impulse, I grabbed the novel Dewey had given me. There were only two other residents down there when I arrived—although at least eight of the sixteen machines were being utilized. As usual, people had left their laundry baskets on the floor in front of their machines to mark their spots.

I would've expected the spot to be a lot busier on a Saturday afternoon, but to be fair, I hadn't spent very many Saturday afternoons at home, so I really had no idea what 'normal' actually was. One of the two people down there was a guy wearing ear pods. He was kicked back in a chair with his eyes closed, listening to an audiobook—which I was amazed I could hear so distinctly when I walked past him. It sounded like some kind of whodunnit, and it appeared to be reaching a crescendo of sorts. I hoped the drama would last long enough for his whites to finish their final rinse cycle. The other person was standing with her back to me, wrestling with a fitted sheet atop one of the folding tables. I staked out a spot near the back wall so I could sit discreetly with my book—I really didn't want to be discovered reading something so . . . glaringly romantic.

I got all three of my loads going and sat down to begin reading *Prognosis for Love*. Dewey hadn't been kidding. There was a scene on page nine depicting a nurse and an intern having stand-up sex in a storage closet. Even though the storytelling was every bit as predictable as Dewey had said it would be, I was impressed by the acrobatics the two lovebirds managed while navigating mops, buckets, and gallon-sized containers of pine-scented phenolic disinfectant. The description of their encounter was so graphic, I was tempted to turn the book sideways to get a better look.

"I thought I recognized you."

It was Harper—the foodie from the elevator. I realized she'd been the one fighting with the fitted sheet. She must've given up on it. It was now balled into a big messy wad beneath her arm.

"Hi," I said belatedly. There was no way I could hide the fucking book without being obvious, so I lowered it—open—to my lap as nonchalantly as possible. I figured I could at least conceal the suggestive cover. "I didn't notice you when I came in."

"That's okay. I usually fly beneath the radar, so I'm used to it."

"Have you been down here long?" *Oh, great one, Izzy . . .*

24

you sound like a space alien attending your first sock hop . . . no pun intended.

Harper just rolled with it. "Sadly, yes. These are the rich and full details of my life. Didn't Eliot say we measure our lives with coffee spoons? I measure mine with dryer sheets."

"At least you'll always smell good," I offered. "Not like that flute-fisk thing in the elevator last night."

"*Lute*fisk." She sounded amused. "And our trusty maintenance workers seemed to have eradicated all traces of it by this morning."

"You noticed that too?"

"Oh, yeah. Kind of hard not to. The doors opened and I thought I'd made a wrong turn and ended up inside a supply closet."

Her analogy was so on target I got flustered and dropped the damn book. I scrambled to grab it, but she picked it up before I could reach it and laughed when she read the title.

"Where on earth did you get this?"

"You wouldn't believe me if I told you."

"Wanna bet?" she dared. "Dewey?"

I was surprised. "What made you guess it was him?"

"Oh, I had a hunch." She smiled. "We're in the same book club."

"You mean you read this?"

"Most of it."

For a second, I felt irrationally surprised. Although I didn't really know her, I wouldn't have pegged the magazine editor as someone who'd just thumb through a book looking for the sex scenes. Much less a sapphic book. Friends of Dorothy sure were getting harder and harder to pick out of crowds these days.

"Just prurient interest in an eclectic topic?" I queried.

"Oh, no. I lay claim to the literature honestly. This one just wasn't my cup of tea."

"Too much disinfectant?"

"In fact, I think it would've benefitted from a bit more."

"Not your cup of tea?"

"Not so much. I go to the book clubs with Dewey more because I enjoy his company than I enjoy reading the books."

"I haven't read many, either. Since I appear to have a night off, Dewey suggested I might give it a try."

"Think you will?" She seemed genuinely curious.

"I'm not sure," I demurred. "I haven't read the book, and I don't want to seem like a lurker."

"Did Dewey tell you about the cheese?"

Mention of the tasty comestible perked me up. "You mean he wasn't lying?"

Harper shook her dark head. "Oh, no. It's good, all right—like little hunks of heaven on toothpicks. I have no idea where they get it."

"The Crack Cheeses R Us store at amazon.com?"

"Or Costco—right next to the flats of motor oil and kitty litter."

I nodded. "All household staples, in my opinion."

Her smile returned. "You should come. Dewey and I tend to sit in the back row and gossip about other tenants of the building."

"Isn't that . . . inappropriate?"

She nodded energetically. "Of course, it is. But it beats staying in with a stack of bad prose to edit and nothing better to watch on TV than reruns of *CSI: Las Vegas*."

"I suppose that's true."

"And again, there's that cheese . . ."

A dryer dinged. Harper looked over her shoulder, then apologized. "That's me. I'm gonna scoot." She turned and headed back toward her folding table. "Hope to see you later on." She waved her free hand.

I watched her walk away, then looked down at the book on my lap. What was I going to do? Stay in and keep reading a

26

book that a group of people really didn't seem to care about—
but were still willing to spend a Saturday evening discussing? Or
go out and eat some seriously great cheese?

I dropped the book back into my laundry basket.

It was really a no-brainer.

It was after nine when I got back to my apartment.

The book club only lasted an hour, but Dewey and Harper
had been right about the quality of the gossip in the back row.
I'd learned more about my neighbors in ninety minutes than I'd
picked up in twelve years of living in the building. Neither of
them had any new intel on the creature called Cujo, although
Dewey said he wouldn't doubt it if Aldo and Luz were the
ones hyping people up about the possible threat posed by some
amorphous creature with an expressed fondness for used sports
footwear.

"I think it's those two morons who are getting high on
something. They probably huffing cans of Lysol in the storage
room."

"At least you wouldn't need to worry about them having
impure thoughts," Harper mused.

"Just make sure I don't read about this in your damn
magazine."

She considered his comment. "Now that you mention it, this
would be one hell of a human interest story . . . terrified residents
of a city high-rise under siege from the predatory marauding of
an unseen creature that roams desolate hallways in the dead of
night."

"Don't go there, Miss Thing. There ain't enough antacid in
the world to manage the heartburn I'd get from that kind of
drivel." Dewey popped a cheese cube into his mouth and made
happy moaning sounds. "Damn, this shit is good."

I agreed. "What do you think this is?" I held one up to the light to examine it more closely. It was clearly a blend of several somethings. "Cheddar and . . . what? Parmesan, maybe? Definitely a hard cheese. It's a remarkable combination."

"Who gives a fuck?" Dewey nudged me. "This ain't one of your damn 'biomimicry' projects. Hunks of cheese on toothpicks ain't gonna make the world a better place. They're just gonna help you get through another twenty-five minute conversation about a book nobody'll even remember the title of by the time they get off the elevator in the lobby. So, get on up there and score us some more. I can't go. I've already been up there three times."

"Me? They'll think I wandered in off the streets for the snacks." I was aghast. "Nobody even knows who I am."

He nudged me again. "No time like the present."

"Oh, dear god." Harper pushed her glasses up her nose and stood up. "Relax you two. *I'll go.*" She scooted past us and headed for the refreshment table at the side of the room.

"Now that's what I call a good woman." Dewey elbowed me again and nodded his head in the direction of Harper's retreating back.

"Will you quit doing that." I rubbed my arm. "It's going to leave a mark."

"Yeah? Well maybe it's time for *you* to start leaving a mark."

I looked from him to Harper and back again. "With her?" I whispered.

He shrugged. "Why the hell not?"

"Well for one thing, she's expressed zero interest in me."

"So?"

"So . . . I'm not gonna make a fool of myself and jump at the first woman who crosses my path. Besides. I don't even know if she's unattached."

"She is."

I was unprepared for that revelation. "She is? How do you know?"

"Because I know *everything* about the people in this building." He looked around the room. "See that blonde in the second row? The one with the buzz cut wearing the Keith Haring sweatshirt?"

I nodded.

"Well, she and her ex got into a knockdown drag-out one night up in the rooftop pool. Turns out little miss buzz cut had been stepping out with Wynona there, in the fourth row." He pointed at a buxom woman with big hair and a lot of shiny bling. "Thing is, Wynona is apparently just bi-curious and didn't ever intend to leave her drooling husband, Frank, who showed up at the pool madder'n a hornet's nest when he found a two-headed dildo nailed to their door with a note that read, 'Tell your wife her girlfriend in 1508 wanted to return this for a refund.'"

I knew my eyes were like saucers. "Are you kidding?"

"Nope. Want me to go on? I got stories like that about every person in this room."

"Shit . . ."

Harper was making her way back toward us with the cheese.

"Trust me." Dewey elbowed me again. "She ain't attached."

I managed to resist his entreaties. It wasn't that I didn't find Harper attractive. I did, actually. And it was rare to meet a woman with a triple digit IQ *and* a sense of humor. But I was a staunch believer in the theory of relationships brilliantly expressed by Olympia Dukakis in the film, *Moonstruck*: you did not shit where you ate. Translation: you didn't date women who lived in your apartment building.

Been there. Bought the T-shirt.

Tonya and I had lived here on separate floors for all four years of our on-again, off-again relationship. When Tonya finally moved back to her apartment on the tenth floor—with the cat—she'd made it clear that there'd be no more . . . commingling of assets. It wasn't too bad at first, but then it seemed that I'd manage to run into her every time I left the apartment. She'd be in the trash room, the mailroom, the laundry room—anywhere I went. It was particularly difficult when I'd return from trips, bedraggled and bleary from long overnights, and Tonya would come in and waltz across the lobby with her latest, younger model draped across her frame like a bedsheet.

I didn't need those visceral reminders of my failures. But it still hurt when Dewey told me one night that Tonya and her cat had decamped for the allure of trendier digs at Jessup House in midtown. It was a relief to know I wouldn't keep running into her—but having her move out was still like being hit with another level of loss.

Déjà vu all over again.

Dewey's brand of tough love didn't do much to snap me out of my depression, either. He finally gave up and quit haranguing me for moping around the joint.

"You're just like the poor jokers in every one of those damn country songs," he opined. 'If You Won't Leave Me, I'll Find a Woman Who Will.'"

I didn't even have the temerity to be offended.

So, for the next couple of months, I licked my wounds and more or less hibernated in the apartment between trips. I spent most of my days and all of my evenings watching old movies on TCM. It was a passion I'd learned from *maman*, who'd developed the same obsession during all the years she'd had to travel for the railroad. She said watching the old black and white classics kept her company on the nights away from home. She called them, "*sa famille* éloignée"—her extended family. When we were kids, Zoé and I would rush to haul out our fleece blankets on Saturday nights and huddle on the floor in front of the television with our bowls of popcorn to watch the classics with her. Zoé quickly lost interest when she grew older and discovered makeup and boys—not necessarily in that order.

But me? I loved staying at home and watching sad movies with *maman*. We probably saw the same ones dozens of times, but neither of us cared. When our favorites—films like *Mildred Pierce, The Maltese Falcon, Double Indemnity,* or *Notorious*—played, we'd squeal like banshees and plan our entire night around the movie—even down to what we'd make for supper. Papa would just grimace, snap up a tome-like history of the War of 1812 or something equally dense, and disappear into his study for the evening.

But life on the extra board at USRail quickly overwhelmed my commitment to moping in solitude. I was always on the go—and as the months went by, I cared less and less about it. I even started volunteering for extra shifts. Why not? If I was destined to remain a hostage to riding the rails, why not earn some bank in the process? It would serve me well when I finally finished the graduate degree in sustainable engineering at Villanova I'd been working on for more than two years. All my course work was complete; I just had to finish writing the dissertation—and progress on that was slower than molasses in January. It was a colossal push-me, pull-you. I griped about never having the time to write it—but I continued to schedule myself to ensure that I wouldn't.

I stared over at the piles of paper and the closed laptop on the small kitchen table I used as an office.

Yeah. That's not happening tonight.

I dropped into my reading chair with resignation. My cellphone sat on the end table along with the book I'd mostly *not* been reading. It was one of Erik Larson's creations—this one about Churchill and England during the blitz.

Great bedtime reading. Not.

My phone sat there quietly pulsating like Poe's *Tell-Tale Heart.* I imagined I could hear the cacophony of sultry voices all calling out to me—chanting that I should take a shot and swipe right.

I picked it up and sat staring at it. When it started buzzing it scared the crap out of me and I nearly tossed it to the floor. It was a text from crew scheduling, of course. Notifying me that I'd been placed on a line departing 30th Street Station tomorrow morning at 9:20 a.m. I was going to be working the Green Mountain Zephyr, with overnights in St. Albans, New Haven, and Springfield. I wondered idly which crew member had called out. USRail had four crews that typically worked this line—two staffing the northbound runs, and two staffing the southbound trains.

It didn't matter. It was one of the routes I genuinely liked— although I doubted I'd have enough time to connect with anyone from my family. Although the train overnighted in the yard at St. Albans on the second night, we began the long trek south promptly at 9:15 a.m. the next morning.

Still . . . the final overnight in Springfield would be the longest one, which meant I'd have all of an evening to kill before my next duty day began on Tuesday. Possibly long enough to arrange a meeting?

I recalled what Sofie had said about the SheDate app being useful to find someone to fuck, marry, or just kill three hours with.

Maybe it was worth a try?

I reasoned with myself. *How bad could it be?*

Better not to think too long about that one.

Before I could talk myself out of it, I launched the app, logged in, and began exploring. Sofie had already completed my rather exhaustive profile. I was amused to learn that I was a Leo (accurate), into ice skating (not since high school) and pickleball (I'd played it exactly twice, two years ago—under duress), an omnivore, a nonsmoker, was fully vaxxed (true), I lived in Philadelphia, I had a postgraduate engineering degree (sort of true), I worked in interstate "transportation" (which I thought made me sound like a long distance trucker), and traveled a lot for work, I liked cats—a lot (which made me sound like a loser), I spoke French fluently, and that my communication style was "better in person."

Then there was that ridiculous profile photo.

On the whole, I thought this was a summary that screamed run like hell. But thanks to something called SheDate Passport, I could search for matches in any defined city or area. So . . . I already knew every place I was going to be next week—why not start my search where I'd be doing my longest overnight?

So, Springfield it was. As soon as I entered the location, the app loaded a ton of possible matches based on my profile. I began to scroll through them and read their profiles.

I had to hand it to SheDate—the profile matching had worked pretty well. I wouldn't have said nay to the company of most of the women—at least for dinner. But then, I was a novice at this, and I didn't have the requisite skill set yet to know how to read the tea leaves of each profile.

For instance, profile one was someone who is "insanely into cats," stated that their favorite Spotify anthem was "Psychosocial" by Slipknot, and insisted they "enjoyed quiet evenings building models." So, was that clumsy code for the prospective match probably being a teenage incel living in his parents' basement somewhere in central Massachusetts?

Swipe left.

Profile two was less rife with inconsistencies. A forty-four-year-old woman who was tired of the dating and bar scene. Enjoyed hiking and riding bikes. Loved to travel. Vacationed in the mountains. Was a voracious reader. Had two dogs. Was passionate about green energy. Loved Coltrane and anything by Ella Fitzgerald. Just got out of a long-term relationship and was looking to start fresh.

Yeah. "Just out of a long-term relationship" equaled I am wounded and still hung up on my ex.

Swipe left.

Profile three had promise at first, but quickly deconstructed when I looked at her portrait gallery. Each photo showed her wearing less and less and her fairly comprehensive array of body art tended toward the exotic . . . I mean, unless you think krakens and black roses are easy to accessorize.

Swipe left.

Next up was someone who could've doubled as an understudy for Skipper, Barbie's little sister. If I'd ever wondered what happened to cheerleaders when they grew up, came out, but staunchly refused to hang up their pom-poms, here she was. "Chrissy" was a plucky insurance agent in Hartford (where else?), and she was looking for someone to share her love of chardonnay, Pilates, eating keto, and tournament pickleball. Oh . . . she also loved Taylor Swift *and* Billie Eilish.

And they said civilization peaked with coffee pods . . .

Swipe left.

The following six matches were all women with very flimsily disguised desires to find their next hookups versus wasting time playing twenty questions.

Swipe left.

Swipe left.

Swipe left.

Well . . . this one is actually kind of cute . . .

No.

Swipe left.

Swipe left.

I went back and took a second look at that cute one . . . *No.* I knew it would only end in disaster if I allowed my sleeping libido to wake up and manage this process.

Swipe left. Again.

Okay. Number ten didn't set off *any* creep warnings. I even read the profile three times to be sure I hadn't overlooked some glaring clue. Nope. She seemed perfectly, uninspiringly normal. Even a bit dull. And eureka—she lived and worked in Springfield, where I'd be overnighting on Thursday.

I studied her photo. It seemed . . . appropriate. Engaging.

Not overhyped or posed. It looked . . . natural.

Her profile said her name was Jane—which dovetailed nicely with the rest of her presentation. She was a hospitalist (I had to look that up) and worked for a regional healthcare system. She said she'd been married more than a decade before she finally came out. Now she was involved in all kinds of PRIDE organizations. And she volunteered weekly at a local animal shelter.

I kept scouring her bio to see if she'd also done a stint healing lepers. But no. Everything about her seemed to be in balance. Even her zodiac sign. Libra.

I sat tapping my fingers against the arm of the chair.

Was I going to do this?

What was the worst that could happen?

Going down that rabbit hole was a mistake. After a full fifteen minutes of imagining all the Technicolor ways this enterprise could quickly become a first runner-up in the Worst That Could Happen category, I steeled my resolve and decided to risk it.

Besides, if this did end up being a gargantuan mistake, I could imagine even more graphic ways to make Sofie pay for it.

Swipe right.

I was packed and ready to go by 7 a.m. on Sunday. I won't deny that I woke up several times during the night and plucked my phone off the nightstand just to see if, by chance, Jane had swiped right on my profile, too.

No such luck. At least not yet. I wondered what the typical turnaround time was for this kind of thing.

I was so damn pathetic . . . fumbling around with a social networking app that I knew next to nothing about. It was like being airdropped into a strange country where I didn't understand the language or customs. I recalled Dewey's advice: if you want to catch a fish, learn to think like a fish.

Okay. *What did fish* think *like?*

I mean, I assumed they mostly thought about ways to avoid being caught by some drunk in a hopped-up bass boat or eaten by some other underwater predator. The perversity of SheDate was that its reason for existing was to facilitate *precisely* these activities, versus forestall them.

It was a paradox.

But I had spent the last six years of my life studying traits in nature and looking for ways to replicate that trait or functionality in human technology and product design. The curriculum was really like "Today's News Flash from Planet Obvious." Because often, the best solutions were the simplest ones that were already around us every day. The creation of Velcro was a marquee example. It had been invented when an engineer spent hours pulling burrs out of his dog's fur. The tenacious burrs succeeded in sticking as much to him as to his dog's coat as he tried to dislodge them. An idea occurred to him. Why not replicate the design of the highly effective burr to create fasteners for a whole range of human products?

Same thing for our prized puffy winter coats and bed comforters. Why not stuff them full of down feathers so we can all stay warm without having to spend our winters in Boca?

So as a student of nature, it should've been a cakewalk for me to observe the patterns and behaviors of my fellow wayfarers on SheDate. What could they, collectively, teach me about better ways to manage or solidify relationships? Nothing? Anything? Or would the message be, simply, that I was taking my biometric shopping list to the wrong store?

I was still pondering these metaphysical quandaries when I left my apartment and made my way toward the elevators. When I rounded the corner, I saw Aldo and Luz bent over some kind of makeshift contraption. It wasn't clear if they were assembling or dismantling it.

"Morning," I called out as I approached them. "What's going on?"

Luz looked up at me. "Hey, Miss Lebrun. Me'n Aldo are just checking our traps."

Traps?

"Really?" I looked more closely at the gizmo they'd erected. It reminded me of the Mousetrap game Zoé and I used to play whenever we visited our grandmother. She kept a big bin full of ancient toys and board games in musty boxes beneath the stairs in her tiny house. Mousetrap had always been my favorite because you got to build elaborate contraptions that towered over the carpet, using all kinds of connectors, chutes, and random-shaped tubes. "Any luck?"

Aldo got to his feet. He was holding some kind of shoe. "Nope. We set these up on four different floors. So far, we ain't caught nothin'."

"Except for that pack of smokes on 19." Luz looked at me. "Unopened, too. We figured maybe Cujo is trying to quit?"

"Stealing shoes?" I asked.

"Nope. Smoking." Luz pulled the hardpack of Salems out of her pocket. "Too bad Dewey don't like menthols."

I pointed at the shoe. "What kind of . . . *bait* are you using?"

"This one's a tennis shoe that belonged to my nephew, Stefano. It ain't new, but he only used it twice. Stefano don't stick with shit for long. And tennis was hard for him on account of he's missing two toes on his left foot from that motocross accident up in Butler."

"I still don't think we should've tried a *used* shoe. Cujo is too smart for that."

"He won't know it's used," Aldo insisted. "Besides, I fogged it with Lysol."

"That's what I'm saying. He probably thought it was a damn bowling shoe." Luz tsked. "Them things are so full of chemicals they probably rot your insoles."

Behind them, the elevator dinged, and the doors opened. It was my cue to beat a hasty retreat.

"Later, you two. I gotta scoot."

"Where you headed this time?" Luz asked.

"Vermont, mostly. By way of an overnight in Massachusetts."

"Hope you packed your wool underwear. You'll freeze your bits off up there in that frozen tundra." Aldo imitated a shiver. "Big storm heading for the Northeast this week."

"What'd they name this one?" Luz asked.

"Beats the hell outta me. Some weird-ass name like Esmerelda. Who names these damn storms, anyway? Some doofus reject at Disneyworld?" Aldo shrugged. "It don't make any sense."

I made it to the elevator just in time to stop the door from closing.

"Good luck," I called out before the doors closed and I began my descent.

Dewey was working the desk when I entered the lobby. I was surprised to see Harper standing there with him. She was wearing a coat and scarf and holding her characteristic armload of folders, so I figured she was either coming or going. Probably going, since it was barely past seven.

"Hey, you two. You're both up and at it nice and early for a Sunday."

Dewey took in my uniform and suitcase. "I see they finally tagged your ass."

"Yeah. I knew I couldn't dodge a bullet for long."

Harper was staring at my hat. I felt self-conscious . . . I knew it probably made me look like an idiot. I raised my hand to adjust it. "They make us wear these," I said to cover my embarrassment.

"It's pretty cute, actually," Harper said. "It inspires confidence."

"Been a long time since you traveled by train."

"Not so long," she stated. "I generally prefer it over flying."

"Where are you headed this week?" Dewey asked.

"North." I pointed up. "I'm on the Zephyr."

"Gonna see the family?"

"Not this trip. The overnight in St. Albans is too short to connect with them." I looked at Harper. "My parents and sister live in Québec."

"I gather from your pronunciation that it's your home?"

I nodded.

"So, your family is French speaking?"

"*Oui*," I replied. "I mean, if you're among the few who consider the Canadian dialect to be French."

"*Oh, je pense que cela compte.*"

I was impressed. "*Ton accent est parfait.*"

"*Merci.*"

"Hey," Dewey raised a hand, "if you two are gonna talk dirty to each other, at least do it in English so I can enjoy it."

Harper laughed. "My French isn't that great. I cut class on all the 'talk dirty' days."

I was tempted to say, "too bad," but thought better of it.

That was because my Olympia Dukakis rule had bolted awake and was busily waving all kinds of red flags. I obeyed its strictures and retreated to safer terrain.

"I need to hustle. I've got a butt-ton of paperwork to complete before heading out."

"Have a safe trip," Harper enjoined.

"See you when you get back on . . ." Dewey waited.

"Thursday," I replied. "Hopefully before midnight."

I waved goodbye and left them standing there. I never felt happy when I left home for these long trips, but today, for some reason, I was more despondent than usual. Maybe because I still hadn't received any response from the elusive Jane.

Not that I'd checked my phone three times on the elevator ride down from twenty-six. I hadn't.

I'd checked it four times.

Bupkis.

Who was I kidding? It wasn't like I was God's gift to online dating, either. I mean . . . hadn't I cavalierly swiped left on a few dozen potential Ms. Rights just because I focused on one ridiculous thing that summoned up a panoply of potential Doomsday scenarios? It was entirely possible that *I* was the one leading the swipe left derby on the damn app.

Oh, well, I thought. *Maman* had called me yesterday afternoon and asked if I knew that *The Lady Eve* was showing on TCM tomorrow night. The Barbara Stanwyck comedy was one of our favorites.

"*Nous pourrions le regarder ensemble,*" she'd said. *Maman* and I frequently would watch movies together—especially when papa was off golfing, or she was visiting with *tante* Estelle in Sherbrooke.

Aunt Estelle was a talker, and *maman* would usually retreat to her room early, just to get some peace and quiet.

So, if Jane flaked out—or worse, since I'd never know—had already swiped left, I could always hunker down with Barbara Stanwyck and Henry Fonda and let Preston Sturges drown my sorrows.

Why not? It had always worked in the past.

William Gray Station was humming when I arrived. Sunday mornings weren't usually heavy travel days, so I wasn't sure what was different about today. Snow had started falling during the short drive from Hopkinson House to 30th Street, and I wondered if Aldo's prognostication about an impending winter storm might prove accurate. This was the small, insistent kind of snow, too—the type that tended to stick to everything and not melt on contact.

40

Great. That meant helping seniors on and off the trains would be more involved than usual—and it was especially important during inclement weather. Slippery steps and cracked concrete station platforms became doubly hazardous during snowy and icy conditions. It also meant I'd be tossing a lot of suitcases. Sometimes, I thought my job as a conductor was more akin to the work of a baggage handler at an airport. I figured I'd be due for shoulder replacement surgery before I turned fifty—if I never finished my damn dissertation and got the hell off the rails.

The train was packed this morning. I noticed a preponderance of millennials in coach—all carrying impressively-padded duffel bags stuffed with high-dollar skis. I had to help at least twenty of them properly stow the bags—without knocking out any other passengers who were not-so-patiently waiting for them to take their damn seats so they could get to the café car and order their double Bloody Marys before the great unwashed beat them to it.

Sunday morning. The morning after Saturday night.

I hoped Anthony made sure the café car was stocked with enough tequila.

This looked like a hardcore crowd to me. I figured at least half of the riders would be with us all the way to Stowe. They'd be able to toss back a shit ton of José Cuervo in nine hours and forty-nine minutes.

The train was so crowded it took both JoAnn (the senior conductor on this route) and me (her assistant conductor) twenty minutes after we'd departed 30th Street Station to scan everyone's ticket and tag the racks above their seats with the names of their arrival stations. JoAnn did the front half of the train—which was generous because it had twice as many passengers—and I got the back half, including business class, which was rarely full. This time, however, we had one passenger who was already demonstrating that she was going to be a serious PITA.

J.S. Oliver was a self-described special needs traveler and her small, transport wheelchair had to be stowed in front of the emergency exit. It wasn't up to me to determine under what circumstances the cranky septuagenarian required the chair—but I did notice that she seemed to have *no* problem elbowing her way to the café car and returning with her complimentary cup of Starbucks. Three times. It was widely known that special needs USRail travelers benefitted from the railroad's equivalent to priority boarding. Requiring a wheelchair guaranteed that you'd get off and on the train first. Most of our stations had special chair lifts we could pull out and use to help them board the train. And, of course, we'd carry their bags for them, too. None of us *ever* had a problem with that when it was clear the passenger had a genuine need. This woman, however, gave no outward sign that she was in any way impaired. In fact, the only disability she manifested in my view was her rabid aura of self-importance. She kept flashing her medical I.D. whenever she asked for some concession—like lowering the temperature on the heat that was blasting in the business class car. Or asking us to have someone come and clean the window beside her seat.

Sadly, she wasn't getting off the train until fucking Springfield, so we'd be stuck with her for the better part of five hours.

As a result, JoAnn and I played rock, paper, scissors whenever it was time to make another circuit through that last car on the train.

It was nearly 1:30 p.m. when we reached New Haven. This stop was always somewhat frenetic because we not only had to off-board and on-board passengers—we had to manually switch tracks so the AEM-7 electric engine could be decoupled and replaced by a Genesis diesel, which would take us the rest of the way north. On a good day when it wasn't snowing—and it was snowing like hell that day—this process only took about fifteen minutes. But it could only happen after either JoAnn or

I hopped off and manually threw the track switch. Since JoAnn had a bum knee, I offered to do the deed. It took some strength to pull the lever on those old manual switches.

She looked at me with narrowed eyes.

"Is this your slimy way of forcing *me* to deal with Cruella in 2B?"

I beamed at her. "How'd you guess?"

I pulled on my foul weather gear and prepared to hop off the train before it reached the switch point. JoAnn flipped me off as she headed for the front of the train to oversee the decoupling of the electric engine.

"Paybacks!" she hollered back at me. But I'd already jumped off the train and her threat quickly got swallowed up by the swirling snow.

These mechanical switches were the worst—especially when it was below freezing, and the stiff old gears refused to engage. It made pulling the big lever that actually moved the tracks about as fun as opening a window that had been painted shut. But I threw all of my weight into it and, eventually, the damn thing lurched forward just as the decoupled engine reached the cutoff. That allowed the big Genesis engine that had been waiting to roll forward and connect with the passenger cars.

I sprinted to jump back aboard just as the train began to roll out of the station.

JoAnn met me in the vestibule between coach and the café car.

"Nice job, A.C." She brushed snow off my jacket. "That was a record turn. Eight minutes. Keep this up and you'll be putting Harrison out of a job."

Harrison was the conductor who'd called in sick for this trip. "Is he really under the weather?" I asked.

"Who the fuck knows? He could just have a bad case of the brown bottle flu."

"I hear it's going around."

"Don't get any ideas, whiz kid. You're stuck with this gig for the week."

"It might surprise you to learn that I'm really okay with that. This would be my first pick for a permanent line."

"No shit?" JoAnn sounded surprised. "Most of you young guns bid for the more glamorous routes."

"*Glamorous?* Do we work for the same railroad?"

JoAnn laughed. "True. But some of the East-West lines have better overnight venues. Not, mind you, that I don't enjoy every minute of my stay in the opulent, downtown Hampton Inn in St. Albans."

"Yeah," I quipped, "I heard they finally got a four slice toaster in the breakfast lounge. Pretty swanky."

"You don't know the half of it. The ice machine on the fourth floor now puts out an astonishing eight cubes an hour."

"Damn. I might need a moment."

"Yeah?" The voice came from behind me. "Well, don't take too long—Cruella de Vil is up my ass about no butt gaskets in the head."

It was Anthony, the café steward.

JoAnn had just about had it with Miss White Privilege in 2B. "What does she expect us to do? Come wipe her pampered ass?"

"Something like that." Anthony looked morose. "I don't know what to tell her."

"Tell her to take a stack of Kleenex and shove it up her withered—"

I cut JoAnn's tirade short. "I'll talk to her."

Anthony looked relieved. "Thanks, Lebrun. I owe you. This bitch is gonna make me start chain-smoking."

"No worries. I got this."

I left them both standing there and made my way back the entire length of the train toward business class. Our special needs traveler was impatiently drumming her needle-like fingers

44

against the padded arm of her seat.

"Hello, Miss Oliver," I began.

"*Dr.* Oliver," she corrected me.

I counted to three. "Pardon me, *Doc-tor* Oliver." I looked into her deep-set, watery blue eyes. "The steward said you had a complaint about the lavatory?"

"If you call that disgusting affront to humanity a lavatory then, yes, I certainly do have a complaint. You may have noticed that this ill-kempt and unrefined tin box your company brazenly refers to as a 'business class accommodation' is actually little better than a cattle car. We are crammed in here like sardines and are forced to breathe germ-laden recycled air that offers less than a life-sustaining supply of oxygen. Add to that the indignities of the disgraceful conditions in your so-called lavatories—which have all the appeal of a stockyard on a hot summer day. It is not to be borne."

"The steward said you had a particular complaint about the lavatory?"

Doctor Oliver turned a lovely shade of affronted purple.

"There are no," she lowered her voice, "liners."

"Liners? I'm not sure I take your meaning."

"*Liners,*" she hissed. "For the toilet seat."

"Oh. You mean *seat protectors*. I'm sorry Dr. Oliver. Most of our preferred passengers travel with their own. It's a carryover from the pandemic. USRail stopped stocking them after the second round of Economic Injury Disaster Loans ran out. I share your disappointment. My best advice is to reach out to your congressperson and lodge a formal complaint. I am sure everyone at USRail will applaud your efforts on our behalf. Now," I magnanimously doffed my cap, "if you'll excuse me, I have to tend to the other 286 passengers on this godforsaken train."

I didn't hear Cruella's muffled response—and I didn't much care. She could file a complaint about me if she wanted to. I wasn't really worried. USRail didn't give a rat's ass about how we behaved as long as crew scheduling could still call extra board bottom feeders like me out to work with less than two hours' notice.

Mercifully, Cruella and her transfer chair got off the train two hours and change later in Springfield. Even the remaining passengers in business class cheered when they saw her wheeled across the platform and into the station building.

The rest of the trip was uneventful. Most of the riders, as predicted, got off in Waterbury/Stowe and headed out into the accumulating snow, weighted down with skis, and offering up audible expressions of glee. It was a nearly empty train that finally pulled into St. Albans at ten minutes to nine.

It took about fifteen minutes to throw the track switch and roll the empty train off the main line into the yard for overnight storage, allowing the train to be cleaned and reversed for southbound travel in the morning.

JoAnn, Anthony, the engine crew and I all made the short, frigid walk through the snow to the station hotel on Lake Street. We were all tired after the long day, so we retrieved our room keys and dispersed. There were next to no restaurants within walking distance that were still open at nine thirty on a Sunday night. Sometimes, we'd all hang together downstairs in the lobby and order pizzas from a local delivery place called Pie in the Sky. But tonight, most of us were tired from fighting the snow and the ensuing delays along the route. But I'd scored a couple of hot dogs and two cans of Space Dust IPA from the café car, so I was set. We all agreed we'd meet downstairs at six thirty for breakfast.

I got off the elevator on my floor and asked JoAnn if she'd mind lending me three of her ice cubes from the high rent district on the fourth floor.

A laugh and, "Fuck off, A.C," was all I heard before the doors closed.

For my part, I couldn't wait to get into my room, take off

my wet socks, and check the SheDate app to see if my luck had changed and my potential Miss HEA had swiped right.

CHAPTER THREE

*Age Gaps—and how mine was wider
than a railway platform.*

Jane finally got around to swiping right sometime on Monday afternoon. I only knew this because my cellphone slid out of my bag when I tossed it onto a bench seat in the café car just after Northampton, on the southbound trek to New Haven—where we'd have our second overnight. When I crawled beneath the small table to pick the phone up, I noticed two things: there were an inordinate number of white cheddar chickpea crisps down there—and that I had received a notification from SheDate. It took every bit of strength I possessed not to launch the app and check it out. For one thing, using our phones for personal business on company time was strictly forbidden. But nobody ever paid much attention to that rule. The real reason I didn't check it was because I didn't want to look like a loser to Anthony, who was sitting across from me at the small table.

"You want something to eat?" He asked me. We were allowed twenty minutes to grab lunch during our shifts, and I'd taken the later slot.

"No. Thanks, man. Those hot dogs I ate last night are still repeating on me."

"I *told* you not to eat that relish. I think that shit turned. Aramark keeps sending expired crap out to our distributors and passing it off as discounted. And as long as it's not moving or covered with hair, USRail doesn't care. If they can keep making a buck, they're happy."

"It wasn't the relish. I just didn't sleep well."

"I hear you." He nodded in solidarity. "I hate the mattresses in that dump. I think they're holdovers from the St. Albans Raid in 1864."

I smiled at him. Anthony was a good-looking kid from Trenton. He'd been with the railroad for less than two years. His aspirations extended beyond being a steward. His ultimate goal was to apply for engineer training. I knew he came from a large family, and he sent a big chunk of his paycheck home to help them cover expenses. "Were you reading those brochures in the lobby again?"

"What the hell else was there to do? The cable in that joint is for shit. I could only get two channels—some lame-ass local station in Plattsburgh, New York, or back-to-back reruns of *Walker, Texas Ranger*. Pathetic."

"Life on the rails, my man."

"Don't I know it. My mother keeps wanting me to quit and go to work selling cars for my cousin Carmine, in Woodland Park."

"But that's not for you?"

"Selling overpriced muscle cars to a bunch of *burloni* who wear too much jewelry? Hell fuck no. Besides, I get squirrelly if I'm off the rails for very long. The only time I feel like I'm in a place I belong?" He pointed at the floor of the car. "It's when I feel *that*—the vibration of those wheels rolling over the tracks. It's like my heartbeat now."

I felt guilty sitting there with him. It wasn't that I didn't love the railroad—I mean, it was in my blood, too. But I viewed it as a means to an end—an end that didn't consign me to a life riding the rails. And a life that didn't require me to take abuse from people like Cruella, simply because they'd bought a ticket to ride.

"You're gonna make a great engineer, Anthony."

He looked hopeful. "You think so?"

I nodded. "You already know where you're going—and nobody can teach you that."

JoAnn entered the café car from coach and dropped down on a seat. "My goddamn knee is killing me. I think it was wrestling with that wheelchair lift yesterday."

"Did you use any of your eight ice cubes on it last night?" I asked.

"Yeah." She laughed. "That and about fourteen Tylenol."

"When are you gonna get that thing fixed, Jo? It ain't gonna get better on its own."

"I know." JoAnn looked at Anthony. "But I can't afford the time off."

"You think you might lose the line if you're out too long?" Anthony shook his head. "I've heard that corporate's hosed a few people by putting them back on the board if they're out too long."

"I'd like to see their asses try." JoAnn stretched her leg out and grimaced. "This ain't my first rodeo."

"Why don't you ease off today, Jo?" I touched her arm. "Let me take the next rotation. We've only got five more stations—and I'll handle the switch in Springfield."

"You did it yesterday."

"So?" I shrugged. "It was exhilarating."

"It was snowing like hell."

"I liked it."

JoAnn shook her head. "Fine. You can do the switch—but I'll do my share of the rotations."

I didn't push my advantage. JoAnn was hardcore. She didn't tolerate assholes or slackers—and she was no novice to hard work. Before joining USRail, she'd worked twenty-five years as a station manager for American Airlines.

You didn't fuck with JoAnn.

A couple of passengers from business class entered the café car and stood at the counter perusing the menu. Anthony got up and went to serve them.

JoAnn nudged me as she watched him. "He's a good kid."

"He is," I agreed. "He'll be running this company one day."

She made a disgusted sound. "Not a chance. He's too high functioning to run this failing empire."

I stared out the window at the passing landscape. Everything in sight was covered in about eight inches of snow and more was predicted for this evening. Schedulers for the northeast corridor were already alerting us that we'd be experiencing significant delays tonight and tomorrow.

Great. And we were barely into December.

I'd been absently fiddling with my phone as I sat there, and JoAnn noticed.

"You got a hot date or something, Iz?"

I looked at her with surprise and a trace of embarrassment.

"Ah, I was *right*." She laughed. "Dish."

"It's nothing like that. I mean . . . not yet anyway."

"Intriguing. What's the story?"

I sighed. "In a moment of weakness, I gave in to a complete lapse of sense and allowed a friend to set me up with a SheDate account."

"No shit?"

"No."

She gestured at my phone. "So, you got a live one?"

"I honestly have no idea. I noticed when I sat down here that I had a notification . . . finally."

"And?"

I shrugged. "And . . . nothing. I haven't checked it yet."

JoAnn rolled her eyes. "What the fuck is wrong with you?

51

Look at it and see."

"We're not supposed to use our personal devices while we're on duty."

"Right. And we're not supposed to pad our expense reports or smuggle hooch into our hotel rooms, either. Oh—and I forgot about *never* disabling inward-facing cameras during deadheads."

"Okay, okay." I pulled out my phone. "I'll check it."

It only took about twenty seconds to launch the SheDate app. Sure enough, Jane had swiped right on my profile. *I even had a message from her!*

> Hi. I'm happy you stopped
> on my profile to say hello.
> I apologize for taking so long
> to respond. It's been a hectic
> few days at work. Tell me a
> bit more about yourself. I see
> you work in transportation. Does
> that mean you travel a lot?

I tried to keep my face impassive but must've failed miserably. JoAnn busted me immediately.

"You got a hot one, I see."

I stuffed the phone back into my bag. "It's not anything yet. Just a note saying nice to meet you."

"Aren't you going to write back?"

JoAnn's scrutiny was making me feel uncomfortable. "I will. Later when we're done for the day."

The PA system roared to life, announcing that we'd be arriving at the next station in fifteen minutes.

"Time to make the donuts." JoAnn groaned and got to her feet. "You wanna do north or south?"

"I'll take north. You can start back here and meet me in the middle."

After I'd finished my rounds, notifying travelers that their arrival station was next, I made haste getting back to the station-side exit before JoAnn arrived so I could open the door and be the one in place to toss bags to the platform. It pissed her off, of course, but I knew she appreciated it.

It was obvious the platform in Hartford had been cleared earlier, but it was snowing again, and the surfaces were still slick with a light dusting. It was a busy stop, and that made getting passengers off and on the train take longer than usual. We were now running a good ten to twelve minutes behind schedule. The closer we got to the larger, metropolitan stations, the harder it would be to make up the time. That invariably led to a trainload of crankier, more harried riders.

On days like this, we all wished USRail would hand out free drinks to *all* riders—not simply the ones in business class.

We were only twenty minutes north of Springfield when we received the following train order.

ON BOTH TRACKS DO NOT EXCEED 5 MPH

AT MP 235.2

BETWEEN MERIDEN AND NEW HAVEN

ACCOUNT STATES THAT BEAVERS HAVE BEEN CUTTING ON A LARGE COTTONWOOD TREE AND IT COULD FALL ON TRACK

NO TRACK FLAGS DISPLAYED

JoAnn and I looked at each other morosely.

"Beavers?" she repeated. "What the serious fuck?"

"Five miles per hour will set us back more than an hour.

Maybe ninety minutes."

"And," I added to her assessment, "that's *only* if the tree doesn't fall across the tracks before we get there."

"Little fuckers. Why can't they get their damn lumber at Home Depot like everyone else?"

Anthony immediately started tallying how much beer and wine he had left. He was sure however much it was, it wouldn't be enough to meet demand if the train was stopped for more than an hour.

It was snowing steadily now. Stopping the train for ninety minutes also meant no heat. "This day keeps getting better and better."

"Gird your loins," JoAnn told us. "It's about to get real." She walked to the PA system to make the announcement. As she explained the situation, we could hear a chorus of groans spreading out along all four hundred and twenty-five feet of passenger cars.

It looked like Jane was going to have to wait a while longer to learn more about me.

It was after seven before I finally checked into my room in New Haven. Overnights here were at least more tolerable than they were in St. Albans. The station hotel was in an area within walking distance of more than a dozen restaurants and bars. Granted, those were usually choked with college students from Yale, but it beat the hell out of trying to stay awake while you waited on the delivery of an indifferent pizza.

That night, I walked the short distance to a pretty good Italian restaurant called Olives and Oil on Temple Street. The last thing I wanted was to be outside in the snow—again—but this place was less than a block from the hotel. The rest of the crew was heading to a local watering hole to watch the Bruins game. All of them except JoAnn, who said she just wanted to head to her room and get off her feet. I asked her if she wanted to accompany me to Olives and Oil, but she took a pass. I told her to look up the online menu and text me her order if they had anything she wanted me to bring back. When she demurred, I insisted. So she promised she'd do it and thanked me profusely.

The Italian *cucina* was hopping when I arrived. But I was lucky enough to score a table without having to wait. I didn't realize how hungry I was until I sat down and took in all the enticing smells coming from the open kitchen. I quickly decided on the goat cheese carbonara with a house salad and a bottle of Barbera—knowing I could take what I didn't drink back to the hotel.

I had a feeling JoAnn would not say nay to it, whether she ordered dinner or not.

Once I'd had my first glass of wine poured, I set about rereading Jane's message on SheDate. I tried to be realistic about it and not read too much into her response. To be fair, it had been friendly, but not overly engaging. Although she did ask me to tell her more about myself.

I was in a quandary. I didn't know how much to share was *too* much. I really had no idea how to navigate this terrain. So, I did the only thing I could think of to do.

I texted Sofie for advice.

Knock knock?

Isabelle? Where are you?

I'm in New Haven on an overnight.

Are you getting laid?

Hardly. If I were, why would I be
texting you?

Because you're riddled with self-doubt
and want assurance you're doing
it right.

Whatever. I do have a question for you,
though.

It goes into the second hole.

WTF does that even mean?

If you have to ask, you haven't graduated
to that level yet.

May I just ask my question?

Oui. Poses ta question.

So, I had a woman swipe right on me after I
swiped right on her profile. She asked me to
tell her more about myself. How much do I
share without looking desperate?

It's usually better at this point to send
naked photos. It saves more time and idle
chitchat.

Seriously? Could you give me advice I can
actually use? You're the one who got me into
this.

Ne te mets pas dans tous tes états.

The only reason I'm worked up is because you won't answer my question.

> Tell her the truth. It's refreshing and she won't believe anything you say, anyway, so you have nothing to lose.

Okay. But how much truth?

> I wouldn't tell her about your abortive relationship experience. But if you want to talk about your job or your family or your Cayman Islands bank accounts, then go for it.

What if she thinks I'm a nerd?

> Then you'll have done a good job telling the truth.

Thanks a lot. What if she doesn't write back?

> Then you go looking for the next Ms. Right and be happy your ELO is ticking up.

What the fuck is an ELO?

> It's the algorithm SheDate uses to rate your relative desirability. The more swipe rights you

get, the more your stock soars.

If she does write back, when do I suggest meeting up?

Depends. How horny are you?

Really?

My guess is that if she writes back, it means she's just as interested in you. So, she might suggest It first.

Okay.

Go forth, young squire. Be bold. Tell her you want to meet and fuck like snow rabbits.

I am metaphorically hanging up now. And I have no idea what a snow rabbit is.

D'accord. Bonne chance. Be sure to let me know what happens.
Je t'aime.

Love you, too.

I decided to go ahead and roll the dice. Why not write back to Jane and tell her about my job? I mean . . . how many people would she know who wrestled with work stoppage because of marauding beavers? That would be amusing if nothing else. Right?

Hi, Jane. It's so nice to hear back from you.

It's been a busy week for me, too. I am a
conductor for USRail, and I work lines mostly
in the northeast corridor. Travel has been
tougher than usual because of the snow,
which keeps on coming. I am on the road
until Friday of this week. My home and crew
base are in Philadelphia. Does your job ever
take you there?

I hesitated for only a moment before hitting send. If she wrote back, she wrote back. If not? Well. I'd do what Sofie suggested and keep on searching.

The server arrived with my salad and entrée and apologized for bringing them both at the same time. I assured her that was fine—I was famished enough to eat the tablecloth.

I hadn't taken more than two bites of the goat cheese carbonara—which was excellent—when my phone dinged. I picked it up and was amazed (and elated) to see that Jane had already written back.

Hello, Isabelle. You are right about the
snow. I just got back from a weekend of
cross-country skiing in Stowe. It was very
beautiful and the new snow was welcome.
I've done a fair amount of traveling in
it this week, too—and some of it by rail!
We'll have to share war stories. I live
and work mostly in the Springfield area,
but I do get to Philadelphia and D.C.
occasionally.

Are you ever in this area (Springfield)? It
would be nice to meet for coffee or drinks.

I had to hand it to Sofie. She sure knew her stuff. I was amazed that Jane was already suggesting a meetup. Why not? I would be in Springfield overnight tomorrow. I wondered if that would be too soon to suggest?

On the other hand, I had no guarantee when I'd next land a stint on the Zephyr.

I decided to go for broke.

> **Hello back! In fact, I'll be in Springfield tomorrow. I should be free and clear by 5:30 p.m. Would you like to meet for drinks someplace?**

> **We're staying at the Marriott Downtown. If this works for you, could you suggest a place within walking distance of that? If not, I am sure I'll be back this way at some point in the near future.**

> That would be lovely. How about we meet at Bridge 22? It's a very nice cocktail bar and restaurant on Boland Way that I think you'll find very walkable from your hotel. Shall we say 6 pm?

I told her that sounded great, and I looked forward to meeting her on Thursday. My head was reeling at the prospect. I'd never gone on a date like this before, and I had no idea what to expect. But it was about time for me to embrace life in this damn century. I'd been too much of a prude—too much of a believer that if there were a Miss Right for me, she'd simply pass right in front of me. The world didn't work that way anymore. Today, if you wanted something, you had to go out and find it.

Maybe this would work out. Maybe it wouldn't. But at least I'd be giving it a shot.

I had nearly finished my entrée and was well into my second glass of the Barbera when my phone chirped. It was JoAnn this time.

> Hey, kiddo. I decided to take you up on your offer and get some takeout. Would you kindly order me the Caesar salad and the Sausage Risotto?

Sure! Any dessert?

> Nope. That'll do it.

Got it. I'll put the order in now. I'm nearly finished. It shouldn't be long.

> I owe you big time. I'm in 1406.

See you shortly.

JoAnn answered her door on the first knock.

"Dear god, that smells great." She took the bag from me and waved me inside. "Let me get my wallet."

"Forget about it. This one's on me." She started to argue but I cut her off. "You've single-handedly taught me more about this job than I learned in all eight weeks in Wilmington at the training center. Popping for a meal is the least I can do to say thank you. Oh . . ." I held out the bottle of Barbera. "I saved you some of this, too. It's actually pretty good."

"Well, shit fire. I don't know whether to drink it or use it to make a poultice to wrap my knee."

61

"Hurts pretty bad tonight?"

"This weather isn't helping." She went into her bathroom and retrieved two plastic cups. "Have you seen the forecast for tomorrow?"

"No. And I'm now afraid to ask."

"Let's just say it's more of the damn same. And this time, it's gonna come packaged with forty mile per hour sustained winds and gusts up to sixty."

"Well, fuck a duck."

She poured us each a cup of the wine. I was reluctant to take it from her, but she insisted.

"I'm not pathetic enough to drink alone—at least not yet. I swore that if I ever reached that point, it'd be time to hang up my trainman's hat." She gestured toward a chair near the window. "Sit down."

I obeyed her and looked down at my shoes. They were pretty much trashed from two days of sloshing around in the snow. I'd be lucky if they dried out by morning. I should've been smart enough to pack an extra pair.

"Kick 'em off," JoAnn ordered. "No reason to sit there with wet feet."

"This has to be the worst part of the job," I complained, as I unlaced my shoes and set them near the heater in her room. "I hate having cold feet."

JoAnn gave me a sly smile. "Are we talking about your socks, or your upcoming SheDate encounter?"

"What makes you think I have a date?"

"Well, for one thing, your facial tic is gone."

"I have a facial tic?" I raised a hand to my cheek.

JoAnn made a happy moaning sound as she dug into her risotto. "Dear god, is this good."

"Yeah. I like the food there. It's consistent and the place isn't usually filled with Yale students."

"I'd think you'd get along well with them. I mean, since

you're a perpetual graduate student, yourself."

"I guess I'm a failure at that, too."

"What are we talking about now?"

I dug my phone out of my jacket pocket and held it up. "I did make a date to meet her tomorrow. Now I'm wondering if I made a mistake."

"Why?"

"I dunno. Doesn't it seem kind of . . . desperate to you?"

"No." JoAnn laughed bitterly. "*Desperate* is me thinking I could have a second career after ruining my marriage and both of my knees working for that goddamn airline. *Desperate* is hoping that every time I return home after a trip, I won't be going into an empty house." She pointed at the TV screen. Chris Hayes was talking about the way Donald Trump's team was gutting the leadership of the RNC. "*Desperate* is believing that my vote counts when we all know that orange anus is gonna be swept right back into office again. You going out on a blind date with someone you met through a phone app? That's not *desperate*. That's just a new operating procedure."

"I guess you're right." I felt embarrassed by my self-obsession. "Maybe I ought to be going out with you, instead, Jo," I suggested. "Think of the time we'd save not having to make small talk."

"Yeah. But at the end of the night, you'd expect me to put out—and that ship has sailed. The only thing I put out these days is the trash. Besides," she ate another large forkful of the risotto, "I could never have a relationship with another woman."

Even though I'd been joking when I'd quipped that Jo and I should go on a date, her stark dismissal of the idea stung a little bit.

"Ouch."

She looked up at me. "Don't misunderstand," she explained. "I don't say that because I find the idea of being with another woman repugnant. I don't. In fact, it makes good sense. But

63

women? Women are . . . *complicated*. They ask too many questions. They care too much about feeling and connection. Men? Men are simple. Stupid and simple. Men are *un-*complicated. Men care about three things: their dicks, their stomachs, and their hairlines—in that order. Men are *easy*—as long as you don't ask them for anything they don't have to give, which is just about anything. And at my stage in life? I don't need complicated. I need easy. Which is why I go home to an empty house."

"Come on, Jo. You can't be that much older than me."

"Like they say in the movies, kid—it ain't the years, it's the mileage."

I couldn't really think of a good comeback, so I didn't say anything. We sipped our wine in silence.

"So, tell me about your date. Where are you meeting up?"

"Some cocktail bar that she said was an easy walk from our hotel. Bridge 22?"

JoAnn choked on her wine.

"Shit. Are you okay?"

"Izzy . . ." JoAnn was still clearing her throat. "Bridge 22 is *in* the goddamn hotel."

I was dumbfounded. "Our hotel?"

"Yes, *our hotel*. Have you never been there?"

"I guess not." I closed my eyes in mortification. "*Je suis une idiote.*"

JoAnn narrowed her eyes in confusion.

"Sorry. I said I'm an idiot."

"I gathered that. What I don't understand is why this bothers you. It's a clear indication that your date thinks the two of you will probably have dessert upstairs. A classic booty call."

Dear god.

"Isn't that what you wanted?"

"I don't know. I thought it was. But now?" *What did I want?* I no longer knew. "Maybe I should pray the snow will keep piling up and prevent us from getting into Springfield before midnight."

"Yeah. I don't think so. The system is supposed to move out by tomorrow evening. So, unless you wanna do the decent thing—call her out for being the hound dog she obviously is, and bail with your integrity intact—it looks like you're stuck."

I sank down into my chair. "Why am I such a loser?"

"Tell you what. How about we arm you with a little insurance policy—your personal get out of jail free card?"

I was intrigued. "Say more."

"It's a thing we used to do back in the early airline days. When any of us had a blind date, we'd make arrangements in advance to have one of our crash pad roommates call us at the twenty minute mark. If the date was going great—no problem. They'd say goodbye and hang up. If the date was going south? Well, roommate would have an extreme emergency that gave us an excuse to get up and flee the scene. End of story."

"And that really worked?"

"All the time."

It was brilliant. "And you'd do that for me?"

"Of course. Paybacks—remember?"

"What'll you use as an emergency?"

"It's best not to plan those in advance. You don't want your reaction to be too rehearsed. It tends to have more authenticity if it's spontaneous."

I looked at her with gratitude.

"I guess we'll find out."

Jane and I exchanged a few more messages before our appointed meeting on Thursday evening.

Some of the anxiety I'd felt after my talk with JoAnn began to moderate a bit. Jane's texts were easy and unaffected. She

65

seemed genuine and personable. I did ask her about why she chose a bar in the hotel where I'd be staying, and she explained that it had been a practical consideration, since she'd be passing it when she left the hospital—and she thought I'd appreciate her humor when she told me she thought I'd find it "walkable."

I had to admit that, without JoAnn's suggestion about "dessert upstairs," it had been kind of funny. So, I chose to accept Jane's more innocent explanation.

Even with the annoying delays caused by the weather, I was only ten minutes late when I arrived at Bridge 22. I could see why JoAnn had laughed like hell when she realized I had no idea where the restaurant was. This was my first overnight in the newly renovated downtown Marriott. Previously, I'd stayed across the street at the Sheraton. The first thing I noticed when we arrived at the hotel was the wide open entrance to the restaurant—inside the lobby opposite the street door.

It would've been impossible to miss.

I felt awkward when I ascended the steps and waited for the hostess to greet me. She seemed preoccupied with a server and the bartender. They were trying to keep their voices down, but I could tell they were talking about a customer—a very difficult customer who was unhappy with . . . something. The bartender was holding some kind of martini in one hand and holding up three fingers with the other. "Third time," was all I could make out. I began to wonder if the drinks here were really as good as reported.

Finally, the hostess noticed me and hurried over.

"Hello," she said. "I am so sorry to have kept you waiting. You can take a seat anyplace—here at the bar or at one of the tables."

"Thanks, but I'm actually here to meet someone . . . for the first time. I think she may have left her name with you for when I arrived?"

"Oh. Sure." She quickly scanned a sheet of paper. She looked up at me before consulting the sheet a second time. "Um . . . are you Isabelle?"

I nodded. "That's me."

"Okay. Your party is seated in the Bonvoy Members Club. Follow me?"

We walked through the open space past a huge copper mural of a vintage motorcycle diagram to the private club room at the back. There were only a smattering of people inside, sunk into massive couches with deep seats. A few small tables ran along a side wall facing the entrance, and a dour-looking, white-haired woman wearing some kind of wool Pendleton creation in black and teal plaid sat there. I didn't notice until we reached her table that a small, transport wheelchair was discreetly stashed behind her.

Ohmyfuckinggod . . . it was J.S. Oliver—the harridan who'd terrorized business class on Sunday.

No. Way. It wasn't possible that this was Jane. There had to be some mistake . . . this woman had to be Jane's . . . mother? Grandmother? Eccentric great-aunt?

The hostess extended a flat hand to indicate that this was my party.

"Your server will be back soon," she said to the woman who was already fixing her with a disapproving glare. "Enjoy your evening," she said to me before gliding away. Her tone was tinged with just a hint of sarcasm.

I continued to stand there awkwardly. "Jane?" I finally asked. When she nodded I felt the floor give way beneath my feet. I'd been . . . what did they call it? *Catfished.*

Oh, Jesus Christ . . . It hadn't even been a full minute and I had nineteen more to wait until JoAnn called with my lifeline.

Nineteen minutes? It might as well have been a decade.

"Sit down, Isabelle." Jane's invitation was delivered with the authority of a drill sergeant ordering me to drop and give her fifty.

"It's . . . nice to meet you," I said, magnanimously.

"You don't look at all like your profile photo." Jane made the observation like she was delivering a terminal diagnosis.

"No . . . I . . . apologize for that. A friend of mine set up my profile for me and she selected it."

My explanation sounded lame as fuck. And why was *I* the one on the damn hot seat when Jane's profile photo *clearly* had been taken more than forty-five years ago? Make that fifty-five years ago.

Don't get me wrong. I wasn't an ageist—far from it. Jane's age wouldn't have been immediately disqualifying for me—but the extent of her full-scale deception was completely disarming. Well. That coupled with what I knew firsthand was her rude-as-fuck public persona.

The demoralized-looking server I had seen at the bar returned carrying another dark martini.

"I hope this one is more to your liking, ma'am," she said as she set the drink down in front of Jane.

"It had better be." Jane did not bother to thank her. "I am not used to having to send my drinks back three times."

"This time, the bartender used Yellow Chartreuse, as you requested." The server shifted her attention to me. "May I bring you something from the bar?"

"Um . . ." I hesitated, not sure I'd be there long enough to drink anything.

"She'll have the same." Jane took the liberty of ordering for me. When I looked at her in surprise, she explained, "It's a Doppelgänger—my signature cocktail. A martini made with whiskey instead of vodka."

I had to bite my tongue not to observe that she'd chosen well.

The server hurried off and I was, once again, left alone with my very first swipe right.

"So," I began belatedly, "you're a . . . doctor?"

"A hospitalist," she corrected. "It's not the same thing. Most people make that mistake. It's wearying to always have to explain the difference."

"I admit I had to look it up, myself."

"How long have you worked for the railroad?" She asked the question like she was demanding to know when I'd had my last period. It was clear that I'd been beneath her notice when we'd had our *tête-à-tête* on Sunday. She had zero recollection of meeting me previously.

"I . . . about twelve years."

"Do you find working on the actual trains . . . fulfilling?"

It felt like a trick question. It was clear to me that she'd had an answer in mind—and it probably wasn't that I liked being on the *actual* trains—which I assumed she saw as tantamount to flying coach on a cut-rate airline.

"Yes. I love it. It's the realization of a dream for me."

"A dream?" She sounded incredulous.

I nodded energetically. "It's a wonderful way to see the country . . . I mean, if you don't mind seeing towns from their bleakest aspects. I do wish USRail would place their stations in the higher rent districts, instead of always choosing desolate locations that look like they've been bombed. Don't you agree?"

She took a moment to reply. I couldn't tell if she knew I was being sarcastic, or whether she just thought I was an idiot with poor taste and low aspirations.

"Wholeheartedly," she finally declared.

The server arrived with my . . . *second* . . . Doppelgänger of the evening. I thanked her when she set it down. She gave me a look that said, "I am so sorry you're stuck here," before backing away.

I felt bad about the cocktail. As challenging as Jane was, I really didn't want to stick her with the tab. I figured I'd just drop a twenty on the table since I had no idea how much the drink cost. It seemed like a low price to pay for my ticket out of purgatory.

"So . . ." I took a sip of the cocktail. It was cloyingly sweet and herbaceous, all at the same time—like it couldn't commit to a single profile. Jane had chosen her signature drink well. "You said you just got back from a weekend, skiing in Stowe."

Her wizened chin went up. "Yes. That's true."

"Did you find it . . . challenging?"

She didn't seem to take my meaning. "Challenging? How so?"

"Well," I pointed at the space behind her, "with the wheelchair and all . . ." My cell phone rang—right on cue. I pulled it from my jacket pocket and looked at the screen. "My apologies. It's work. I have to take it." I answered the call. " Hello?"

"This is room service. Is everything to your liking?" JoAnn asked.

"No. Not at all," I replied. "It's good you called me."

"Ahhhhh," she intuited. "Ardor cools. And so quickly. So . . . it appears I have an emergency and need your help."

"My *god*—what happened?" I did my best to sound wholly engaged.

"Well, I decided there was nothing good on TV, so why not give myself a home perm? Problem is, I spilled activator all over my trousers, and they're rapidly turning into Capri pants. Can you rush right up here and lend me something to wear? I'm on the night shift."

It took every ounce of composure I possessed not to laugh out loud. I was going to kill JoAnn—right after I fell to my knees before her in gratitude.

"Oh. Of course I can." I looked at Jane apologetically. "Hold tight, I'll be right there!"

I hung up and immediately got to my feet.

"I'm terribly sorry, Jane. But a colleague is in crisis, and I have to rush upstairs to help her." I dug a twenty dollar bill out of my pocket and laid it on the table. "Thank you so much for meeting me here. It was . . . an education."

Jane sat there with her mouth gaping open.

When she finally spoke, her tone was frosty. "What on earth is going on?"

"It's an environmental emergency," I explained.

"And *your* assistance is required—how?"

"Oh. I neglected to tell you that I come from a long line of people with vast experience in chemical intervention."

"You mean *engineers?*" she asked, dryly.

"No." I pushed my chair in. "Dry cleaners."

I was sure some blistering rejoinder was imminent, so I quickly laid a patch escaping the rarified air of the Bonvoy Members Club.

Fuck you and the skis you rode in on, lady.

I practically sprinted to the elevators.

CHAPTER FOUR

*Fake Relationships—and why you
should never try one at home.*

I didn't see Dewey when I finally made it home. It was just as
well. I knew he'd want to hear about my trip, and I was too
exhausted to share all the gory details. And after the whole Jane
debacle I wanted nothing more than to retreat to my apartment
and binge watch reruns of *The Big Valley*.

Barbara Stanwyck always made me feel better. There was no
situation that Victoria Barkley couldn't manage—usually just by
staring down the upstart baddie *du jour* who thought he could
run roughshod over any of her "boys."

I felt ridiculous about what I'd taken to calling "The Jane
Incident."

Catfished.

By my first damn swipe right. What a loser I was! I had no
idea how I was going to tell Sofie. There'd be no way to avoid it.
She already knew I'd had a live one and would never rest until I
filled her in on how it went. I could already hear her cackling at
my misfortune. She'd never let me live this one down.

Fuck it. I'd do my best Scarlett O'Hara and worry about
that tomorrow. I knew I was free from having to obsess about
another call up for at least two days, so I turned my phone off

and left it in the kitchen overnight. The last thing I felt like doing was going on another fishing trip, SheDate style. In fact, I wasn't sure I even wanted to try again.

When I woke up, I was famished. I hadn't eaten anything for supper. It had been too late to think about cooking when I got home, and this time, the elevator had smelled like onion pizza—which either meant Mrs. Dahlby had had another late-night craving, or Aldo and Luz were on a Cujo stakeout and got the munchies. Either way, the smell killed my appetite. So, after showering, I decided to treat myself and head out for breakfast at the *J'aime* French Café on Pine Street.

Eating a *pain au chocolat* and washing it down with a large *macchiato* always made me forget my troubles.

I expected the café to be crowded on a Saturday morning, so I resolved to arrive promptly at eight when they opened because they only had a few tables, and I was determined to snag one. It was too cold to eat outside and most of the park was still covered with snow. Even though I arrived at 8:03, all the tables were already taken, and there was a long line at the counter.

Merde. Oh well . . . I could just order and take it back to the apartment. I figured I'd pick up a chocolate pretzel for Dewey, too—he was a sucker for them.

"Isabelle!"

I turned around, surprised that someone had called my name. It was Harper, seated at one of the small tables toward the back of the café. Predictably, she had a stack of folders on the chair beside her. She waved me over.

"Hi," I said after reaching her table. "I didn't expect to see you here."

"Are you kidding? I love this place. Are you going or staying?"

I looked around the crowded space. "Going, I guess."

"Why don't you join me?"

"Aren't you working? I don't want to bug you."

"Oh, no." She began collecting her folders. "Don't be silly.

Go get your stuff and come on back."

"Are you sure?"

"Go!" She fluttered her fingers at me.

I smiled and left her to place my order. By the time I returned to her table, she had packed up the papers she'd been going over. I felt guilty about intruding on her work and said as much. Again.

"Don't be ridiculous. I always bring paperwork or a book with me when I go someplace alone. It prevents people from feeling sorry for me."

"Why would anyone feel sorry for you?"

"If you have to ask, then the explanation will make me feel even worse than I already do."

I had a hard time imagining anyone with the name Harper Abramowicz *ever* felt unsure of herself. After meeting her on the elevator, I'd looked her up at the *Philadelphia Magazine* website. She was a senior editor and had responsibility for several departments at the publication.

"I don't think that makes you look *worse*. I think that makes you look . . . prepared."

"Prepared?" She thought about it. "I'll take that. It makes me sound like a Girl Scout."

"Isn't that their motto?"

"Beats the hell outta me. I got kicked out before we got to the motto part."

"You did?" That was an intriguing admission. "What for?"

She leaned across the small table and lowered her voice. "I stole two boxes of Tagalongs."

"Gasp." I pretended to be shocked. "I'm sharing a table with a felon?"

She laughed. "It wasn't that bad. We were selling cookies at a shopping center in King of Prussia. I chased after a kid who cried after his mother told him they couldn't afford them and gave him two boxes. I fully intended to pay the money back once

I got my allowance later that week. But our den mother was a real stickler, and I got bounced instead."

"Well, that story sucks."

"It was pretty Dickensian, I'll grant you."

"I always wanted to be a Girl Guide—or *Les Guides Catholiques du Canada*. But my father refused."

"Why?" She asked.

"I think it was the uniforms. He's always had an aversion for closed societies—an offshoot of his grandfather having lived in Belgium during the Nazi occupation. Of course, the uniform was the only reason I *wanted* to join." I smiled. "I've always had a thing for uniforms, too," I added.

"Really? I hadn't noticed."

"What about you?" I asked. "Any more felonies in your background?"

"Not yet."

"Did you grow up in King of Prussia?"

"Sadly, yes."

"Why sadly? It's pretty swanky, isn't it?"

"It was a lot of things. I suppose you could say swanky was one of them."

"Poor little rich girl?"

"Something like that."

"May I ask you something personal?"

Harper looked amused. "Sure."

"Why'd your parents name you Harper?"

"Oh. My mother was a big *To Kill a Mockingbird* fan."

I nodded. "I figured it was either Harper Lee or Rhoda . . ."

Harper laughed. Then her expression abruptly changed. She suddenly looked . . . *panicked.*

"What is it?" I asked with concern. "You look like you've seen a ghost."

"Pretty good guess." She threw her hand across the table and grabbed my hand with a desperate grip. "Please, please just go along with what's about to happen? *Please?* I'll explain later. I promise."

"Okay . . ." I said, warily.

She got to her feet just as two women approached our table.

"Harper!" One of them bellowed. "How are you, girl? It's great to see you."

The larger woman pulled Harper into a bear hug.

I heard Harper's muffled "I'm fine" against the puffy, salmon-colored North Face jacket her friend was wearing.

"It's awesome to run into you." The boisterous woman released Harper but still held on to her arms. "I was just saying to Nina that we should give you a call and try to get together." She looked at me and extended a hand. "Hi. I'm Gina."

Gina and Nina?

I wondered if they'd left the Santa Maria parked outside.

I took her hand and shook it. "I'm Izzy. Nice to meet you."

"And I'm terribly rude." Harper had recovered enough to finish introductions. She gestured at Gina's companion. "This is Nina, Gina's . . ."

"Squeeze." Gina put her arm around the more petite Nina and pulled her close.

"Nice to meet you, Nina."

"Likewise," Nina said in a waifish voice.

"So, Harper—you didn't tell me you were seeing someone new." Gina fist-bumped her. "Nice going, girl."

"Well . . ." Harper began.

"I'm the lucky one," I spoke up. "She put up quite a fight, but I persevered."

I didn't see Harper's expression, but I'm pretty sure she was baffled. But, hey? She begged me to play along so I was playing along.

"That's great!" Gina's eyes widened. "I just got a great idea. Why don't the four of us go out together?"

"Oh," Harper shot me a worried look. "I don't think . . ."

"*Come on.* It'll be *awesome.* Like old times!" It was clear that Gina was used to getting her way. "We've got extra tickets to the Flyers/Maple Leafs game tonight. Primo seats. *On the glass.* You two join us. It'll be a hoot. We can go out for beer and wings after." She squeezed her companion again. I expected to hear the snap of poor Nina's bones cracking. "Won't it be great, Nina?"

"It sure will, honey."

I had to strain to hear Nina's thin response.

"It's set, then," Gina declared. "We'll meet you out front at the Broad Street entrance—seven sharp."

"I don't know if . . ." Harper began.

"That sounds great," I said. "We'll be there."

"Fuckin' A!" Gina beamed at both of us. "See you tonight."

They wandered off to order god knows what—probably a couple of quiche Lorraines for Gina and a spring water for Nina—no ice.

When we retook our seats, Harper looked at me like I'd lost my mind.

"Care to explain to me what *that* was?" she demanded.

"You told me to go along with whatever happened. So, I went along."

"Oh, you more than went along—you took the wheel and drove us off a damn cliff."

"Hey—beggars *cannot* be choosers."

"What if I already had plans for tonight?"

"Do you?"

"That's beside the point." Harper sat slowly shaking her head. "Now we're stuck going to this goddamn hockey game."

"I'll admit I was praying we wouldn't get roped into doing anything with them. But then she mentioned the hockey game . . ."

"Do *not* tell me you're a Flyers fan . . ."

"Hell no."

"I didn't think so."

"I'm a Maple Leafs fan," I added.

77

"Excuse me?"

"Hello?" I pointed at my chest. *"Canadian."*

"Of course." Harper actually rolled her eyes. "Well. Now we're good and stuck. Unless you can come up with a sudden ailment." Her face brightened. "Maybe you'll get called out for a trip?"

"Gee, *thanks*. I just got back from a six-day jaunt. They won't be tapping me for at least two days."

"Fuck."

"Sorry to disappoint you."

"I'm sorry . . . It's not that. Gina has just always been a bully. I've never been able to stand up to her when it comes to something she wants. That's what led to our breakup."

"How long were you together?"

"I'm embarrassed to tell you." She met my eyes. "Eight years."

I was surprised. "That sounds like a lot of hockey games."

"You have no idea."

"If you don't mind my asking, how'd you meet?"

"I don't mind. I owe you an explanation after roping you in." She picked up her fork and poked at her last bit of spinach and feta *feuilleté*. "The magazine was doing a feature on the Flyers. I was on the writing staff then and, although I didn't do sports reporting, I got assigned the story. Part of my research involved going to several games and I met Gina there. She worked in marketing for the Wells Fargo Center and was very involved in sports promotion. She was instrumental in teaching me everything I needed to know about hockey to write about it credibly. I found her to be fun and vivacious. She lived life out loud—very unlike . . . well . . . everything I grew up with. We eventually started dating, and the rest is history."

"Any idea when she started seeing Nina?"

Harper shook her head. "But I think a while ago. Nina works for Wells Fargo, too. I think they're actually a good fit. Gina needs to be in charge, and Nina lets her be."

"It's a good division of labor, I guess." I was curious about something else. "You said Gina was unlike what you'd grown up with."

"Yes. She was."

"So, does that mean she was your first relationship?"

Harper gave me a half smile. "Gina was my first *girlfriend*. Yes."

"Late bloomer?"

"You might say that."

"Compared to you, I was an upstart."

"Oh?"

I nodded energetically. "I had my first girlfriend at age nine."

"*Nine?*"

"Uh huh. Marie-Denise. She was a friend of my sister, Zoé's. Marie-Denise was a figure skater at John Rennie High School in Pointe Claire and competed in competitions across Canada. Of course, *she* never knew we were girlfriends—but *I knew*. And after my first, great love, I never looked back."

"Very inspiring."

"I thought so, too."

"Apart from the hockey inducement, what led you to agree so readily to the date tonight?"

"It's embarrassing to admit, but I had nothing planned. I was just going to go to the Film Center on Chestnut Street and watch an old classic."

"Really?" Harper sounded genuinely interested. "What're they showing?"

"*Die! Die! My Darling!*"

"Seriously?"

I nodded.

"Have you ever … um … *seen* it?" Harper asked.

"Of course. About six times."

"And you're going again … *why?*"

"It's a classic."

"It's *old*. I'll grant you that. But I wouldn't call it a *classic*."

"It's Tallulah Bankhead."

"In what is arguably one of her worst roles."

I sulked for at least an entire twenty seconds. "Okay," I admitted. "You busted me. It's because Stefani Powers is really hot in it."

"I kind of suspected."

"I never said I wasn't shallow."

"As much as you seem to love this movie, have you ever seen the Charles Busch drag version of it?"

I was stunned. *There was a drag version of* Die! Die! My Darling! *and I didn't know about it?*

"No? For real?"

"For real. Yes. It's called, *Die, Mommie, Die*. Look for it. I am sure it's streaming someplace."

"Somebody up there hates me."

"Well, now I don't feel as badly as I did. If I can prevent you from wasting another two hours' worth of gray matter watching a supremely indifferent movie, I'll consider the evening a success."

"Oh, I see. And watching twelve grown men on ice skates slap the shit out of each other is a more refined use of my gray matter?"

"Well ..."

"I thought as much."

"The least I can do is drive. Meet me in the lobby at six fifteen?"

"Can't we just take the bus?"

"We could. But I haven't taken my car out in a month, and I need to run it before the oil coagulates."

"Okay." I smiled at her. "It's a date."

Dewey was all smiles when I handed him his chocolate pretzel.

"Well, you sure know the way to my cold, dead heart." He held the bag up to his nose and inhaled like I'd just handed him his weight in white truffles.

"I figured you could eat it on your break."

"Which," he looked at his watch, "commences right now. Come with me and get a cup of coffee."

I had nothing else to do—at least not until six fifteen—so I followed him to the tiny office behind the welcome desk.

"Take a seat." He gestured toward one of the battered chairs. "Want some?" He held up the ancient staff coffee pot. The prehistoric contraption had been around since my father lived here.

I shook my head. "When are you gonna replace that thing? I swear it browns out the building every time you turn it on."

"You are just like the rest of your generation. You don't throw things out just because they're *old*. This unit still works *fine*. And, P.S., it makes great coffee."

"Dewey," I pointed at the handle, "it's held together with duct tape."

"And my ass is held together with Advil and bailing twine. You wanna throw me out, too?"

"Of course not." I thought about my impending faux date with Harper. "You're a classic."

He poured his mug of coffee and, after adding four packs of sugar, sat down facing me.

"How was your ride on the Zephyr?"

"Still rocking and rolling. The snow sucked, but we managed."

"Uh huh. See any action along the way?"

"We had a ground stop because some enterprising beavers were landscaping with cottonwood trees. Apart from that, it was pretty uneventful."

He looked at me with wonder. "I was asking about *action*—not beavers." He chuckled. "At least not the kind that eat trees."

"Meaning?"

81

"Meaning . . . did your little forays on that dating app net any fish?"

"Unfortunately, yes."

He was in mid-bite but stopped short. "Unfortunately?"

"Oh, yeah. I met someone. And it didn't work out—which, believe me, is an understatement."

"What the hell happened?"

I threw up my hands. "Beats the hell outta me. I did my diligence. I read all the profiles very carefully looking for anything suspicious or off kilter. And this one woman sounded . . . normal. I mean, she had zero creep factor. So, we agreed to meet for drinks in Springfield, where I had an overnight."

"And what happened?"

"For starters, she picked a bar located downstairs in my hotel."

Dewey chuckled. "Pretty good economy in that. No cab fare."

I gave him a withering look. "I had never stayed in that hotel before, so I had no idea where the bar was when she suggested it."

"But she knew where you were staying?"

"Of course. I asked her to pick a place within walking distance."

"So . . . you met her and?"

"And . . . she wasn't what I thought."

"Meaning you didn't find her attractive?"

"No. Meaning she wasn't at all like she presented in her profile."

"Well, that ain't uncommon. Didn't you say Sofie picked an older photo of you to use?"

"Yes. But my photo wasn't thirty-five years old."

"Whoa." Dewey was genuinely taken aback. "She was thirty-five years older than you thought?"

"No. She was thirty-five years older than Methuselah."

"Damn."

"And that wasn't the worst part. I'd already had a bad interaction with her two days earlier on the damn train. She'd been a passenger—one of those castrating, high-maintenance, creature of privilege types. She complained nonstop about everything from the moment she got on until we lowered her wheelchair to the station platform in Springfield."

Dewey held up a long index finger. "Did you just say *wheelchair?*"

I nodded. "You heard me correctly. And that would've been no problem if she hadn't just bragged about spending the previous weekend skiing in Stowe."

"Hot damn, girl. When you fuck up, you don't mess around."

"Hey." I took umbrage at his assessment of the situation. "In what way was this *my* fuck up?"

"Maybe you should've taken more time to talk with her—get to know her a bit better before jumping at the first opportunity to get jiggy with her."

"*Jiggy?* I'm not even going to dignify that with a response."

"You said you'd already met her earlier—on the train. That happened, and you didn't know who she was?"

"Hell no. If I had, I would never have agreed to meet her for drinks, believe me."

"Because she was a fossil *and* a bitch?"

"Not just that. She also lied about everything on her profile. And posted all those misleading photos. I don't even know if they were actually pictures of her. They could've been pulled off the Internet. Or they could've been pictures of her granddaughter."

"That would've been damn creepy."

"No kidding."

"Well." Dewey reached into his inside coat pocket and withdrew a small notebook. And a scrap of worn-down pencil. "We can definitely mark this one off."

I was confused. "This one ... what?"

"This trope. You done blown right through it—so no need to reinvent the wheel." He was busy writing something down.

"Do I even want to know what you're talking about?"

"Tropes. You know . . . we talked about them at book club."

Book club? All I remembered discussing at book club were some rather eclectic door hangers . . .

"I don't remember anything about tropes."

"Then allow me to enlighten you." He tapped his pencil on the notebook. "Romance is all about tropes—the types of relationships and situations the stories follow. There are a lot of them—and most of the books fall into one category or another."

I wasn't sure I liked the direction of this conversation. I didn't want my love life—or potential love life—to follow some foreordained script.

"You mean every one of those books you read follows one of these plots?"

He nodded. "They all have different details, though. In one, the main character might be a corporate big shot. In the next, she might be a brain surgeon or a secret agent—or even a train conductor. But the point is that everybody is looking for love within the rules of one or other of the tropes."

What the hell was Dewey saying? That my life—that all of our lives—were lived in adherence to some kind of overused literary device?

"Well, that idea sucks out loud." I didn't try to hide my consternation. "Talk about life imitates art."

"Where do you think all the great ideas come from? Watching the world around you. Ain't that what your whole damn Ph.D. is about? Mimicking?"

"*Mimicry,*" I corrected him. "Biomimicry to be exact."

"Same shit, different trope, is what I say."

Dewey was right. He was right in boldfaced, italicized, *and* underlined all caps. Life and romance—especially romance— *did* mimic art . . . *even if these pulpy books* were *an example of the art being imitated.*

Hell. Whatever extension of art they formed, these tales were part of the narrative literature of sapphic culture. *My culture.*

And I'd just been blindsided by the fact that I—a woman who was wholly enmeshed in studying the ways nature can improve and enhance the human relationship to the physical world—had missed one of the biggest clues of all. I'd become a walking *trope.* A mobile science experiment. And the worst part?

I didn't really care.

"What are you thinking about?" Dewey asked. "You look like your hamster just died."

"Not my hamster. My delusions."

"They ain't nothing wrong with looking for love. We all do it—even when we lie and say we aren't. And who cares if the paths we take to get there are already worn down by the feet of a thousand other travelers? That's just the way things are. Now," he held up his tiny notebook and pencil, "let's start your checkoff list."

"Seriously? You're going to graph my failed relationships?"

"Did I say graph? We're not making a damn graph. We're making a list. Let's see what we've got so far. Okay. Tonya. How would you characterize that one?"

"A complete lapse in judgment?"

"I'd be the last person to argue with you about that. But you have to look more broadly. How'd you meet her?"

"At work." I shrugged. "She was a dispatcher. We met when I first went on the board."

"Okay. There you go." He made a note. "*Office Romance.* Done."

"Office romance is a trope?"

Dewey huffed. "A *big* goddamn trope. Okay. Now . . . this lying catfish you just met in Springfield. You really outdid yourself on this one. You got yourself a bona fide double truck."

"What's that supposed to mean?"

"She was a two-fer. That means we can knock off *Age Gap* and *Fake Identity*." He wrote the items down. "At this rate, you're gonna blow through the whole damn lexicon at light speed."

"Very funny." I thought again about my date with Harper. If every kind of foray into relationships with women fell into one of these categories, which category did pretending to be Harper's girlfriend fall into? I watched Dewey make his notes while I deliberated.

Did I want to tell him?

On the other hand, why not tell him? It's not like he wouldn't find out. Dewey knew everything that happened in this building—and in most cases, predicted it before it occurred. He was like the reigning Sybil of Hopkinson House.

"So, I have this thing happening tonight . . ." I began.

He looked at me—*through* me, was more like it—while he waited for me to continue.

"I ran into Harper at *J'aime,* and we shared a table. Her ex, Gina showed up—with her new girlfriend in tow."

"Uh oh. Did Harper freak out?"

"Not exactly. But it was clear she was agitated. She begged me to go along with her pretense that we were a couple. I guess she didn't want Gina to think she was alone?"

"Not surprising. That was a hard breakup for her. Your first is always tough."

"Breakup?"

"First girlfriend." He made a note. "*Toaster Oven.*"

"Isn't this supposed to be *my* list?"

"You're tangentially involved, so it counts."

"Whatever. So, Gina invited us to go on a double date."

"And Harper said no?"

"Not exactly. I kind of spoke up first and said we'd love to."

"Say what?" Dewey sat back in his chair and picked up his mug of coffee as if he were readying himself for a longer explanation.

I waved a hand through the space between us. "What else was I supposed to do? Gina was being so brutishly insistent—totally oblivious to the fact she was making Harper miserable. So, I thought I could save Harper the obvious—and in my view, ill-founded—humiliation she was feeling, and accept."

Dewey was shaking his head. "I can imagine what Harper said about that."

"Can you?"

"Let's see . . . she told you to stay in your own damn lane?"

"Words to that effect. What she actually said was that I'd taken the wheel and driven the car off a cliff."

Dewey laughed. "I do love me some Harper."

"No doubt."

"So, when's this 'date'?"

"Tonight."

"*Tonight?* Damn, Lebrun. No flies on you."

"I did not pick the night nor the venue. Gina did. In fact, I begin to wonder if Gina also controls the tides."

"She *is* one bossy-ass jock. What's this date? *Wait.* Don't tell me . . . you're going to a hockey game."

My eyes widened. "How the hell did you guess that?"

"Deductive reasoning. Gina works for the Wells Fargo Center. The Flyers are playing the Maple Leafs tonight. Ain't no way in hell she'd miss that match. The Vegas odds are plus 115."

I looked at him in wonder. "Do you *ever* sleep, man?"

"So, you and Harper are going out with Gina and Skeletor—and you'll have to spend the entire night being all lovey-dovey. Make sure you buy her one of those Choco Tacos. She loves that shit."

"Okay, wise guy." I pointed at his notepad. "How are you gonna mark this one down?"

"Easy." He wielded his pencil with a flourish. "*Fake Relationship.* Check." He did a rapid calculation before looking up at me. "*Five.* Damn, girl. At this rate, you'll blow through the

87

teens by the end of the weekend."

For some reason, Dewey's use of the term "fake relationship'" bugged me. Even though I knew I wasn't going out on a real date with Harper, calling it "fake" felt . . . disappointing.

"I do have one question for you," I told him.

"Shoot."

"What happens if you get lucky and find the right one? You know . . . the one that doesn't make you want to change your identity and go into hiding."

"Well, that's easy." He closed the notebook and stuffed it back into his pocket. "You put a damn ring on it and throw the list away."

I met Harper in the lobby at six fifteen, just like we'd planned. I kind of thought I might run into her at the elevators, but instead, shared the ride down with Aldo and Luz, who were hot on the trail of a new infraction in the Cujo saga.

"Did you hear about what happened on sixteen?" Aldo asked me. The excitement in his voice was almost tangible.

I said I had not.

He held up a mangled object. It looked like someone had tried to run a Christmas wreath through a shredder. "Mrs. Christakos in 1612 opened her door this morning and found this in the middle of the hallway." He showed it to me before glancing at Luz, who was cleaning her thumbnail with a bent paperclip. "Luz noticed that the blue and white ribbons were all in shreds."

Luz nodded. "Mrs. Christakos thinks it was a hate crime. Me 'n Aldo know it was Cujo. Those ribbons hanging down were how he got hold of it to pull it off her door."

I was confused by this new hate crime thesis. "I thought he was only interested in sports footwear."

"Could be he's getting bolder—going for more high-value targets."

"Christmas wreaths are more high value than golf shoes?" I asked.

"It's about *volume*," Luz explained. "Try counting the number of wreaths you see when you walk down any one of the hallways in this building. This could turn into an epidemic."

"I suppose that's true." I nodded in agreement. "Although it might spell record profits for Hobby Lobby."

Aldo looked like someone had turned on the lights. "I didn't think about that angle." He nudged Luz. "Maybe this Cujo is all tied up with those Christo-fascists. They don't want any Christmas decorations that ain't traditional . . . you know . . . all red and green like they were in Jesus's time."

"Jesus didn't have Christmas decorations, you moron."

Aldo was clearly offended by Luz's comment. "Well then, how do you explain that every damn thing associated with Christmas is always red and green?"

Luz looked at me for help.

"I think it's related to the woven crown of holly branches Jesus wore at the crucifixion," I explained. "Green leaves and red berries—representing everlasting life and the blood of Christ."

Aldo looked at me with wonder. "Well, damn. You sure do know a lot about Jesus."

"What is twelve years of Catholic school?" I said it as if it were a daily-double *Jeopardy!* question.

"Well, me'n Luz think Dewey needs to tell people to take in their Christmas wreaths at night."

"He ain't gonna do it, Aldo." Luz looked at me. "Dewey doesn't want to stir the pot."

Aldo nodded. "He's real conservative that way."

Mercifully, we'd reached the lobby and the doors opened. I saw Harper right away, standing at the desk talking with Dewey.

"Good luck," I said. "I hope you catch him."

I waved at Harper, and she excused herself from Dewey and walked over to meet me. Behind her, Aldo and Luz were making a beeline for Dewey—intending, for sure, to show him what was left of Mrs. Christakos's eviscerated wreath. I could tell by his body language that Dewey was already gearing up for this latest installment of *Tales from the Crypt*.

"Ready to meet your fate?" Harper asked.

"As I'll ever be." I took in her ensemble. She looked . . . nice. Jeans and a black V-neck knit sweater. She smelled good, too. Like . . . nutmeg and ginger cookies. It was a fresh, holiday kind of scent. Not too cloying. Just right. "You smell good," I said, before I could think better of it.

Oh, great one, Lebrun. Really smooth.

Harper seemed amused by my observation. "Thanks. I wanted something that had a shot at standing up to the aroma of five thousand Campo's cheese steaks."

"God. Will we have to burn our clothes?"

"Probably. That's why I wore this ancient sweater."

"It doesn't look ancient. It looks brand new."

"I have good load sense," she explained. "It's why I'm always in the laundry room."

"It is?"

"Small loads means many trips. I try not to mix fabrics or colors."

"You're way ahead of me. I mix everything." I held the door to the parking garage open for her. "Especially metaphors."

She laughed. It was a silvery sound. It seemed right for the season, too.

I was thinking about my conversation with Aldo and Luz. "Are you Jewish?" I asked.

She looked at me with a puzzled expression.

"Sorry," I explained. "The boys were telling me about some wanton destruction of a Christmas wreath on sixteen."

"I heard about that," she said. "I ran into Mrs. Christakos in the mailroom. She was pretty pissed. She said that wreath cost her seventy-five bucks."

"Hobby Lobby?"

"Amazon."

"Oh." I wondered if I needed to amend the Christo-fascist theory the next time I ran into the duo. I'd have hated to have them going down the wrong rabbit hole in their investigation of Cujo's motivation to wreak such wanton destruction.

"Yes," Harper declared.

"Yes?"

"The answer to your question. Yes, I'm Jewish." She laughed. "With a last name like Abramowicz, I wonder why you had to ask."

"It was an academic question, really. Apropos of Christmas wreaths."

"Well, I have one of those, too. I just don't have it out yet. It's too early."

"You do?"

"Sure. I come from a little-known subset of Ashkenazim— or what my father lovingly calls 'ham-eating Jews.' We aren't . . . fussy about traditions. At least, not in private. In public, however, it's a different story. They all toe the line to protect the family business."

"It's great when your faith doesn't get in the way of the finer things in life."

"You mean like scrapple?"

"Spurious pork products were exactly what I had in mind."

"This is me." Harper aimed her key fob at a sleek little BMW. Its lights flashed and the doors unlocked.

"Nice ride." I was impressed. My own car was a beater diesel Peugeot that was a family hand-me-down. I inherited it from my sister, Zoé, before she landed the high-dollar insurance gig and needed to impress clients with a quieter conveyance. The Peugeot smoked and rattled like a Parisian cab—which it actually had been in a previous life. The thing now had more than 227,000 miles on it and was "just getting broken in"—according to our father, who'd acquired the car from a colleague who'd had it shipped to Montréal from France in 1999.

"It's just a car," Harper said as we climbed in. "I get a constant ration of shit from my brothers because I have no respect for machines that, in my view, only exist to serve us."

"Yeah? Well, I don't think my car got that 'serve us' memo. It drinks oil and only runs on odd-numbered days—except for leap years."

"What happens during leap years?"

"It doesn't run at all."

"Why don't you replace it?" We were exiting the parking garage and turning onto 6th Street.

"I'm not home enough to really even need it. I mostly use SEPTA to get around town."

"I guess that makes sense."

We rode along in silence for a couple of minutes. Then we both began speaking at the same time.

"Sorry," I blurted. "You go first."

"No—I interrupted you. Please. What were you going to say?"

"Well. I was wondering . . . if we needed to, maybe, rehearse anything for tonight?"

Harper looked over at me with a surprised expression. "I was going to ask the same thing."

"So, maybe we should? I mean—at least invent a story about how we met and when we started dating? That kind of thing."

"Agreed."

"Do you have any thoughts?" I asked.

"I suppose we could say we met in the building?"

"That makes sense," I agreed. "In the laundry room—while you were down there monopolizing half the machines with your tiny loads?"

She smiled. "That could work."

"Love in the rinse cycle," I quipped.

"For me, it would have to be love in the optional *second* rinse cycle."

"Boy, you really are hardcore, aren't you?"

"I don't fuck around when it comes to laundry."

I was tempted to say I didn't fuck around at all—especially not lately. But it seemed too soon in our friendship to share intimate details like that.

"Okay. Laundry room it is. When did we start dating?"

"Six months ago? That sounds long enough to be serious but short enough to cover us for any gaffes."

"Gaffes?"

"Sure. Like the fact that we know nothing about each other's families—apart from the fact that I know you have a sister named Zoé who sells insurance, and you know I grew up in King of Prussia and have brothers."

"How many brothers?" I asked.

"Two. Peter and Jacob. Both younger. Both assholes."

"What kind of work do they do?"

"They both work for our father—like all good Jewish boys." She looked at me. "One guess what the family business is."

"Um . . ." I pretended to give it deep thought. "Hat blocking?"

Harper laughed so hard she nearly ran the car off the road. "Close. What's your second guess."

"Some kind of finance? I was going to say diamond merchants, but that seemed too . . ."

"Culturally insensitive?"

"Well, yes. But I was intentionally going for obvious stereotypes—which I suppose is even more culturally insensitive."

"You might say that."

"Okay. I give up. What's the family business?"

"We design and install custom halachic mikvah spas."

Okay. I'd never heard of that one before.

"What's a . . . mikvah spa?"

"It's a ritual bath—very important in orthodox Judaism. Women make use of ritual baths each month, seven days after their menses. It's a ritual to restore purity."

"No kidding?"

"Nope. It also means the husband can hit it again—once all the woman's business parts have been purified after her failure to become pregnant."

"Damn. Talk about no respect for the machines that serve you."

"See why I told you I'm not religious?"

"This seems like a very specialized market."

"Oh, it is. But you'd be amazed at the number of people with enough money to invest in these. And to be fair, the prep work to install one isn't that much more than the cost of putting a hot tub inside your bathroom."

"Good to know. I mean, you never know when you're going to feel good and dirty."

"Opinions on that might vary."

"True." I considered her response. "Think we might need one after the hockey game?"

"Count on it."

We reached the Broad Street entrance to Wells Fargo Arena and began looking for a place to park. We were early enough that it didn't take long. I spotted Gina and Nina right away.

Correction. I spotted someone right away who turned out to be Gina.

"What the serious fuck is that?" I whispered to Harper as we got closer to the entrance where dozens of people were milling about.

"What?" Harper asked.

"That clown-person over there. The one with the . . . orange and black face and the matching two-tone wig."

"You mean Gina?"

I did a double-take. *Dear god* . . . it *was* Gina. I looked at Harper in horror. "She's a . . ."

"Face painter?"

I was too stunned to speak, so I just nodded stupidly.

"See why I didn't want to come?"

"*You* dated a face painter." It was a statement of fact—not a question.

"Hey . . . in fairness, I did *not* know this about her when we met. It was summertime."

"How soon afterward did you find out?"

"Fuck you. Let's just get this over with." Harper grabbed my hand and led me toward her ex and poor, waifish Nina.

"There you are!" Gina bellowed "Like my getup? It's called The Full Gritty."

"Gritty is the Flyers mascot," Harper explained.

"Some of those jokers inside would pay upwards of a hundred bucks to get made up like this. I can do it myself for free. Isn't that right, Nina?"

Whatever Nina replied was swallowed up by the crowd noise, which gained in intensity as we stepped inside the massive arena.

Gina noticed my outfit—blue jeans and a blue- and white-striped sweater.

"I see you're wearing your team colors."

To be fair, I hadn't really thought about it. The sweater just happened to be one of the clean ones on the top of the pile.

"Oh. Yeah," I replied. "I guess so. But I'm actually from Québec, not Ontario. It would be tantamount to heresy in my family to support the Maple Leafs over the Canadiens."

"Well, you might want to keep your jacket on, so you don't end up with a quart of mustard on your head. Sometimes when the fans get pissed, they start throwing shit—like pretzels."

I looked at Harper with surprise. "I didn't realize I needed hazardous duty pay for this date."

"One time," Gina continued, "I got nailed by some asshole's prosthetic leg. Can you believe that? He got so mad he took off his fucking leg and threw it at the ice."

"My god. Did he get it back?"

"Not from me," Gina scoffed. "I finished the job for him and hurled it the final ten feet. Those jackoffs were playing like shit."

"Note to self: keep jacket on." I heard Harper stifle a laugh.

It took us fifteen minutes to make our way to our seats which were, as Nina had promised, at center ice on the glass.

"You'll see the real shit good and up close here," she told me. "Hope you're not squeamish when you see blood."

I turned toward Harper who was busy pulling something out of her bag. It looked like . . . a book.

"What the hell is that?" I whispered.

She showed it to me.

Anna Karenina.

"You have *got* to be joking. You brought a Tolstoy novel to a hockey game?"

"Well . . ."

"Well, what? If I have to watch this shit, so do you."

"But I *always* read at these games."

"Nuh uh. You do *not* get to retreat to some salon in Imperial Russia and fantasize about getting hit by a train to end your torment. That's *my* gig." I shoved the book back into her bag. "We're stuck in this little costume drama together." I took hold of her hand. "Aren't we . . . *dear?*"

Out of the corner of my eye, I saw Gina nudge Nina. "Look at those two, honey," she gushed. "They're just like us."

It was then I wondered if Anna could find us *two* trains.

By the end of the second period, I was really beginning to feel queasy.

I'd never seen so many smashed faces up close. The glass separating us from the ice was smudged like a filthy windshield and smeared with blood. At one point, I was sure I saw a bicuspid sail past my ear. After about the sixth time five faces were plastered together against the glass in front of us—displaying an unhappy array of broken teeth and bad bridgework—I leaned over to Harper and whispered, "Too bad neither of us are dentists. We could tape our cards against the inside of the glass."

She slapped me on the arm and hissed, "*Behave.* This is hard enough as it is."

Every time the Flyers missed a shot or failed to block one, Gina would roar to her feet and scream abuse at the team.

She wasn't alone in those expressions of frustration and disappointment. The crowd behind us wasn't very pleased with the performance of the home team, either. I'd never heard such crude expressions of disgust delivered at ear-splitting decibels. And Gina hadn't been kidding about the pretzels. I saw more than a baker's dozen of them soaring over us. There were so many game stoppages to clear the ice of debris the referees finally slapped the Flyers with two delay of game penalties.

Of course, Gina had nothing but contempt for the officials for *that* indignity.

At one point, between periods, she and Nina headed for the concession stands for more beer. Harper took advantage of the break to apologize profusely for the experience.

"I am embarrassed and humiliated about subjecting you to this classless and shameful display."

"It's okay," I assured her. "I'm Canadian. I grew up going to bad hockey games."

"I meant Gina."

"Oh." I smiled at her. "Yeah. You might owe me one."

"Only one? You're letting me off easy."

"Truthfully? This is the best fake date I've had in . . . well. Longer than I can remember."

Harper looked dubious. "The best? I'd hate to know what the worst was."

"Oh. That's easy. It just happened on Thursday night in Springfield."

"Interesting. Care to share?"

"Maybe later, when we're not surrounded by 18,000 angry drunks."

"Deal." Harper clearly had something else on her mind. "Listen. We do not have to go out with those two after the game. I can plead a brain bleed or something so we can make a quick escape as soon as this thing is over."

"Okay. That works for me. I mean . . . *not* the part where you have a brain bleed—but the part about not spending any more time with The Full Gritty would be welcome respite."

"It's the least I can do. I promise I'll have you safely back home by nine forty-five at the latest."

"Well, you haven't eaten anything since we got here. Do you want me to go and get you something?"

"No. I'm fine."

"Not even a Choco Taco? I teased.

She looked surprised. "Who told you I liked those?"

"One guess."

"Dewey." Harper sighed. "That man never stops."

"Fact."

"I think I'd rather grab something guaranteed not to kill me later at home."

"Okay." I became aware of a nagging sense of disappointment. The prospect of sitting down with Harper for a quiet bite to eat—with the operative word being *quiet*—had really appealed to me. But she seemed set on escaping the arena and heading straight home. I stole a look at her. She caught me and I quickly dropped my eyes.

"What?" she asked.

"It's nothing."

98

"I recognize that look. It's not nothing. What were you thinking?"

"I was . . . well. When you said we could ditch out as soon as the game ended, I thought it might be nice to go and get dinner someplace quiet. You know . . . take some time to detox from prolonged exposure to this profane, stentorian rabble."

"*Stentorian?*"

"Hey . . . you aren't the only one who reads Tolstoy."

"Right."

"So? Bad idea? It's okay if you're too tired."

"No. On the contrary. I think it's a great idea. I was just trying to think of a good place to go."

I brightened up at once. "Do you like Asian food?"

"I'm Jewish. What do you think?"

"Ever been to Miss Saigon?"

"On Walnut Street?"

I nodded.

"I love that place. Do you think we can get in?"

"Let me call right now and see if I can get us a table. I know one of the owners—he used to ride the metro from D.C. every day when they were working on opening the place."

Harper waited while I placed the call. I was in luck, and Choung was in the restaurant. He said it was tight, but he could squeeze us in *if* we could get there by eight forty-five. When I told Harper, she said no problem—we'd make our escape early.

"Just roll with it when they get back," she said.

Gina and Nina returned, loaded down with enough food to feed everyone in the first four rows. For the life of me, I had no idea how she thought they'd be ready to go out for wings and beer after the game. Correction: more beer. By my count, Gina had already downed at least six.

Of course, two of those had ended up hurled at the ice, so I suppose she was still running a deficit . . .

About five minutes into the third period, Harper began to

complain about having a headache. She moved closer to me and tucked her head beneath my chin.

"Take me home, baby," she cooed. "I need to lie down."

I belatedly put my arm around her.

"What's the matter pumpkin? Are you sick?"

She nodded. I realized that she hadn't been lying about her perfume. It really did stand up well against the total sensory onslaught of Gina's steak sandwiches.

"Don't worry, love muffin," I assured her. "I'll take you home."

Of course, Gina had been oblivious to Harper's plight—but Nina noticed and poked her companion in the ribs with a bony elbow. She pointed at the two of us, huddled together in our seats.

"What's wrong?" Gina demanded. "Is she sick?"

"I think so." I pulled Harper closer. "She wants to go home." I looked down at Harper. "Don't you, poodle?"

"Well that sucks out loud." She peered closely at Harper. "Did you eat one of those Mission burritos?" She looked at me. "Those things always cramp her up."

"*No*," Harper muttered. "I have a splitting headache. I need to go lie down."

"Come on, kumquat." I helped Harper stand up. "Let's get you to the car."

"Hey, give me a call if you still want to meet up with us later, okay?"

I couldn't tell if Gina was truly magnanimous or simply a colossal prick. Either way, it was impossible to imagine that she'd been Harper's girlfriend. Correction. Her first girlfriend.

"Will do," I assured her. "Thanks for the evening. It was a . . . blast."

"Yes," Harper added in a small voice. "It was good to see you both."

"Bye, Harper." It was the first thing I'd heard Nina say out loud. "I hope you feel better."

In that moment, I wanted to grab Nina and take her with us. I wondered if she were suffering from Stockholm syndrome. She had all the earmarks of a hostage.

We were about five rows away when someone screamed, "PIPE!" and everyone ducked. I looked to my left quickly enough to catch a glimpse of something that resembled a muffler hurtling toward the penalty box.

Who the fuck were these people?

And how the hell did you smuggle a goddamn muffler into a place like this?

"What was that?" Harper asked when we regained our feet.

"I think it was a muffler."

"Like a scarf?" she asked.

"No. A *muffler*—as in that thing that goes beneath your car and terminates at the tail pipe."

"Someone threw a muffler at the ice?"

"It appears so." We were finally nearing the exit.

"So much for the Midas touch," she quipped.

I wanted to hug her.

We'd been at our table for less than ten minutes and were already halfway through our cocktails. Harper ordered a sparkling Negroni, and I went for a barrel-aged Manhattan.

I took the liberty of ordering our second round as soon as the server set the first drinks on the table. I noticed that Harper didn't argue with me.

"Before we go any further . . . I do need to ask you about something."

"Shoot," I said.

"Pumpkin? Kumquat? *Love muffin?*"

I shrugged. "I was improvising. You know . . . like Brando."

"You mean method acting?"

"Right."

"Well, for the record—it doesn't work very well for you."

"Story of my life. See why I went into conducting?"

"Moving right along . . ." she sat back against her chair and regarded me. The red and gold light cast by the basketed globes above us gave the scene a theatrical flair. It was like stage lighting, carefully crafted for use on a reduced scale—perfect for intimate conversations. "So. Which one of us gets to go first?"

"Go first about what?" I asked.

"Worst—and best—dates. You said you'd dish once we got to someplace quiet. We're in someplace quiet. And I know I probably owe you a gazillion explanations for how I ended up in a relationship with Gina—and worse, why I stayed in one for so long. So . . . I reiterate—which one of us goes first?"

"Wanna flip for it?"

"Okay. What are we gonna flip?"

"Um." I looked around. "Hold on a second."

I got up and walked to the bar. When I returned, I had the perfect thing. I held it out to Harper.

"Here you go."

She looked the bottlecap over. "Lucky Buddha Beer?"

I nodded.

"Pretty inspired." She held the bottlecap up. "Buddha is heads, back of Buddha is tails. What's your call?"

"Heads."

She flipped the cap expertly and slapped it down on the table.

It was tails.

"Tsk, tsk, tsk. I win." Harper propped her elbow on the table and rested her chin on the back of her hand. "Go ahead. I'm all ears."

I drained my cocktail. "Sure, you are."

"Let me help realign your stream of consciousness. You said the worst date of your life was on Thursday night in Springfield?"

I nodded. "Good memory."

"I do try. It's useful in my line of work."

I was resigned to my fate. But if Harper was going to make me reveal the most mortifying aspects of my first foray into the land of SheDate, I knew I could exact an equivalent pound of flesh from her when it was her turn to explain the Herculean flight from reason it had to have taken for her to spend—what was it? *Eight years* with Gina.

Eight years. *My god.*

Finally, something made my relationship with Tonya look less pathetic. Well. Maybe not *less* pathetic. I mean, it *had* been pretty epically bad. But at least, with Harper, I'd found a horrific equivalent that didn't make me look like the only loser on the planet.

"So," I began. "I have this friend—my best friend, actually—Sofie. We grew up together and we were college roommates at McGill. She lives here in Philadelphia now, too."

"Really? Where does she work?"

"Marsh McLennan. She's an actuary."

"Interesting. That's one of those jobs you've always known about, but never met anyone who's actually done it."

"You don't know the half of it. Sofie is . . . a human contradiction. Professionally, she's buttoned-up as hell. As good and steady as they come. Personally? She's a lightning rod for the surreal. The weirder and less traditional the experience is—the more avid a practitioner she becomes. Together, we are like oil and water. But she's always been my confidant, and she always pushes me to move outside my comfort zone. So, after my relationship with Tonya fell apart—which is another story and one you won't get tonight—it was Sofie who pushed me to crawl out of my cocoon and create a profile on SheDate."

Harper's eyes betrayed her. I could tell she was surprised by my revelation.

"What?" I asked. "You've never tried a dating app?"

"No. I confess. I'm far too . . ."

"Sensible?" I offered.

"No. I was going to say chicken."

"To be fair, Sofie did all the work. I pretty much sat there and looked at her stupidly while she filled out the answers to the profile questions. And then she dug out this ridiculous photo of me that had been taken at a pool party when I was about twenty years old. I mean, I knew I was cruising for disaster, but I just sat there and went along with it."

"Why?"

"Why'd I go along with it?"

Harped nodded.

The server arrived with our second round of drinks.

"Oh, god bless you," I practically hummed.

"Mr. Chuong wanted me to tell you that he has taken the liberty of ordering your meal for this evening," the server informed us. "So please relax and enjoy yourselves. The first course will be out soon."

"Well, I'm impressed as hell," Harper declared. "You must've given this Mr. Chuong some hellaciously good rides back and forth from D.C."

"I slipped him extra Chiclets from the café car . . ."

"I see. Well, I am gratified to be the recipient of your largesse." She sipped her new drink. "But you were saying?"

I was confused. "What was I saying?"

"You were about to reveal why you went along with Sofie's scheme to set you up on SheDate when you had a premonition it would end in disaster."

"Wow. Great tracking skills. You should've been a shrink."

"I thought about it."

"But decided against it because?"

"Nice try. This is your inquisition, not mine. Please proceed."

"I guess I went along with it because part of me agreed that, left to my own devices, I'd never do *anything*. I mean, the right person would just have to pass in front of me. And how was that ever going to happen when I spend most of my days walking the aisles of moving passenger cars—never spending more than eleven minutes at any one station. All I ever do is switch locations."

"What about graduate school?"

"What about it?"

"Dewey said you are nearly finished with your Ph.D. Won't that change things for you? Open up new avenues for social exploration?"

"'Nearly finished' is a euphemism for seemingly incapable of completing the damn thing. Done all the coursework, taken the prelims. Just have to finish writing the damn dissertation. And that's hard to do when I'm constantly on call and rarely at home for even two days together. I've been working on it for nearly six years now."

"That's not uncommon."

"It hardly equates to being on the cusp of a brighter future burgeoning with prospects for wealth and felicitous relationships."

"Okay. So, you decided to try SheDate. I am assuming you made at least one connection—the infamous one from Thursday night."

"Yeah. I made a connection, all right."

"What happened?"

What had happened? I'd been catfished by an arrogant septuagenarian with a wheelchair and an insane aptitude for lying. How did I share that without looking like a complete idiot? There didn't seem to be many benign options.

I chose candor.

"I got catfished. By a woman who pretended to be a zillion years younger than she was. And even if I'd been able to deal with that, she made it impossible by showing up with an ego the size of Texas and a narcissistic obsession with her own importance. Oh

... she'd also been a passenger on the train two days earlier and ran roughshod over every one of us—including the other passengers. And even though I was the one who ultimately confronted her on behalf of the crew, she had zero recollection of meeting me when we met for drinks at my hotel on Thursday night."

"You met her for drinks at your hotel?"

"It wasn't like that. *She* picked the location—not me. I'd never stayed in that hotel before, and I didn't even know it had a cocktail lounge right off the lobby. Of course, she was a Bonvoy member, so we sat in the rarified air of a private club away from the riffraff." I closed my eyes in mortification. "She was absolutely horrible. And she never owned up to lying to me about every aspect of who she was. Instead, she took exception to the fact that I had posted a younger photo of myself."

"God. That all sounds awful."

"Trust me. If we didn't share the sanctity of the laundry room, I'd never have revealed this much to you."

Harper smiled. "Your secret is safe with me. I won't tell anyone. Not even Dewey."

"Oh, worry not. Dewey already knows."

"He does?"

"Oh yeah. He's already keeping a log of all the tropes I've managed to explode."

"Tropes? You mean like ... *trope* tropes? In fiction?"

"Yes. Precisely. Apparently, I have an aptitude for this. I'm already up to five."

"Five?" Harper sounded impressed. "He told me I'd only blown through one."

"Toaster oven?" I suggested.

She actually blushed. "I guess that secret is out."

"Don't worry. Apparently I share that one with you ... some kind of guilt by association."

"Now I'm doubly sorry."

"Don't be sorry. Get back out there." I said it like I meant it—although I wasn't yet sure I did. "Think of all you're missing. There have to be, what? Twenty? Thirty more tropes to explore? And some of them are *bound* to be good, even if they fail miserably like all the rest."

"I think the point is not *to* fail," Harper said with intent.

"Oh yeah? You got a strategy for that one?"

"Nope. But when I come up with one, you'll be the first to know."

"You mean after Dewey?"

She thought about it. "Okay. You'll be the second to know."

We raised our glasses and clinked rims just as our server arrived with two steaming cups of pho.

"I have a question for you."

"I just bet you do." Harper sat back and folded her arms.

We'd finished our meal and were sharing a dessert of poached pears topped with candied jalapeño, basil, and lime. Harper's turn at the wheel to explain her relationship with Gina had been fairly straightforward. She'd been raised in a regimented environment with very controlling parents. The family, although not devout, was so steeped in the appearance of orthodoxy that Harper's coming out was greeted with shame and hostility. She'd been a student at Bryn Mawr when she'd had her first romantic encounter with another woman—although she was quick to note that this experience was *not* unique at an august ivy institution where at least a third of her classmates were LUGs—Lesbians Until Graduation. But, she said, her parents freaked out when she told them and threatened to yank her out and send her to Gratz—the Jewish college in Melrose Park.

"Like *that* would've made any difference." She laughed bitterly.

"What did you do?"

"Nothing. I knew they were blowing smoke. My mother would rather die than have her only daughter graduate from some off-brand college. So, I stayed, and I graduated. And Hayley dumped my ass the night before commencement and rode off into the sunset with her childhood sweetheart, Todd. I think she lives in Sherman Oaks now, with her two kids and three plastic surgeons."

"And then you met Gina?"

"Not quite. And quit jumping ahead. We'll get to the featured attraction, but first you have to sit through a few more words from the sponsors."

I shoved the dessert plate across the table. "The rest of this is yours."

"What are you talking about? You've hardly had any of it."

"That's not true. I ate, like, two thirds of it."

Harper was picking through the detritus of the elegant dessert. "I see you kindly saved me most of the jalapeños."

"I figured they might light a fire under your storytelling so we could get to the good part."

"Believe me, Gina is not the good part."

"Okay, then. What is?"

Harper thought about it. "I don't think I've had it yet."

"Fair enough." I felt bad about being so flippant. After all, I barely knew her. "I don't mean to be an asshole."

"It just comes naturally to you?" she teased.

"Something like that. My mother calls me *hérissonne*."

"A hedgehog?"

I was impressed. "Your French is very good."

"It should be halfway decent. It was my major in college."

"No way? *Wow*. We have a lot in common. I'm told that Canadian French is halfway decent, too."

She laughed. "Your French is just fine. But why does your mother call you a hedgehog?"

"Because I'm pricky and roll into a ball when I'm threatened."

"Good coping mechanism."

"Except when it happens at cocktail parties."

"Or on blind dates?"

"Oh, I didn't roll into a ball on *that* date," I clarified. "I shook the dust from my feet and strode out, trailing my garments like an affronted queen."

"A la Esther and the Persian king?"

"I was thinking more of RuPaul."

"I can see that." Harper studied me for a moment. "So, let me simplify the Gina interlude for you."

"Okay. But you call eight years an *interlude?*"

"You know, I *could* say something about six years and your dissertation . . ."

"Fair enough. Please continue."

"Gina appealed to me because she was the exact opposite of everything I'd experienced before. She was loud and brash and didn't give two flying fucks about what anyone thought of her. Her overall . . . *bigness* appealed to me because she was strong in all the areas I was weak. And, as I've already explained, having others make my decisions was not a departure from the norm. So that part of the equation felt normal. It wasn't an aberration."

"So, what finally changed for you?"

"For starters—Dewey. Gina and I rented an apartment in the building—not the one I'm in now—and I got to know him. It didn't take long for us to become dear friends." She nodded. "You know how he is . . . he's like the oracle at Delphi. Only he operates behind a desk in the lobby, not from a hole in the floor. In typical fashion, he quickly zeroed in on the . . . toxic perversity of my relationship with Gina—who, for all her enlightened bravado, always regarded Dewey as 'the help.' That was the first thing that pierced the armor of our shared existence. After that, a slow drip led to the floodgates opening, and I found it more and more impossible to overlook all the ways we were different. It was like getting hit by the flash of a camera—throwing everything into a kind of bold relief I'd never recognized before. Things that once had seemed fresh and innovative at the beginning morphed into a sustained case of progressive claustrophobia. But I was such a weenie, it still took me more than two years to break up with her—even though I knew in my viscera it was over." She paused in reflection. "Way over."

"So, you changed apartments? Why?"

"Gina was unwilling to move out—but I knew I wanted to stay in Hopkinson House. It was the first place I ever felt like I belonged. I loved the quirky community. It fit me like an old pair of gloves—perfectly molded to the shape of my hands. And I knew the pace of life there wouldn't appeal to Gina for long. She didn't enjoy playing 'what's cooking on twenty-eight' during elevator rides. And she had zero patience for the antics of Aldo and Luz—who I find to be . . . charming—in a Monty Python kind of way."

"African or European?"

Harper shot me a withering look. "So, what was the question you wanted to ask me?"

"That night we first met on the elevator? You knew about the extra board. And when I asked you how, you said it was a long story."

"Right. I was being ironic. It was a long story—literally. The magazine did a feature on the railroad when USRail announced extended service from Philadelphia to eight new cities and unveiled plans for four different Christmas Train packages. The rather prolix article included details about holiday staffing shortages and how the railroad scheduled crews to cover the bases."

"Wow. I don't know how I missed that one."

"I do. Most of it ended up on the cutting room floor, as they say. I had to shorten the piece by sixteen hundred words and those sections were among the parts that didn't survive the final cut."

"Story of my life."

"I am sorry. No slight intended." Her apology felt genuine. "But while we're on the topic of questions—I have one for you."

"Okay."

She cleared her throat. "Poodle?"

"Hey . . . you wanted Gina to think we were a couple, right? Isn't that how couples talk to each other?"

"Not in my experience—or they wouldn't remain couples for long."

"I was improvising—and, I might add, doing a pretty fine job of it while dodging car mufflers and mustard-soaked soft pretzels."

"That is true."

I sighed. "It's getting late. Are you ready to blow this pop stand?"

"I am."

Harper insisted that she be allowed to pick up the check. She called it the hazardous duty pay I'd requested earlier. I quickly realized that arguing with her was pointless. But I made her promise that she'd grant me equal opportunity in the future.

It only took us fifteen minutes to get back to Washington Park. For once, the elevator ride to the twenty-sixth floor was uneventful. There were no signs of Aldo or Luz. I figured Dewey had ordered them to take the night off and give their quest to find the elusive Cujo a rest.

We stepped out of the elevator on our floor and stood there stupidly, not really saying anything. After so much easy camaraderie, it made no sense that we now were behaving like strangers at a cocktail buffet.

"Thanks for a great evening" felt like an inane comment to make. And Harper seemed to be at a loss for words, too. The awkward moment was made even more awkward when we both started speaking at the same time.

"Well . . ." I began.

"I suppose . . ." she began.

We both smiled shyly.

I don't know which one of us started it, but suddenly we were bending toward each other. *STOP!* My brain was screaming. *NOT WITH SOMEONE IN THE FUCKING BUILDING!*

But I didn't care. And a twenty-mule team couldn't have stopped me from what I was about to do. We were scant millimeters away from setting the next natural disaster in my life into motion when the elevator doors dinged, and we both shot apart like we'd been caught playing spin the bottle beneath the pews in church.

The doors opened, and Aldo and Luz appeared—*of course.* And this time, they were carrying the most bizarre-looking Christmas wreath I'd ever seen. This one was enrobed with billiard ball-sized bulbs of garlic.

And it was redolent as fuck.

"Dear *god.*" I waved a hand back and forth in front of my face. "What the hell is that?"

Luz held it up for closer inspection—which neither Harper nor I cared to undertake.

"It's a trap," she explained. "If Cujo avoids this wreath, then we know we're onto something."

"That's right," Aldo added. "Garlic always keeps evil spirits away. So, we figure if Cujo doesn't mess with this one, we can go on and hang garlic on all the rest of the wreaths in the building."

"Problem solved." Luz sounded confident about their idea.

"That sounds . . ." I looked at Harper.

"Like an idea with some merit," she supplied. Then she smiled at me. "I'll say goodnight now. Thanks for the evening. It was . . . an experience."

"To say the least." I gave her a small wave. "See you around the chapparal."

She nodded and turned to head toward her apartment. I

watched her go with a feeling of . . . emptiness. It was hard to quantify.

I didn't realize that Aldo and Luz had been watching her egress, too.

"That is one fine lookin' woman."

I looked at Luz with surprise.

"What?" She said. "Just 'cause I work here doesn't mean I'm dead."

Yeah. This was not a conversation I needed to have. Not tonight—and not with the Don Quixote and Sancho Panza of Hopkinson House.

"Goodnight, you two," I said. "Good luck with your latest . . . *trap.*"

I headed back to my apartment, wondering vaguely where scheduling would send me next—and whether, when I got there, if I'd be brave enough to test the dating waters again.

CHAPTER FIVE

Love Triangles—and other lessons in plane geometry.

Predictably, I did get a call from crew scheduling on Sunday—but wonder of wonders, I didn't have to report at 30th Street Station for duty until Monday morning at seven.

Apparently, miracles still happened.

I was going to be on The Nor'easter this time, and I knew from experience that this line was a real ball buster. I'd have nonstop overnights and wouldn't arrive back in Philly until Friday afternoon. To make a sucky schedule even worse, the trip back home was a deadhead. Which meant I wasn't working—so no pay—but I still had to ride the damn train for nearly three hours to get back.

I decided to celebrate by inviting Sofie over for dinner. She'd been texting me nearly nonstop for details about my date in Springfield. The mortification of having to relate all the gruesome particulars by typing a narrative with my index finger held little appeal for me. So, I finally just asked if she had plans for the evening. For once, she didn't, so she agreed to come by for an early dinner and a movie—as long as we picked something shorter than *Oppenheimer*.

I made sure I was packed and ready to go long before Sofie arrived at four. Then I spent the better part of six hours working on my dissertation. It took me the first hour and a half to get reacquainted with where I'd left the damn thing the last time I worked on it—which was more than three weeks ago. My work schedule of late had been so horrendous I hadn't had the time or the stamina to focus on it during my normal thirty-six hours at home. As much as this rankled and unnerved me, I knew there'd be nothing I could do about it for at least the next six weeks. Low seniority conductors on the extra board had no ability to avoid being tagged for every rotten trip—especially in the run-up to the holidays. It would only get worse until after New Year's.

But I'd lucked out and had an entire day to at least try and accomplish something. So, I made hay while this brief burst of sun shone down on my kitchen table, covered with books and papers all detailing the finer points of how dung beetles collect fog inside their shells and convert it to water they can drink in extremely dry climates. My thesis was an exploration of how to use this process to design ways we might be able to draw fresh water from sources like fog and dew.

Maybe not the most riveting topic . . . but it was either this or the influence of humpback whales on the development of wind turbines.

I'll admit that, although I actually made some measurable progress on my magnum opus, I had to fight the impulse to keep thinking about Harper and our non-date last night. And what the fuck with my behavior at the end of the evening? I'd nearly kissed her in front of the elevators. What an epic *mess* that would've created . . . Neither of us needed another damn dalliance in this Peyton Place of a building.

Besides—it violated my prime directive: The Dukakis Rule.

Still . . . Harper hadn't seemed to mind. In fact, I thought she was leaning into it as much as I'd been.

Enough! Back to work. *Where was I?*

There were three categories of dung beetles: Dwellers, Tunnelers, and Rollers. Dwellers, which I was focused on, lived on top of the heap and thrived on fresh cow patties. Dwellers, like all varieties of dung beetles, were commensurate recyclers, loosening and nourishing the soil and magically transforming the fog that emanated from the heat of decomposing dung into fresh, clean water.

There was something epically Frostian in the symmetry of beetles turning manure into water.

Of course, the great poet would've found a more lyrical way to describe the exchange.

Thankfully, that wasn't my job. *My* job was to explore ways the process could be replicated in a sustainable manner—especially important as the planet continued to heat up and rampaging climate change increased the salinity of water bodies—and groundwater—through the sustained intrusion of saltwater.

Nice work if you can get it in the MAGA era.

I knocked off a little before four so I could shower and begin my prep work for dinner.

I decided to make skillet-roasted cheese ravioli in a lemon and brown butter sauce, topped with fresh ricotta. The choice of ravioli had been a practical one for Sofie. It would spare her the onerous task of cutting her food into equal-sized portions.

She said she'd bring the wine and I made sure to tell her just *one* bottle since I was on the clock beginning at o'dark-thirty tomorrow morning. Of course, when she arrived at the crack of four (actuaries were always very punctual), she was bearing two bottles that were French and, I was sure, very expensive. I noted that she'd brought one white and one red.

Sofie always covered all the bases.

I took them from her. "What are these? And why are there two of them?"

"*Bonsoir, grincheuse.*" She kissed me on both cheeks. "Since when do I obey your orders?"

"I am *not* cranky," I insisted. "At least, not yet."

I would've said have a seat, but she was already perched on

a stool in the kitchen.

"What are you making?" she demanded to know.

I was a pretty good cook—unlike Sofie, who had zero patience for anything that required planning. A characteristic completely at odds with her career.

"Skillet ravioli with brown butter sauce and lemon. Sound good?"

"Oui." She was busy reaching for the corkscrew. "Kindly fetch me two white wine glasses?"

I did as directed and retrieved the glasses from the cupboard. Like the good *Québécoies* I was, I had a kitchen fully equipped with all appropriate stemware.

Sofie extracted the cork with a pop dramatic enough to have registered on a seismograph.

"Are we a bit anxious?" I asked.

"Long ass night."

"Care to elaborate?"

"Non," she poured two very generous glasses of the straw-colored wine, "I really don't."

"Intriguing. How come my life is always an open book, but yours requires a Yankee White security clearance to access?"

Sofie took a healthy gulp of the wine. "Because, white rabbit, details of my private actions would make your virgin ears bleed."

"Noted." I tried the wine. It was, indeed, very good. Superb, in fact. I picked up the bottle to examine it. It was a *Pascal Cotat Sancerre La Grande Cote*. A stalwart from the Loire region and, I'm sure, a bargain at over a hundred bucks.

Sofie didn't drink anything that cost less than fifty dollars.

"Shall I put this into the fridge?"

"Non." Sofie took the bottle back from me. "It won't be around long enough to warm up."

Okay. It was going to be one of *those* nights.

I resumed readying the ingredients for our dinner.

"So. Regale me with details about your first tour of the

117

SheDate playground."

I took a deep breath and spilled my guts. There was no need to try and soft-pedal the details. Sofie would've just pulled them out of me with the dexterity of a dentist extracting an infected molar. When I finished my tale of woe, I expected her to ask me to hand her my phone so she could uninstall the app. Instead, she just sighed and said, "Back to work, then."

I was stunned. "What do you mean 'back to work'? There's no way I'm going for another voyage on this Flying Dutchman of dating apps. So, you can just forget it."

Sofie refilled her wine glass—for the second time. "Don't be an idiot. Of course you are. You're just developing a healthy set of sea legs."

"Even if that were true, I certainly don't intend to acquire them walking the plank of misery that awaits me at the end of each fucking swipe right."

"Nothing in life worth having has ever been easy, Izzy."

"Yeah? Well," I quoted, "I'm not sure I agree with your policework there."

"Name something."

I searched my mind to come up with a few candidates—things I'd learned without suffering or humiliation. "What about knitting? I picked that up in two seconds—and I'm *good* at it. Ask my grandmother."

"I am sure this ability will make you a very desirable catch among toothless crones in the nursing home. *We're* talking about skills that can get you laid."

I gave up. I knew she was right. "I don't think I'm any good at knowing how to decipher the profiles. I must've missed some obvious clues with Jane."

"Doubtful. Some people are just very skilled at how they present. She sounds like an experienced catfisher."

"How do I know I won't make the same mistake again?"

"You don't. You just have to keep working it. And maybe

don't agree to meet someone in your own goddamn hotel again."

"Hey, that was not my fault. I'd never stayed there before."

"And looking up the suggested venue on your fucking phone never occurred to you before agreeing to meet her?"

"Well . . ."

"Do you know yet where you'll be next week?"

I nodded. "I just got my crew assignment a few hours ago."

"What days and cities for overnights?"

"Um . . ." I picked up my phone and looked up the details of the line. "It looks like Monday is Boston, Tuesday is D.C., Wednesday is Providence, and Thursday is a half day to Stamford."

"Seriously? They really pick some armpits for overnights."

"Ever been on a train, Sofie?"

"Only under duress. Hand me your phone."

I gave it to her. "Why?"

"I'm going to find you another date for one of these nights."

"*You* are?"

"*Oui.* I'm more experienced."

"You just said I needed to keep working it."

"You will be the one working it. I'm going to get you into the starting gate—you'll have to run the race on your own."

I watched in amazement as her fingers flew across the app, swiping left every two seconds. Finally, she slowed down and seemed to examine one more closely. Then I saw her swipe right. She handed the phone back to me.

"Done."

I looked at the screen. "What do you mean, 'done'?"

"I mean I found a hot prospect in Providence. I hope you hear back from her."

"Who is she?"

"Someone dull enough to make your heart go pitty-pat. A schoolteacher. Sixth grade. Was married to a man but got out of it more than a decade ago. Likes to cook, read, and watch old

119

movies. Hates flying but *loves* to travel by train. You're welcome."

"Are you kidding me? What's her name?"

"Who cares?" Sofie waved at my phone dismissively. "It's Bridget, or something equally Catholic. I'm sure you'll get married and have nine kids."

"Wow. You're good."

"News flash. This is why I'm worn out from last night."

"Jeez. I'm glad I picked up something decadent for dessert."

"*Qu'as-tu acheté?* Not more of that horrible cherry pie you had the last time, I hope."

"*Non.* I picked up some *merveilleux* at the French Café."

"Ohhhh. Talk dirty to me . . ."

"I knew you'd be pleased."

I was just about to start cooking when my doorbell rang. I excused myself from Sofie and went to answer it.

I hoped it wasn't Aldo or Luz asking if they could hang garlic on my door.

It wasn't. I was surprised to see Harper standing there. She was carrying a basket containing laundry, and something else.

"Hi," I said. I was genuinely happy to see her.

"Hi. I apologize for just showing up like this—but it occurred to me that I don't have your cell phone number. So, I thought I'd take a chance you were home and just pop by on my way to the laundry."

"No. Please." I stepped back and held the door open. "Come on in."

"No. No, really. I just had something to give you."

"Come in," I commanded. "You can give it to me inside."

"Isabelle?" Sofie's voice rang out from the kitchen. "*Qui est là?*"

"It's my friend, Harper," I answered her. "*Elle vit dans l'immeuble.*"

"You *have* to come in now," I told Harper. "Sofie will insist on meeting you."

"Oh?" Harper looked amused—and curious. "The infamous Sofie is here?"

"You mean notorious." Sofie had joined us. "*Not* infamous."

"*Mes excuses.*" Harper extended a hand. "Very nice to meet you. I'm Harper . . . *la blanchisseuse.*"

Sofie shook her hand warmly. "Every building needs a French-speaking laundress."

Harper smiled. "Just like every woman needs a best friend who is notorious."

"I like you," Sofie declared. "Come in and have some wine."

Harper looked quickly at me. "Oh, no. I really can't. I didn't come by to intrude. Just to give you this." She reached into her laundry basket and withdrew a DVD. "I didn't even realize I had it until I saw it on the bookcase last night."

It was a copy of the Charles Busch classic, *Die, Mommie, Die!*

I was ecstatic. "No way! You had this? *Fantastic.* We were looking for something to watch tonight."

"*Qu'est-ce que c'est?*"

"It's a drag remake of *Die! Die! My Darling!*" I explained to Sofie. "By Charles Busch."

"How perfect. We can all watch it together." She faced Harper. "You'll stay for dinner?"

"No." Harper was aghast. "I really did *not* come here to beg for an invitation."

"Beg?" Sofie said. "Who said anything about begging? Do you really have something more pressing to do this evening? I mean, apart from line drying your lingerie?"

"Take my advice and give it up, Harper. Once her mind is set on something, you cannot change it. Besides," I took her laundry basket from her and set it down on the floor by the door, "I really want you to stay, too."

"It's decided." Sofie turned and headed back toward her stool. "Come and join me in the kitchen, Harper, while

Izzy serves us."

"It's bigger than both of us," I said to Harper. "It's best if you just embrace your fate."

Harper sighed. "*Okay*. Although I still feel like a schmuck."

"Don't." I took hold of her elbow and steered her toward my Pullman kitchen. "On the upside, I'm a pretty good cook."

"She speaks the truth," Sofie declared. "Now, Izzy . . . kindly fetch me another glass."

I did as directed and Sofie poured Harper a glass of the *Sancerre*. I watched her eyes grow wide as she tasted it.

"My *god*." She held the glass up to the light and examined it. "What *is* this? It's divine."

"Sofie doesn't drink the cheap shit," I explained. "Too bad she's already inhaled most of this bottle."

"Pish posh. I am sure that if you scour the dark recesses of this domicile you can cough up another bottle of something halfway drinkable."

"Only halfway drinkable?" I asked. "I am sure I can find something in that category."

"I'd rather ingest bile."

Harper seemed amused by our banter. "At the risk of sounding impertinent, I do have a *Château Suduiraut Vieilles Vignes* that I think is fit to drink. I could go fetch it?"

"Fly little blackbird, fly!" Sofie made fluttering motions with her hand. "Do please, hurry back."

"You really don't have to go get it," I assured her. "We have a bottle of red."

"No, please . . . if I'm going to crash your party, at least allow me to contribute."

"Okay . . ." I still wasn't very happy that Sofie had pushed her into coughing up what was undoubtedly a good bottle of wine.

She left to go back to her apartment and get the wine, stopping to pick up her laundry basket on the way.

As soon as she was out the door, Sofie trained her eyes on

me like the crosshairs of a shotgun.

"Okay. *Dish*. Who the hell is *that*, and why have I heard nothing about her until now?"

"She's . . . just a woman who lives in the building. I met her on the elevator last week."

"And you're already talking about drag remakes of *Die! Die! My Darling!*? Did we fold space and end up in a new dimension? You are renowned for moving at glacial pace in relationships."

"It's not a *relationship*. It's . . ." I wasn't sure how to characterize my . . . whatever with Harper. "We're just friends."

"Friends?"

I nodded. "That's it."

"Izzy. She speaks French."

"I'm aware of this."

"She drinks good wine."

"So it seems."

"She's uncommonly easy on the eyes."

"Also true."

"She uses three-syllable words."

"I noted that."

"She's single?"

"Oui."

"And queer?"

"Obviously."

"Why the fuck hasn't she moved in, yet?"

"Precisely because she lives in the *same* goddamn building. I am not going down that road again, Sofie. *Not ever*. End of story."

"That is an arbitrary and ridiculous standard."

"Look, just because you'd have no scruples about sleeping with anyone who passes in front of you, regardless of the mine fields they're towing in their wake—doesn't mean I can do the same thing. We've discussed this before. I will *not* go through a repeat of what I endured with Tonya."

"Why are you persuaded that the ending you had with her is the only possibility?"

"Because I'm a realist."

"More like you're delusional and have no sense of self-esteem. Me?" She pointed at her ample chest. "If I weren't straight, I'd *totally* be hitting that."

"Let's change the subject, shall we?" Sofie's comment irked me—mostly because I'd been having the same thought but was too chicken to act on it. "She'll be back any minute—she lives on this floor."

"All right. But I want to go on record stating that this position of yours is stupid and short-sighted. Women like that don't happen along every day. You're nuts to pass up one who literally landed right on your precious doorstep."

"I'll take that under advisement."

"You're welcome."

"If you'll pardon me, I'm going to start cooking now, so we have time to watch the movie."

"Don't say I didn't try." Sofie reclaimed her seat on the stool. "How about some music?"

"Sure. What do you feel like?"

"I don't know . . . something seductive, perhaps?"

"Not a chance. Alexa?" I called out. "Play French cooking music."

The air filled with the sultry voice of Melody Gardot, singing "Your Heart is as Black as Night."

"Nice." Sofie nodded with approval.

"It should be your theme song."

Sofie gave me the finger.

"Well, we need to support native Philadelphians, don't we?"

"*Oui*. Especially when they also sing in French."

The doorbell rang. Harper had returned.

"I'll get it." Sofie jumped off her stool. "You keep cooking."

When they reentered the kitchen, I noticed that Harper was

carrying something besides the wine. It looked like . . . garlic.

"What's that?" I asked.

"You tell me." She handed me the large bulb. It was attached to a length of shiny green ribbon. "This was hanging on your door when I got back."

"Oh, dear god." I dropped the garlic into a bowl on the counter. "It's the dynamic duo."

"Aldo and Luz?" She asked. "Why on earth would they put a huge bulb of garlic on your door?"

"*Loup-garou?*" Sofie volunteered.

"I don't think we have a werewolf infestation in this building," I replied. "At least, not yet. Besides, garlic doesn't repel werewolves, it repels vampires."

"Really?" Harper sounded confused. "What do werewolves hate?"

"Wolfsbane. And, I think, silver."

"Noted. Remind me not to wear cheap jewelry when I come over here." Sofie stashed Harper's bottle of wine in the fridge—presumably to keep it cool until we opened it. "Apropos of the undead," she queried, "how do you know so much about these creatures of the night?"

"You mean Aldo and Luz?" Sofie flipped me off and Harper laughed. "You're kidding, right? You don't remember when Zoé dated that goth Blitz Kid from Toronto? They watched horror films nonstop." I looked over at Harper. "Zoé thought it was beyond cool that he was so obsessed with the occult and black and white cinema. In reality, he was obsessed with goth *fashion*. Tim Curry was his idol . . . right after Lily Munster."

"To be fair, she *was* a classic." Sofie seemed lost in thought for a moment. "Those diaphanous gowns are a killer if you miss even one Pilates class."

"You'd know this of course."

"I *beg* your pardon." Sofie faced me and lifted her sweater. "Have you *seen* these abs? I have a rock-hard core."

125

"Good for you," I said. "It matches the granite between your ears."

"*Vas te faire foutre.*"

I smiled sweetly at Harper. "Isn't it nice when we all get along?"

She looked amused. I liked that her eyes were crisscrossed with smile lines.

"May I help you with something?" she asked.

Sofie choked on her wine. I quickly shot her a warning look. *Don't even* think *about going there.*

"Sure." I nodded toward the baguette on the counter. "How about you slice the bread?"

Harper quickly joined me and set to work. I appreciated that she didn't ask me where anything was. She simply looked around the kitchen until she located the knife block and found a suitable cutting board.

"*Pardon?* Why didn't you ask me to slice the bread?"

"Because I don't trust you with sharp objects."

"*Pourquoi pas?*" Sofie feigned offense.

"It doesn't work out for the upholstery," I explained. "The last time you used a knife here, you flung it while making a point and eviscerated the back of a chair."

Sofie took umbrage at my retelling of the incident. "I did not *fling* it. I dropped it with gusto."

"It flew five feet across the room."

"That chair was in the wrong place."

"Oh? You were aiming at something else?"

"*Oui.* I was *trying* to get it into the sink."

"Yeah? Well, note to self: sinks are usually in the *kitchen*— not the living room."

Sofie waved a hand dismissively. "*Détails.*"

I returned my attention to the ravioli which was browning nicely in the cast iron skillet. This was a great dish—easy to make and delicious. An added perk was that it always turned out, so it was low stress for me. I enjoyed cooking, but tended to be neurotic when I was cooking for other people. I think that derives from what an exceptional cook my mother is. She is always so relaxed and competent in the kitchen. She never worries about a less than perfect performance. She always says cooking for friends is an expression of love—and love is never bad, even when the performance is imperfect.

For the record, I can't recall a single meal of hers that even skated close to the realm of imperfect.

Tonight? All I wanted was for the dish to turn out. I was doubly intense about it because Harper had joined us.

But all the signs were good.

While Sofie was busily employed opening another bottle of wine, I asked Harper to help me clear the kitchen table, so we had a place to eat. I noticed that she stopped to read some of my handwritten notes.

"Dung beetles?" she asked.

"It's . . . complicated. They're an essential component of my research."

"*Oui,*" Sofie chimed in. "This is why I am fond of saying Izzy is always up to her eyeballs in some kind of shit."

"Very funny." I unplugged my laptop and set it atop a stack of folders on a small side table.

Harper was already on her way to the kitchen cabinet to retrieve silverware.

"Plates?" she asked.

"Cabinet to the right of the sink."

We made short work of setting the table. Sofie brought Harper's bottle of wine and our glasses over.

Five minutes later, we were all deep into the brown butter ravioli—which, for my money, tasted pretty damn good.

"My, god." Harper was in transports. "This is delicious."

"Don't rave so much, Harper." Sofie topped off her wine. "We don't want her to get a big head. Although, that ridiculous uniform hat would at least cover it up."

"Hey . . . you always said I looked *good* in hats."

"I meant *millinery*. Not that stove pipe creation they make you wear."

Stove pipe? "It's not that bad." I looked at Harper for support. "Is it?"

"I think it's cute," she said.

"See?" I glared at Sofie.

"Great. Then we'll add 'loves to wear exotic headgear' to your SheDate profile."

"You can't do that . . . it would make me sound like I have external orthodontics."

Sofie shrugged. "If the hat fits . . ."

"Does SheDate really get that . . . *granular?*" Harper asked.

"Hell yes." Sofie explained. "The more granular you get, the likelier you are to find a perfect match."

"I confess, I've always been too chicken to try a dating app."

"*Pourquoi?*" Sofie asked. "Afraid you'll connect with the wrong person?"

"I'm not sure. Maybe I'm afraid I'd connect with the *right* person."

That answer intrigued me. "Why is finding the right person scary?"

"Because I've never had that experience." Harper demurred. "Maybe I wouldn't know what to do with one."

I didn't bother to make a reply—mostly because I shared her view.

"Trust me, honey." Sofie loved to fill a vacuum. "You do the *same* damn things you do with a wrong one. You just do them without angst and with less screaming."

"Well. I think it's better for everyone if I steer clear of the apps." Harper smiled at Sofie. "I wouldn't even know where to begin."

"I'm not sure I agree. But if ever you change your mind, I'm just a phone call away. I feel fairly confident that I could get you set up in two minutes."

I leaned toward Harper. "*Run. Run like hell.*"

Sofie ate her last ravioli with a flourish and pushed her plate away.

"Excellent meal. Why don't we eat our *merveilleux* while we watch the movie?"

I was fine with that suggestion.

"Great idea. Just leave these plates. I can clear everything away later." I got to my feet. "Anyone want coffee?"

"*Oui.*" Sofie nodded enthusiastically. "As long as it's thirteen percent alcohol and comes in a red wine glass."

"Okay. That's *one* no." I looked at Harper. "You?"

"I think I'm fine sticking with wine, too."

"That makes three of us. You two go get comfortable, and I'll fetch the wine and other glasses."

Sofie opened the *Louis Jadot Côte de Beaune Villages* she'd brought, while I put the DVD into my Blu-ray player. I noticed that Sofie had been quick to commandeer the side chair, forcing Harper and I to sit beside each other on the couch.

I shot her a look intended to say, *I'm on to your reindeer games.* But she ignored me. As usual.

"I cannot believe I didn't know about this movie," I complained.

"Me, either," Sofie agreed. "I remember seeing *Looped* on Broadway—and I wonder if that was Busch's inspiration to make this? The play was brilliant."

"No way! You saw that, too?" Harper was animated. "I *loved* it. Valerie Harper was mesmerizing."

"Okay." I held up a hand. "Odd man out here. What was *Looped?*"

"Were you raised beneath a rock?" Sofie shook her red head with disbelief. "*Looped* was Valerie Harper's stunning *tour de force* performance of a drunken and profane Tallulah Bankhead, taking eight full hours to redub *one* line of dialogue from—you guessed it—*Die! Die! My Darling!* Which, by the way, was her final film."

"I even remember the line," Harper added.

"What was it?" I was beyond intrigued.

"'And so, Patricia, as I was telling you, that deluded rector has in literal effect, closed the church to me.'"

Sofie clapped merrily. "Brava! You nailed it in one take."

"Did you say eight hours?" I asked.

"Oh, yes. Eight hours, four packs of cigarettes and . . . how many bottles of scotch?"

Sofie answered Harper's question. "Just the one. But she rolled into the recording studio with a good head start."

The opening credits began to roll, and I was already thinking about orchestrating a date for the three of us to go see the original movie at the Film Center on Chestnut Street.

The difference in pace between the Nor'easter and the Zephyr was enough to make my head spin. I'd worked this line before, but it had always been on the southern route, which terminated in Roanoke, Virginia. This time, I was crewing the northern trains—which all hit stations in high-traffic areas and seemed to stop more than they ran. This meant we were constantly on- and off-boarding passengers. We practically had to sprint between stations to scan tickets and tag arrival destinations.

The train on the first day was running from Philadelphia to Boston, where we'd overnight. Just between Union Station in New Haven and South Station in Boston, there were eighteen stops.

It was exhausting. I had no idea why anyone would want to hold this line. The only good part about it was that the trains ran only during the daytime—so there were no night hours. That meant your overnights all commenced at a reasonable time—at least affording you the chance to get a decent dinner or take in some local attraction, if you were so inclined.

Or, if you had the desire and had done some advance planning, you could even meet up with the person who'd finally swiped right on your profile.

Bridget, the schoolteacher, did eventually indicate that she was at least interested enough to learn a bit more about me. We ended up spending a bit of time on Monday evening texting. I'd had to hand it to Sofie. She really seemed to have done a credible job finding somebody who:

a) hadn't just been cross-country skiing;
b) didn't suggest meeting at the bar in my hotel; or
c) wasn't bothered by my "blue collar" profession.

To say I found Bridget refreshing might sound odd, since I hadn't been on SheDate enough to know what the norm was. But, still, something about her presentation just felt easy. Unaffected. She was pretty, too, in a wholesome and unadorned-looking way—like she could've done ads for milk or yogurt. She seemed so self-effacing that I actually apologized for my misleading profile photo and sent her a more recent picture—one of me with Zoé, taken by another passenger during her train ride to Hartford on the Zephyr. I figured if she thought I looked dweeby, at least Zoé looked great and could earn me a few points by association. Instead of being put off that I'd posted a misleading picture, Bridget laughed it off and said it was what everyone did—and she proved her point by sending me a picture of herself, taken just the week before during a class outing. For my part, I saw next to no difference in how Bridget looked in the newer photo.

She still looked cute as hell. And she was just so . . . nice.

More than ever, I hoped the reality wouldn't disappoint.

She lived in Providence, where I'd be overnighting on Wednesday. I'd been to Providence a couple of times before, and I liked the city. Especially the RiverWalk area, which was home to my favorite restaurant, Bacaro. So, I'd been thrilled when Bridget suggested we meet there for drinks.

Once again, I marveled at Sofie's seemingly effortless ability to find me the right—or at least, a *potentially* right—person so quickly.

For once, we had a week with moderate temperatures and next to no snow—so schedule delays were at a minimum. It was a near-balmy 52 degrees when we got to our hotel at the end of our duty day. So, after changing out of my uniform, I walked along the Providence River and entered Bacaro right on time.

I didn't have any trouble spotting Bridget—she looked exactly like her pictures: petite, fluffy, and sweet. She saw me, too, and waved vigorously from her table by the window. I was more excited than nervous as I approached her table. It was only then that I realized she wasn't alone—another woman sat with her.

I tried to stifle a premonition of dread. *She's probably just an acquaintance she ran into here*, I told myself. *She lives in this town, so of course she knows people.*

"Isabelle?" Bridget got to her feet and extended her hand. "It's so great to meet you."

I shook her hand warmly. "You, too." I looked nervously at her friend, who was just sitting there staring up at me. "Um . . . hi," I said to her.

"Oh." Bridget waved a dismissive hand at her companion. "Don't pay any attention to Freddie. She's just shy and never says much around strangers. Sit down. Let's get you a cocktail."

Freddie continued to stare at me like I was sporting some kind of disfiguring birthmark. She looked a bit older than Bridget—probably closer to my age, or a few years older. She might've been attractive except for the scowl that seemed to be the natural expression of her face in repose.

"So," I began to cover my nervousness, "you two are friends?"

"*Best* friends," Bridget gushed. "We do *everything* together, don't we, Freddie?"

Freddie glanced at Bridget but said nothing. She quickly returned her sober gaze to me.

"I guess 'everything' includes meeting new people for drinks?" I asked.

"Of course." Bridget said it like a head cheerleader being asked to top a pyramid of her squad members. "When I told Freddie about you, she *insisted* on coming along." Bridget slapped Freddie's arm. "You didn't want to miss out, did you Freddie?" She looked back at me. "Freddie just *loves* uniforms. When she saw your USRail photo, I knew I couldn't keep her away."

Okay . . . that was vaguely creepy. I hadn't shared any of my work photos with Bridget.

"Really?" I asked with all the innocence I could muster. "Where'd you find those?"

"Freddie is a whiz on the Internet. She found loads of them—didn't you Freddie?"

Crickets.

"That's . . . impressive," I said, to cover my discomfort.

Bridget slapped her tiny hands together. "Isn't this just so much fun?"

Fun? What about this was fun? Freddie's brooding scrutiny was activating all of my trip wires.

I decided to try again. "So, Freddie," I asked in the most upbeat tone I could manage, "are you a teacher, too?"

Crickets.

I looked at Bridget for help. She nodded vigorously.

"Freddie teaches math . . . algebra and geometry. All that really dense stuff that makes my head spin. But, believe me, she's *really* good with shapes . . ." She laid a hand on Freddie's arm. "All *kinds* of shapes. She says each of us is an empty vessel, just waiting to be filled. Isn't that right, Freddie? And you just *love* to fill things, don't you?"

Crickets.

I began to wish I'd reached out to JoAnn, to ask for my twenty minute lifeline. But alas, I was on my own this time.

What the hell? *Why not cut to the chase and see what these two were really up to?*

"So, what exactly, does Freddie like to fill these empty vessels with?"

"With *pleasure*, of course." Bridget smiled brightly. She had an impressive mouthful of very even, very white teeth. "I *knew* you'd get it! I t*old* Freddie you would." She faced Freddie with excitement. "I told you."

Freddie looked at her again—but this time, she gave Bridget a faint nod.

My god. The moment was electric. I could imagine it being tantamount to the first time moviegoers heard Garbo speak on the big screen.

"We're hoping you'll want to join us," Bridget said, in hushed confidential tones.

"Join you in ... what ... exactly?"

"Exploring our favorite shape."

"And that is?"

"The triangle, of course. But I have to warn you ... Freddie is greedy, and she always wants to be the hypotenuse."

"The ..." I made a straight up and down gesture with my index finger.

"Right! Did you know that in the original Greek, *hypotenuse* means 'down under'? Isn't that perfect?"

I nodded stupidly. "It's beyond perfect."

"And I'm here to tell you that you've never *been* down under until you've had Freddie as your hypotenuse. It's magic."

Magic? As much as I fought it, I could not stop my mind from imagining the spectacle of Freddie sprawled beneath ...

the two of us.

The two of us?

The three *of us?*

"Excuse me, Bridget. I don't want to make a wrong assumption here. And please don't be offended if I'm terribly off base. But are you suggesting that we—that we three—that all of us . . ."

"Have sex together?" She nodded "Yes, please! Isn't it just the *best* idea? And Freddie was hoping maybe you could get us on the train? Just some empty spot—even a table in the club car?" She looked at her companion. "Freddie just *loves* trains. She says all that clacking and rocking are the natural rhythms of the libido. Do you think you can work that out? *Could we go for a night ride?*"

I was too stupefied to answer.

"Don't worry if you can't make it happen. I have a waterbed— and the motion of it is almost as good." She looked lovingly at Freddie. "We like cruise ships too, don't we Freddie?" She looked back at me. "Listening to the water sloshing around beneath us makes me *so* hot."

Bridget's hand had disappeared beneath the table. I had no idea what she was doing, but whatever it was, it appeared to be working just *fine* for Freddie, who looked like she was about to have a seizure.

I had no doubt now that I'd been reading all of Bridget's sines—and cosines—accurately. And this was one angle I had *no* desire to solve for.

I got to my feet. "I just remembered that I have to make a call to . . . report in to scheduling for tomorrow." I looked over at Freddie, who was still locked into some kind of trance from Bridget . . . *measuring her angles.* "Please excuse me."

I turned on my heel and made a hasty retreat toward the bar, then ducked around a corner and exited from the side entrance to the restaurant.

What the serious fuck was that?

I needed a few minutes in private to figure out what the fuck I was going to do. I knew what I *wanted* to do: get the hell out of there. But I didn't want to be a total asshole, either, by just disappearing on Bridget . . . *and Freddie*. And I couldn't stand out here forever making up my mind.

I pulled out my phone and sent an S.O.S. text to Sofie. Her reply came back immediately.

"Driving. Unavailable for the next thirty minutes."

Fuck.

Now what?

Before I could think better of it, I texted Harper and told her I was in a jam and needed advice. Quick.

My phone rang less than ten seconds later.

"What's going on?" Harper asked, with more than a trace of urgency. "Are you all right?"

I quickly, albeit not very articulately, brought her up to speed on my blind date, *ménage à trois* dilemma.

"So, I made an excuse to leave the table," I concluded, "and now I'm standing outside in an alley, trying to figure out what to do."

"To recap . . ." Harper began, "this Freddie person wanted to do . . . *what* exactly?"

"I'd need a protractor to explain it fully."

"And . . . Bridget was giving Freddie a . . . *hand job* . . . when you made your escape?"

"It certainly seemed like it."

"Well," Harper quipped. "I'd say sharing an appetizer is definitely off the table."

"Very funny."

"Sorry. I really can understand your dilemma. On the one hand, you're dismayed by Bridget's apparent false pretenses for the date. On the other, you don't want to be a douchebag and just flee the scene without telling her why."

I relaxed a tiny bit. "Correct. So, what do I do?"

"Are you asking me what I think *you* should do—or do you want me to tell you what *I'd* do in your situation?"

I shot a nervous look back through the window of the restaurant door. "Yes?"

Harper laughed. "Knowing you as I'm beginning to, I think you'd probably feel bound to front-load your apology for leaving early with gifts of flowers or Belgian chocolates."

That sounded about right . . .

"Okay. So, what would *you* do?" I asked her.

"You're already outside, right?"

"Yeah."

"Run. Run like hell."

I felt relief wash over me. Maybe being a douchebag wasn't the worst thing in the world?

"Thank you," I whispered.

"Quit talking to me. Get the hell out of there."

"Yes, ma'am." I disconnected and headed for the RiverWalk.

I was sure of only two things.

I wasn't leaving my hotel room again that night.

And yesterday had been the *last* time I would ever let Sofie touch my goddamn phone.

"It was a fucking three-way. Are you hearing me? A *three-way?*"

"So?"

"What do you mean, 'so'? I about shit my pants, Sofie. I thought you said she was safe?"

"Izzy. Calm down. I don't have time for this now. I have a date."

"Calm down? You weren't there. It totally weirded me out. They were like geeky, sex-crazed math nerds. All into shapes . . . especially triangles. And this Freddie creature was some kind of self-styled human hypotenuse—which clearly translated into liking life on the *bottom*. Who are these fucking people on this godforsaken app, Sofie? They make the Star Wars Millennium Bar look like the Melrose Diner."

"*Izzy. Détends-toi. Calmes-toi.*"

"Don't tell me to calm down! It was surreal as fuck. I felt like I was in the middle of an Ingmar Bergman film . . . one of those uber-weird ones with Bibi Andersson."

"These things just happen. It's a crap shoot. It doesn't make anyone creepy or abnormal. It just means they're less inhibited than you are—and are more open to . . . *experience*." Sofie was beginning to sound impatient. "I told you that when you signed up. Now I really have to go. I'm going to be late. We can talk later."

"I did *not* sign up. *You* signed me up."

"I don't recall you wrestling your phone away from me. You went along with it. Now just relax and trust the process."

"What process? This game of Russian roulette you call online dating? What's next? *Three* bullets in the cylinder instead of two?"

"I suggested a much simpler solution for you, but you wouldn't hear of it."

"*What* simpler solution?"

"The one who lives on your floor."

There was no way I was having this conversation with Sofie again. Thinking about Harper that way just gave me hives . . . I was so sure it would end in disaster—no matter how much I wished it wouldn't.

"*No*. And that's final."

"Okay, then. *Do svidaniya*, baby. I gotta go. I'll call you back later."

The line went dead.

I threw my phone down on the bed and picked up the TV remote.

Maybe there'd be something good to watch until I could fall asleep.

Bingo. TCM was showing *Notorious* at eight. Two hours of watching Ingrid Bergman outsmart Nazis in Rio would make *anything* better. I could order room service.

I could call *maman* and see if she were at home.

We could watch it together.

CHAPTER SIX

Forced Proximity + Reunion—and what
made me think it would work a second time?

True to form, the weather shifted dramatically on Wednesday night. And by Thursday morning, a potential winter storm system they'd been "watching" had decided to follow the least likely path in the lauded spaghetti model and was barreling toward the Northeast. Worse, it was predicted to roar right up the Long Island Sound and take aim at New York City—bringing damaging winds, freezing cold temperatures, and significant amounts of snow and ice.

Great. Just great.

My next overnight was in . . . wait for it . . . *Stamford*—just a scant, fifty-eight minute train ride northeast of the city. Which meant we'd be gliding along the rails smack dab in the middle of the storm as it made its perilous trek south.

I'd be lucky if I got there by midnight.

The onslaught of nasty weather—especially when it hadn't been predicted—put everyone on edge. And the trains were more packed than usual since it was a Friday, and people were eager to get where they were going for the weekend.

By the time we reached New Haven, we were already running more than thirty minutes behind, and the snow was really coming down. Union Station was tied up in knots because so many trains had delays and the transfers were all blown to hell. Several incoming trains had been placed on ground stops until some of the traffic at the station cleared out. We'd lucked out and were one of the last trains to get in before things got completely backed up. Consequently, we ended up taking on a score of extra passengers who had hastily bought tickets to try and get out of Connecticut, hoping they could make better connections to complete their trips to destinations farther south.

I wasn't optimistic for any of them, but my job was to present a positive, can-do attitude. So, I slung bags, helped people find their seats, and gave dozens of them the train's Wi-Fi password—even though it was clearly printed on every seat back. We had a nearly full train, so it took longer than normal to get everyone boarded and settled. When we finally made our slow roll out of the station, we were running forty-five minutes behind schedule. If we even made it to the next stop in Bridgeport, we were guaranteed to face epic rations of shit from frustrated passengers.

Adam, the senior conductor, and I flipped for which halves of the train to check in. I lost the toss and got most of coach—the first three cars after the engine. There wasn't an empty seat to be had. The aisles were full of mud and melting snow and the overhead bins were crammed with suitcases and backpacks. Kids were screaming and lines were already forming by the restrooms. I did not envy Steve in the café car.

There were going to be a helluva lot of pissed-off people paying $7.50 for their cans of Stella.

I made my way down the aisle of each car.

"Ticket, please."

"Ticket, please."

"Ticket, please. Ma'am, you need to stow that bag in the overhead bin."

"Ticket, please."

"Ticket, please. Sure. The Wi-Fi password is USRailGuest."

"Ticket, please. No, sir. This train does not stop in Brattleboro. That's the Zephyr."

"Ticket, please. The Wi-Fi password is USRailGuest."

"Ticket, please." *Oh, Jesus H. Christ . . . It was Tonya.* "Um. What are you doing here?"

She seemed just as baffled to see me. "Dispatch sent me to Rensselaer to train some new hires. I was on my way home when I got bounced from the Zephyr. They helped me make this connection in New Haven. I'm trying to get to Philly. Do you think we'll make it . . . in this life?" There was an awkward pause. "How are you?"

"I'm . . . fine," I lied. I scanned her QR code. "Frankly, I'm not sure about anything farther south than Bridgeport. I'll try to get an update once I finish these check-ins and let you know. It's . . . good to see you."

"You, too." She dropped her eyes to her cell phone. "Thanks."

At least she was as uncomfortable as I was.

I moved on.

"Ticket, please."

What the serious fuck was Tonya doing here?

"Ticket, please."

On this train, of all the goddamn trains trying to get to New York.

"Ticket, please. Yes, ma'am—the Wi-Fi password is USRailGuest."

Just my damn luck.

I finished my rounds and fought my way to the café car to meet up with Adam. We did our calculations and reconciled the manifests. Everything checked out. Including passenger T. Wilkes in Coach C. As Adam and I finished our paperwork, I asked him for the latest on the weather.

"What is control saying about our odds to make it to Stamford?"

142

"You don't wanna know."

Fuck me . . .

"How bad is it?"

"Bad. There is all kinds of debris and clutter on the tracks from this wind. Bridgeport is reporting gusts of fifty to sixty miles per hour. We're going to be lucky if we don't get a ground stop—if we even make it that far."

"What the hell do we do if we can't make it to Stamford?"

"We all get off in Bridgeport, I guess. Don't sweat it. The railroad has to put us up. The problem will be finding a place when there are 275 people on the train who will be fighting for the same rooms. We might end up sleeping on the floor in the station."

"Charming. My trip is over once we reach Stamford. I'm deadheading from there back to Philly. Do you think they'll make me stay with the train until we reach Stamford—or can I get released if we get stuck in Bridgeport?"

Adam gave me a look that seemed to say, *You poor, stupid fuck . . . what do you think will happen?*

"I don't really know. You can always ask, I suppose. Stranger things have happened."

"This is your way of saying I've got a snowball's chance in hell, isn't it"

"Pretty much. Sorry Izzy. I know it sucks."

"Life on the board, man. I knew what I was getting into."

Adam was a great guy. He voluntarily worked the extra board because it allowed him to spend more time at home with his wife and two small kids. And he worked a second job as a policeman in the small Massachusetts town where he lived.

"Yeah. About that," he began, "how much longer do you have to wait until you can hold a line?"

"I dunno. Maybe another year? Maybe eighteen months."

"I saw JoAnn Cooke the other day. She said you were a good crewmember. One of the best she'd worked with in ten years.

She also said you were trying to finish a graduate degree. Do you think you'll stay on with USRail? Or do you plan to bail as soon as you get the degree?"

I was surprised by the directness of his question. Nobody connected with the railroad had ever approached me about my plans in quite that way. I wasn't sure how to answer him.

"Most days, I'd say hell yeah—I'm off these rails as soon as I get that sheepskin. But now?" I deliberated. "Now I honestly don't know."

"Well." he put on his hat and stood up. "Maybe a good night's sleep will help you get some clarity. In the meantime, look at the bright side: some sweet young thing might just offer to share her room with you."

His words sent a shiver up my spine.

"Yeah. From your mouth to god's ear."

"I'm going to make my way up to the front of the train. See if the engine crew has any better information."

"Okay. Let me know?"

"Trust me. You'll be the first person I tell."

In fact, Adam did get news from the engine crew—and none of it was good.

Flow control was preparing to issue a full ground stop for us—but it wasn't going to be at the next station. Conditions had worsened to the point that it would be unsafe to continue. Because we were still about thirty minutes outside Bridgeport and track conditions had slowed us to a near crawl, the decision had been made to stop and reverse course. That meant the train would back up—literally. The engine would push us back the ten miles we'd traveled since leaving New Haven. In New Haven, there was sufficient yard space to safely park the train overnight. Passengers would be issued vouchers to help defray some—but not all—of the unexpected overnight expense. And the station had been contacted to arrange for shuttle services to area hotels.

As for the crew? We'd be transported to a backup hotel because the regular station hotel was already booked solid.

Now the fun part began.

We'd make a general announcement over the PA system, then we'd have to walk the gauntlet, eighty-five feet at a time, to reiterate the same unwelcome information to each car full of passengers. To be fair, most of the riders had been fighting weather delays all day. In some (few) cases, that made them more stoic and willing to accept the bad news. Others? Well. Others weren't as understanding. This was one of those regrettable times when train conductors were imbued with superpowers. And why weren't we able to control the weather? Why hadn't we predicted that this would happen? Why didn't we have the ability to secure space in hotels that weren't already overflowing with other travelers? Why was the Wi-Fi so shitty on this train? And why was the café car still charging $7.50 for cans of beer that should be free because of the inconvenience?

That last complaint was the only one I felt some solidarity with. A couple of Stellas was sounding pretty damn good to me right then, too.

If you haven't had the pleasure of walking forward on a train that's traveling backward, let me clarify the experience for you. It's surreal. It's like freefalling through history and it seriously messes with your head. Even when viewed through the driving white haze of a snow that appeared to be falling sideways, you still recognized things you hadn't really paid attention to before. Boarded up buildings. Abandoned cars. Small, shopworn towns with one working stoplight. The same dog sitting on a sagging back deck, futilely trying to shake the snow off his coat. I watched the dog. He looked . . . familiar. *Why hadn't I noticed him the first time we'd passed?* It hadn't even been that long ago.

Life in that moment became like one of those confounding

time and distance problems . . . a train moving at eight miles per hour travels a distance of twelve miles but has to stop twice for intervals of six and nine minutes each. How long will it take the train to reach its destination?

And when it gets there, will there be better Wi-Fi?

I wondered, as I walked the cars that were gliding back through time, if the same formula could be applied to our lives. *To my life.* If I could walk backward along the roads I'd traveled, what might I see that I'd managed to miss the first time? When I reached my destination, would I know it?

And why did I have an eerie premonition that I was about to find out?

Mercifully, we pulled into Union Station at New Haven without incident. The good news was that the station had all but shut down to other incoming trains, although there still were dozens of stranded passengers milling about, hoping for some kind of transportation miracle.

Off-loading 275 people and their luggage was like another kind of math problem. The best approach was to start with the rear of the train and proceed one car at a time—instead of allowing for the usual crush of riders crowding the exit doors. Ground crew workers were on hand to distribute vouchers and direct passengers to various shuttle buses. To say it was like herding cats would be an understatement.

I didn't see Tonya get off the train—she exited through the door Adam was staffing. But I supposed she'd make her way to one of the area hotels without incident. I'd never known her to be passive when faced with any obstacle, so I was confident she'd land on her feet.

My immediate future was a bit less certain. By the time Adam and I off-loaded the last passenger, we knew our prospects for finding lodging were disappearing faster than the view down the tracks. The blowing snow was making everything disappear—including the likelihood that we'd get space in any of the area hotels that weren't already filled to the gills.

But we got lucky. The station manager had the foresight to hold out a few extra rooms at three of the locations where USRail was billeting passengers for the night. The good news was that we would not be sleeping on the station floor. The bad news was we were being split up and sent to different destinations. That meant getting everyone back to the station on time in the morning would be a cluster—assuming, of course, the weather relented enough to allow us to leave New Haven. How the railroad would recover anything resembling a normal schedule tomorrow was anyone's guess. Stranded trains were like dominoes: the way one fell had an impact on all the others along the line. I was happy I was not the one tasked to figure these flow issues out—it would be tantamount to untangling fifty strands of Christmas lights.

Luck of the draw landed me at the New Haven hotel on George Street. Its location in center city made it very walkable—even in this weather—to a dozen or so restaurants, so at least I wouldn't starve. The registration desk was still crowded with a line of people—some of whom I recognized—trying to check in.

I knew my life would get a lot easier once I was able to ditch my uniform and not be a walking customer service portal. Of course, I felt guilty about that. After all, part of my job was to care for passengers—even when they'd rather hang me in effigy for the transgressions of Mother Nature. Or the railroad.

I was nicely installed in my small room on the sixth floor—right next to the uncommonly loud ice machines in vending—by two o'clock. What a day. I hadn't had anything to eat since six thirty that morning, and I was famished. I spent a few minutes looking up restaurants that were more than a few blocks from the hotel and narrowed the list to three that sounded good. My logic was that the farther out I looked, the less likely they were to be choked with other stranded passengers. So, after changing into street clothes, I grabbed my jacket, gloves and knit cap and headed for the elevators.

Once I got outside, I stood for a minute beneath the portico over the hotel entrance to try and get my bearings.

"Izzy?"

I recognized the voice immediately. Why wouldn't I? I'd heard it every day for more than four years. I turned around.

"Hi, Tonya. Are you on your way out, or going in?"

"Out. I wanted to find a place to eat. What about you?"

"The same. So . . . this is where you landed, too?"

She nodded. "What are the odds, right?"

"I think all the passengers got pretty spread out. Same for the crew. As far as I know, I'm the only one sent to this hotel."

"You got lucky. I was thrilled I didn't get sent to La Quinta."

"You say that like it's Guantánamo."

"Ever stayed at one?"

I thought about it. "Can't say I have."

"Let me put it this way. I used to work with an idiot who said he always loved staying in them when he traveled because he thought 'La Quinta' meant 'Next to Denny's' in Spanish. For the record, he wasn't wrong—at least about proximity to Denny's."

I laughed. "I'd be happy with that right about now."

"Me, too."

"Where are you headed?"

"I looked at a few places online, thinking it would be better to cast a wider net since the closest places are probably already overrun."

"I had the same thought."

"Of course you did. All railroad workers share a brain."

"What'd you decide?"

"There's a Belgian Café about four blocks," she turned around and pointed, "that a-way."

Waffles and beer? That could work . . .

"Sounds . . . inviting."

"Wanna go with me?" she asked. "I'd like the company." When I hesitated, she added, "I'll even walk in front of you so I can block the wind for you."

This easygoing, good-humored Tonya was the person I'd missed. It felt nice to reconnect with her. *With this aspect of her, at least.*

"Sure," I said. "Let's go."

MaisonB, the Belgian Café and bakery, was only a fifteen-minute walk from the hotel. When we arrived, it was busy, but not overwhelmed. It seemed to be a popular destination for the Yale crowd. There were quite a few graduate student and faculty-looking types spread about, huddled over books or laptops. Most of the patrons were drinking elaborate coffee concoctions. The glass pastry cases were filled with fussy, delectable-looking confections that, the sign proclaimed, were all baked on site.

We found a vacant table and sat down to peruse the menu—which consisted entirely of breakfast and lunch offerings—even though they were open until nine at night.

And my prognostication had been accurate: they did indeed serve waffles and beer.

I ordered a *croque madame* and Tonya ordered a smoked salmon omelette. We both got Abbey Leffe beers. They were just right for the occasion—a perfect balance of sweet and bitter. We agreed to visit the pastry case on the way out, thinking we'd each appreciate something sweet later on in evening.

Once we got our beers and were waiting on our food, we sat staring at each other somewhat awkwardly. There seemed, at least to me, to be an embargo on every topic. We could hardly talk about the weather . . . big damn duh. It was the entire reason we were stranded together in New Haven.

I mean . . . what else did I have to ask her about?

How are you liking life in that $3K a month loft apartment?

Are you still dating women with IQs smaller than their shoe sizes?

Does the cat ever ask about me?

I cleared my throat and tried for something less . . . volatile.

"So, how was Rensselaer?"

"It was . . . about like you'd expect. Cold. Gray." She was absently picking at the label on her bottle. "Unvarying."

"Not much nightlife, I suppose."

She laughed. "No. Not much."

"Too bad. You always did like a good nightlife." I knew it was bitchy, but I couldn't resist.

Tonya's chin went up. "There was a time you did, too."

Touché. "You're right. I did."

"I'm not the one who changed." Tonya leaned forward. "You were."

"I know that."

"You don't get to do that and get off scot-free."

"Do what?" I wasn't sure which particular offense of mine she was referencing.

"Change the terms of our contract midstream and just expect me to fall in line without question."

I was nonplussed by her assessment. "We had a contract?"

"An implied one—like all relationships have."

How had I missed *that* detail?

"I guess I never thought about it that way," I said. "I never meant to . . ." *What? What had I never meant to do? Be honest about my feelings?*

"Don't worry about it." Tonya's tone was dismissive. "It's all in the past, anyway—so why dredge it up? Besides . . . it was obvious the hours you were working were taking a toll on you. It made sense that you had no energy for sex when you got home."

Her words landed like hammer blows. I didn't ever recall a time when I'd been too tired for sex—or at least, expressing it if I were. Tonya had been the one who'd withdrawn—to the extent that I finally gave up making overtures. We'd never talked about it, of course. Because not having sex . . . *correction:* not having sex more than three times a week—which was Tonya's minimum—was something we'd never discuss. I always yielded to her nonverbal cues. That's because she'd always been the cruise director of our relationship. I even jokingly called her Julie McCoy.

But, somehow, the demise of our physical relationship had now been recast as a casualty of my job?

This was a brave, new adventure in revisionist history.

"Is that really what you think happened?" I asked.

"No. That *is* what happened. It's why I started looking elsewhere for fulfillment."

It had also been true that Tonya began seeing other women when I was off on overnight trips. I'd been expected to overlook that detail, too.

It was amazing how easily we fell right back into our old, established patterns. Tonya would pontificate, and I would capitulate. But in self-defense, I'd always been conflict averse. It had only been in the last couple of years I'd begun to chafe against always being compliant.

But Tonya was right: it *was* all in the past. None of it mattered now.

And I had bigger fish to fry. Like praying that the weather lightened up so we could all get the hell out of New Haven in the morning. As it was, I was looking at an additional night on the road, and not getting home now until Saturday.

It sucked.

Our food arrived and it looked sensational. We both dug into our entrees with zeal. When we'd finished, Tonya suggested we pick up some pastries and get a couple of coffees to go.

The snow was still coming down hard during our walk back to the hotel. And this time, we were heading into the wind coming in off the sound. I stuck the bag containing our pastries into my backpack to keep them dry, and we set out. The wind and the snow in our faces made it impossible to carry on a conversation. I was tired from the grueling day, and I wanted nothing more than to get back to my room and relax . . . probably nap.

The lobby had settled down a lot by the time we reached the hotel. There were only a few people milling about. As we walked past the registration desk to get to the elevators, I could hear a couple of hotel employees saying they hoped management would shut the place down early so they could get out before dark. It seemed likely to me. There was zero chance they'd be getting any more traffic from Union Station. It was now sealed up tighter than a snare drum.

Tonya's room was on the fourth floor, so I punched buttons for four and six and we made the short ride together. When the bell dinged for her floor, she turned abruptly and gave me a quick hug.

"It really was great to see you, Izzy," she said into my coat. "We shouldn't let so much time go by."

I hugged her back belatedly. "I know," I agreed. "Let's do better."

"Let's." She disengaged and stepped off as soon as the door opened. "See you around." She waved and headed off down the hallway, carrying her double mocha latte.

I had a lot to process when I got back to my room. What a confounding couple of days it had been. It seemed like a year ago that I'd made my great escape from the impending *ménage à trois* in Providence.

Providence?

I found the irony of *that* one hard to escape . . . exploring Freddie's 'hypotenuse' with a willing Bridget would hardly have been . . . *providential*. It would've been more like sitting through a remake of any Freddy Kreuger movie.

I figured a hot shower would do more to relax me than a nap, so I headed for the bathroom and decided to take my time, letting the pulsating water flow over my tired joints for more than twenty minutes. It was luxurious. Afterward, I wrapped myself in an oversized hotel robe, picked up my tepid coffee, and walked to the window to watch the snow. Adam had said he'd call us all later this evening to let us know what time to plan on reporting tomorrow. As much as I wanted to get home, I hoped it wouldn't be too early.

The soft knock on my door surprised me. At first, I wasn't sure I'd heard it, I was becoming so accustomed to the noise of the ice machines next door. But then it happened a second time, and I was sure it was someone at my door. So, I crossed the room, still holding my coffee cup, and looked through the peep hole.

It was Tonya.

What the hell was she doing up here?

I unhitched the security lock and opened the door.

"Hey."

"Sorry to bother you," she said, "but you absconded with *both* of the desserts."

It didn't occur to me to ask how she'd found my room number—or why, once she found it out, she didn't just call me.

"Well, damn if I did. I'm sorry." I held the door open wider. "Come on in and I'll get it for you."

I stepped back so she could come inside. I felt ridiculous to be standing there wearing only a hotel robe. Tonya seemed to just roll with it.

"A shower sounds inspired. I think I'll do the same when I get back."

I was opening my backpack to remove the bag of desserts. "Do it soon, while there's still hot water."

"Great idea."

The voice came from just behind me. When I turned around, Tonya was standing very close. I took a step back and realized I was pinned against the side of the bed.

"I forgot how hot you look with wet hair." She reached up

153

and pushed some loose strands back behind my ear.

"Um . . ." I stupidly held up the bag. "Here are the desserts. Where do you want yours?"

Oh . . . nice one, Lebrun. Real smooth . . .

She took the bag from me and dropped it onto the bed. "I think here is good."

"Here?" I was trying—and failing—to make sense of what was happening. She wasn't really coming on to me . . . was she?

Impossible.

"I really have missed you, Izzy. Missed all the things we used to do. *The things you'd do to me.*"

I opened my mouth to speak, but no sound came out.

She kissed me. I tried to push her away.

"Wait . . ."

She moved in again. Her lips were on my neck this time. Then they began to travel down the open v of my robe.

"Don't . . ." I began.

"Don't what?" she whispered against my bare skin.

God help me. No. This wasn't what I wanted.

Was it?

"Stop." I said. "Don't . . . stop."

Now her hands were in motion, untying my robe.

I couldn't think. Couldn't breathe. I knew in my viscera this was a mistake—that it didn't mean anything to her. I was just a convenient outlet . . . like a USB port in a bedside lamp. Some way to get a quick charge between overnights.

Her mouth was doing things to me. Moving across my chest, across my abdomen. I felt my knees begin to buckle.

"Please . . . *please* . . . don't . . ." I wound my hands into her hair as her head continued its journey. I was lost and I knew it. It was pointless to keep fighting. "Don't," I repeated. "Don't . . . *stop.*"

And she didn't.

I woke up shortly after one. I didn't have to roll over to see if Tonya was still there. I knew for certain she'd be gone.

But I looked anyway.

She wasn't there.

And the bag of pastries was gone, too. She'd even taken mine. As miserable as I felt, and as full of recriminations, I still had to laugh at that. Tonya was nothing if not consistent. Good thing I'd had no illusions about what last night would mean.

It meant nothing. Not to her. I had to search my flagging conscience to determine if it had meant anything to me. Mercifully, after a careful and caustic review of my own weakness, I realized it hadn't.

Did that make me as contemptible as I felt?

Probably.

In fact, I felt like shit. The interlude with Tonya felt like it had taken place out of time. None of this had been in the cards. Running into her this way couldn't have been scripted. It was too unbelievable. It strained credibility beyond the breaking point. Any competent editor would've cut it right out of the manuscript. *Too obvious,* they'd have said. *Nobody would buy it.*

And they'd have been right. I was embarrassed about how fucking textbook it had been. And I hoped, more than anything, that she'd make a different connection today so I wouldn't have to run into her on the train. I mean . . . what would I say? *I guess my dessert was the one not in the bag?*

Yeah. I had no good conversation starters.

Adam had asked us all to be at the station by 7:30, so we could have our debrief and get the train out of the yard. Our normal departure time for New Haven was at 10:35. But control needed to get us out of the station to free up track space for other incoming trains. The one thing we were sure of was that nobody would complain about reaching their final destinations early.

When I looked out my window, the snow had stopped, and the sky was partly cloudy. Very good omens for travel today. The street in front of the hotel had been cleared, which probably meant snowplows had been out running all night to keep ahead. I hope the same would be true for the ground rail crews, who kept the tracks clear of falling tree limbs and other debris. With the winds that had driven this storm down the sound, I was sure there had to have been a lot of clutter deposited along the rail lines.

I grabbed a quick breakfast in the hotel lobby and waited on the shuttle to take me to the station. Mercifully, there was no sign of Tonya.

Even at seven thirty in the morning, the station was as jammed with people as Walmart on the Friday after Thanksgiving—and all of them were vying for the same P.A.-announced specials. I clung to my vain hope that the "last in, first out" principle would apply to our place in the queue of trains waiting to depart New Haven.

For once, lady luck smiled on us, and we got the green light to board and head out at nine thirty—a full hour before our scheduled departure. USRail had sent text messages to all ticketed passengers to alert them to the change. But even with that, I was sure there'd be a score who would show up an hour later and be royally pissed off that they'd missed their connections . . . again.

And Adam had been right about his prognostication that crew scheduling would not let me off the hook in Stamford. I still had to do the fucking overnight before I got released. Their excuse was that things were so knotted up from the delays yesterday they might have to shift me to a slot on another line to work the trip back to Philadelphia. For my part, if I had to stay over, why not work the way back and make some extra coin? I could always use the additional bank for ... well. For something. *Maybe for six bottles of wine Sofie would lower herself to drink without complaint.*

That made me think back over our dinner with Harper on Sunday night. We'd laughed like schoolgirls at the lampoon of *Die! Die! My Darling!* The troubled heroine, played superbly by Charles Busch in drag, fell hopelessly under the spell of ne'er-do-well gigolo Tony Parker, played by Jason Priestly of *90210* fame. The irreverent comedy blended elements from a dozen of the hallmark *femme fatale* genre films. It even had a nod to *Mildred Pierce*—which made me sure *Maman* would enjoy it, too.

I might ask Harper if I could borrow it for my next trip to Frelighsburg.

Sofie and Harper had left together shortly after the film ended. They both knew I had an early start the next morning and didn't want to overstay. I wanted to walk with them as far as the elevator, but Sofie insisted I stay behind.

"Harper can see me off." She shooed me back inside. "You need to get back in there and clean up that monstrous mess in the kitchen."

"What mess?" I'd asked. I prided myself on being a very tidy chef.

She shot me a dismissive look. "I neglected to tell you that I spilled half a bottle of buckwheat honey when I was plating the desserts."

I was aghast. "What the fuck were you doing with that?" The Canadian dark honey was something I only used in baking—which was rare. I didn't even know how Sofie found it.

"I wanted a drizzle on my *merveilleux*."

"For god's sake, why? The stuff is already sweet enough to choke a grizzly bear."

"Don't be a hater."

Harper laughed.

"Yeah. Okay." I waved them off. "You two enjoy the rest of your evenings. It appears I have to steam clean my kitchen."

They were already in deep conversation about ... *something* ... before I closed my door.

That can't be good, I'd thought as I proceeded to embrace my fate confronting the mess Sofie'd left behind.

It occurred to me that I was getting pretty damned good at embracing my fate. For my part, this dalliance with online dating was proving to be nothing more than a master class in dealing with mortification and disappointment—not necessarily in that order. I was becoming sure of only one thing: I didn't need any more of the growth experiences SheDate had to offer.

Fortunately, the rest of our duty day went smoothly, and we rolled into Stamford twenty-five minutes early. I was surprised when crew scheduling contacted me to say they were reassigning me to crew the southbound run on line 93, which departed Stamford less than ninety minutes after our arrival and would get me back in Philadelphia by three thirty that afternoon.

I didn't mind. It got me home a day earlier than expected and paid me for a half day of overtime.

But I was one tired puppy when I finally got back to Hopkinson House.

What a damn week.

I half hoped I would run into Harper, but there was no sign of her in the lobby, on the elevator, or in the hallway on twenty-six.

I didn't see Aldo or Luz either, but I did notice that every wreath I passed en route to my apartment had a conspicuous bulb of garlic affixed to its festive greenery.

I supposed it was good news that we didn't have to worry about an influx of vampires—even though most of them probably preferred the accommodations in Tonya's upscale digs at Jessup House. In my experience, vampires were *always* pretty snooty ... Bela Lugosi, Christopher Lee, Frank Langella, David Bowie *and* Catherine Deneuve ... the list went on and on. I suspected that most of them would've found haunting the halls of Hopkinson House beneath their stations.

But try telling that to our resident Abbott and Costello . . .

My apartment was cold and quiet when I let myself inside. I thought about ditching my bag and scouring the fridge for something to reheat—but it was still too early. I really wanted to nap, because I hadn't slept well the night before. But I was determined to make myself stay awake. So, after changing clothes I cast about for something to do.

I should've immediately made use of the extra time to get reacquainted with my dung beetles.

But, no. That wasn't happening today.

I wondered what Harper was up to? I recalled seeing her around the building previously on Friday afternoons, so I supposed she might work from home on those days. I was happy we'd finally exchanged phone numbers during our impromptu movie night, so I decided to send her a text.

Howdy, stranger!

I only had to wait about ninety seconds for her to text back.

Hi there! Are you back from your trip?

I am. Just got home, in fact.

How was it? Did you get caught in that storm that hit New York?

Affirmative. It sucked. I won't bore you with details. It was pretty gruesome.

Please bore me. I'm in the throes of something truly mind-numbing and

159

could use the distraction.

Believe me. Listening to my tale of woe
would be worse than watching clothes dry.

Really? One guess what I'm doing right now.

No way?

Way.

Dear god. Doing laundry really is pathological for
you, isn't it?

I'd be offended by that crack if
it weren't so true—and pathetic.

How many loads you got going?

I refuse to answer that question on
the grounds it might incriminate
me.

I know this one. Citing the fifth amendment
equates to fewer than six but more than three,
correct?

I will neither confirm nor deny
the veracity of that statement.

Just wondering if there'd be available
space for me to toss in a load of poorly
sorted items.

En tant que blanchisseuse locale, je peux affirmer qu'il y a des machines disponibles.

Wow. Sofie was right.

About?

Texting about laundry in French really is pretty hot.

Maybe you should add this skill to your SheDate profile?

I'd rather add fabric softener to my mixed bag of unmentionables. Okay if I come down and join you? I promise not to interfere with your sorting.

Don't be silly. I never sort down here. There isn't enough space to accommodate all my loads.

Noted. See you in just a few.

It only took me a minute to grab my laundry and head for the basement.

Truth be told, I'd never been so excited to do my laundry. But I was still bruised from the encounter with Tonya—and the near miss with Bridget and Freddie in Providence. Spending some time with a friendly face belonging to someone who had no predispositions about me, or my prospects, sounded very welcoming.

I found Harper in her customary back corner, keeping watch over her four machines. She laughed when she caught sight of my basket, crammed to the gills with everything from towels to sweaters.

"Please tell me you have no intention of washing all of that together."

"Okay." I set my basket down in front of a mammoth Speed Queen washer and slapped my pockets to find my card. I'd just loaded it up with credits two weeks ago, so it should still have enough space left for today. "I won't tell you."

I opened the big door and began cramming my stuff inside. "Wait!"

Harper's exclamation was so determined, I paused in mid-cram.

"What?"

She got up from her chair and walked over to where I stood. "You cannot do that."

"Sure I can. I do it all the time." I reached down for a handful of assorted items.

"Stop." She laid a hand on my arm. "Really. Just stop."

She reached inside the machine and pulled my items back out. "Go stand over there." She pointed at a spot about ten feet away from where we stood. "I'll take care of this."

"Why do I feel like I'm in time out?" I complained. "It's my damn laundry."

Harper was busy sorting my clothes. "Would you expect me to stand idly by and watch you walk down the center of the railroad tracks at night, in the face of an oncoming train?"

"I hardly see the similarity here . . ."

She held up a white T-shirt that had become intertwined with a pair of cherry red briefs. "Clearly."

"Oh, come on." I watched the number of piles increase to three. "At this rate, I'll be here all afternoon."

I thought better of my comment as soon as it was out of

162

my mouth. There were worse things to do than spend the next couple of hours with Harper in a deserted laundry room . . . sorting my unmentionables.

"It won't be *that* bad," she clarified. "You can use three machines on short cycles. These will be small loads."

"Okay." I accepted my fate magnanimously. "Got anything I can read?" It had been my experience that Harper always had a veritable lending library tucked away in her cavernous basket—*probably because she spent so much goddamn time down here.*

"Give me your card," she demanded. She expertly added the requisite amount of soap to each machine before swiping the card to get them going. She handed the card back to me. "In fact, I do have something—the book for our next club meeting. I just finished it."

"Oh, great. What's this one about? Lesbian skydivers who meet and fall in love fifty-five hundred feet above the earth? Wait . . . don't tell me. It's called *Falling for You.*"

"Nice try. But this one is a grumpy-sunshine romance about two large animal veterinarians who clash over the right way to manage an outbreak of anthrax on a Wyoming dude ranch." She paused. "Think an Olivia Cruise taking place on the wide-open range."

"Seriously?" I blinked. "They must be running out of shit to write about. What's it called?"

She walked over to her basket and pulled out the paperback. Again, it featured a pastel composition of cartoon figures posing at opposite ends of a Hereford. The title, written in a large, loopy font, was *A Rare Breed of Love.*

"Dear god. Did you actually read this?"

"What do you think?"

I fanned through the pages of the book. "I think . . . *not.*"

"That would be incorrect. I read the relevant parts."

"But why do you buy them if you don't read all of the . . . parts?"

She shrugged. "It seems like the right thing to do. I mean, it helps the authors out."

"So they can write more books you won't read?"

"Something like that. As a writer myself, I appreciate the work it takes to craft one of these tales—even if it isn't at the top of my must-read pile."

"I am sure people said the same thing about *Das Kapital*."

"Probably. But then, that one wasn't available on Kindle Unlimited."

"Good point. Besides, Marx didn't write that many sex scenes."

"I can guarantee you it would've increased his readership."

I walked over and sat down in a chair near where she'd been sitting. She joined me.

"So, are you going to tell me your horror stories about traveling in the winter storm?"

I stretched out my legs and crossed my ankles. My shoes were dirty. I thought about asking Harper if I could throw them into one of the machines but thought better of it.

I didn't want to spark an international incident.

"The trip was going okay until we left Providence on Thursday morning. That's when the weather shit hit the proverbial fan. Conditions deteriorated all day, and we kept losing time because we had to slow our speed to a near crawl. Finally, they put us on a full ground stop—after mandating that the engine reverse course and push us ten miles back to New Haven, where we had to offboard everyone and find lodging for the night."

"That sounds like a nightmare."

I thought about Tonya. "It was . . . believe me. In more ways than one."

I could tell Harper was taking her time preparing to ask me her next question.

"Sofie thought she'd found you the perfect date in Providence."

I laughed. "So she did."

"And . . . obviously, that didn't go as planned. Was it as awful as you described?"

"It was . . . *an experience.*"

Harper laughed. "To say the least. Any more rich details to share?"

"You mean apart from my amazement that Bridget, the poster child for Catholic middle schools, turned out to be more suited to being the pitch woman for eclectic forms of recreational *discourse?*"

"Yes. Apart from that."

"In retrospect, I suppose her unveiled honesty about her proclivities *was* kind of refreshing. That complete lack of artifice must signify some level of self-acceptance. But I must admit that showing up for our date with her paramour in tow—that ill-tempered geometry teacher named 'Freddie'—was off-putting, to say the least. It was when Bridget quickly explained to me that in their three-way encounters with women, Freddie always played the role of *hypotenuse*, that the event jumped the shark."

Shock and bemusement appeared to be arm-wrestling for ascendency in Harper's reaction.

"So, you fled the scene?" she asked.

"Of course I did. I made a flimsy excuse about having to call scheduling and laid a patch to the restroom faster than rats jumping off a sinking ship."

"Does Sofie know?"

"Oh, she knows, all right. I laid a patch getting back to my hotel and I called her immediately."

"And she said?"

"Before or after she told me I knew SheDate was a crap shoot?" I didn't bother to share that Sofie had also suggested I try dating someone closer to home. A *lot* closer.

"I am sorry." Harper sounded like she meant it.

"I can tell you one thing."

"What's that?"

"It's going to be a cold day in hell before I go fishing on that godforsaken app again."

My phone dinged. I pulled it from my pocket and checked the display.

No fucking way.

Someone on SheDate had just swiped right on my profile.

I wanted to throw the damn thing into the washing machine to see if a heavy-duty Speed Queen could clean up its damn algorithms.

I held it up to show Harper. "Speak of the devil."

She smiled. "No rest for the weary, I suppose."

"I dunno about that." I stuffed the phone back into my pocket. "I'm pretty damn weary at this point."

"Well." Harper got up to go check on her loads. "I could always ask Gina if she knows another face painter."

"Yeah." I agreed. "Maybe I should try that. It would make my escapes from disastrous dates so much more effortless. I mean, slinking out the back entrance of a restaurant is a whole lot more respectful if you're wearing The Full Gritty."

"I've always thought so," Harper agreed. She began pulling items out of a dryer.

"Well, for right now, consider me happy in my solitude. But if that ever changes, I promise you'll be the first to know."

"I hope that I am." Harper resumed folding her clothes, leaving me to wonder if her response had been literal or ironic. Nevertheless, I felt my heart skip a beat.

But I was too chicken to ask, so instead, I sat watching my clothes tumble through the small window of the nearest washing machine.

Dewey was in a great mood when I showed up at the reception desk later that evening, carrying a six-pack of black cherry

Wishniak. I'd been to Whole Foods earlier to pick up some groceries and saw a tower of the iconic soft drinks on an end cap display. I remembered how Dewey used to crow about drinking those when he was a kid, growing up in East Germantown. He liked to complain that the newer, knock-off brands weren't as good as the original Frank's—but I'd never known him to refuse one, either.

He was demonstrably thrilled with the modest gift and promptly popped one open.

"You want one, too?" he asked, magnanimously.

I knew better than to accept. "No thanks, man. I'm sugared out."

"I just bet you are," he chuckled. "Sofie told me about your three-way in Providence."

I was aghast. "I did not have a three-way—not in Providence and not anyplace else, either."

"Uh huh."

"And when the hell did you talk to Sofie? This just happened forty-eight damn hours ago."

"Don't get your panties in a wad, missy. I saw her yesterday when she dropped Harper off."

What? Sofie had been out with Harper?

"Where had those two been?"

"Lunch, I think. At least, Harper thanked her for lunch before heading upstairs in the elevator."

Funny . . . Harper didn't mention it when we'd been doing our laundry together. I wondered if Sofie had entertained her with *her* perspective on my catastrophic date?

I doubted it.

Harper hadn't mentioned anything since my revelation to her about Bridget and Freddie. And as much as she drove me crazy, it would be uncharacteristic for Sofie to do anything that would make me look pitiful in the eyes of a new friend.

"That's . . . nice." I said.

"Oh, yeah? You don't look real happy about it," he observed.

"I'm . . . not *any* way about it. But I wonder why she chose to tell you about my debacle?"

"Probably because she knew you'd come slinking down here to confess your sins at some point, and she wanted to go ahead and grease the skids for me."

I nodded. "That sounds about right."

"So," he continued, "tell me about Miss Sixth Grade teacher and her mixed bag of magic tricks."

"Most of them involved lessons in plane geometry which, she explained, was best understood from the vantage point of her companion, Freddie—who preferred the view from below—if you catch my drift."

"So this Bridget wanted to have a three-way with you and—this Freddie person?"

"You might say that."

Dewey slowly shook his head. "The more I live in this world, the less I understand it."

"Have any of your girls ever used these dating apps?"

"Hell," he scoffed. "If they have I sure don't wanna know about it. It sounds like a damn traveling circus."

"More like hell's funhouse."

"Let's at least update your stats."

"What are you talking about? What stats?"

"Your stats," he reached into his inside coat pocket and withdrew his small notepad. "We gotta update your progress knocking out the tropes."

I rolled my eyes. "Is this really the part that interests you?"

"Ordinarily, something like this wouldn't hold my interest for very long. But with you," he grabbed a pencil off the desk, "the averages are climbing at light speed."

"What the hell does that mean?"

"How many of these SheDate hookups have you had now?"

"Only a couple."

"And for the first two of those three dates we've knocked off," he did a quick calculation, "*five tropes*. That's when we give you credit for the office romance with Tonya—and Harper's toaster oven."

"Yeah . . . I still don't see why I get tagged for that one."

Dewey waved his pencil in the air. "It's a statistical control."

"Whatever."

"Then we add in the fake relationship with Harper. And now the interlude with the twisted sisters in Providence." He laughed. "That one is a real crowd pleaser: *love triangles*."

I had to admit he'd got the triangle part right—but I wasn't sure this idea was what was meant by the trope.

"Are you sure this is the kind of triangle they have in mind?"

He paused in his writing. "Did it have three sides and a hypotenuse?"

I nodded.

"It was a damn triangle." He finished the entry with a flourish. "So, to recap. You've blown through toaster oven, office romance, age gap, false identity, fake relationship, and love triangle." He counted again. "Damn, girl. You've only had three at bats, and you're averaging one point two-five tropes per at bat. Next thing we know, the Phillies scout will be following your ass around with a contract."

"I doubt it."

He took a big swig of his Wishniak. "I can hardly wait to see what's waiting in the on-deck circle."

I wasn't sure I wanted to tell him the switch-hitter had already come and gone.

He must've read my face because he hit me with the full Dewey—which was a lot like The Full Gritty without the hair and makeup. But it was just as intense.

"You got something else on your mind?"

"What makes you think that?"

"Because I've been knowing you ever since you came here

169

with your daddy. You never could keep what you were feeling off your face. Right now, you look just like you always did when he was taking you to the train station to head back home."

"Probably because I knew Zoé would always meet me in New Haven, and she'd steal my window seat."

"Well then, who stole something else you wanted? Because that's exactly how you look right now."

I stood drumming the desktop with my fingers. To his credit, Dewey stayed quiet and just waited me out.

"We hit that rotten weather system that rolled through the upper Northeast on Thursday," I explained. "Actually, it hit us. It got so bad all the trains were running late and, eventually, we got a full ground stop. We had to backtrack to New Haven and spend an unplanned overnight. All the passengers got vouchers and were sent out to various hotels in the area."

"Bet they were all good sports about it, too," Dewey offered.

"Yeah. Not so much. I was still smarting from that horrible experience with Bridget and Freddie in Providence. I felt like such a damn loser—like the universe had my number and just kept shoveling shit into my path. Then everything got worse." I took a deep breath before continuing. "A lot worse."

"How worse?" Dewey sounded suspicious.

"Tonya was on the train . . . *our* train."

"Say what?"

I nodded. "She'd been working up in Rensselaer and was trying to get back when the storm hit. All the connections were hosed so she got a ticket on the Nor'easter hoping to get back." I shook my head. "Luck of the draw."

"I think I got a bad feeling about this . . ."

"Well, you're a wise man, because it gets worse."

"Do I want to hear how?"

"Probably not. But I'm going to tell you anyway. The railroad dispersed everyone—all 275 passengers and our crew—to about five different hotels. Tonya and I ended up at the same place."

"Hell's bells."

"We ran into each other downstairs when we both were heading out to find someplace to get something to eat. So we decided to go together. It was snowing like hell and windy as fuck, but we walked about fifteen minutes to get to a place that would likely be less crowded. After dinner, we went back to the hotel—but not until we'd bought some pastries for each of us to eat later. I stuffed the bag into my backpack to keep it from getting wet—but forgot to take it out when we got on the elevator. She got off on her floor, and I figured that was that."

"I'm assuming that *wasn't* that?"

I shook my head. "Nope. I took a long shower and was just hanging out, watching the snow fall outside the window, when she showed up at my room—auspiciously to get her dessert."

He scoffed. "Is that the new term for booty call?"

"Don't make this harder than it already is."

Dewey's eyes grew wide. "Honey, do *not* tell me you hit that?"

I reached for his bottle. "Gimme a swig of that, please?" He handed it to me, and I took a swallow. It tasted like cherry cough syrup. "God . . . how do you drink this shit?"

He took the bottle back but didn't answer me.

"It wasn't my idea," I said in self-defense.

"So, she just threw herself at you?"

"*Yes*. Well, no. I mean . . ." I flailed around trying to find the right word to describe what had happened. What I had allowed to happen. "I guess I didn't stop her."

"How'd you leave it?"

"Oh, that's the best part." I looked him squarely in the eyes. "I didn't have to leave anything. I think she probably lit out as soon as I fell asleep."

"That sounds like her," he agreed.

"And . . ."

He waited.

"She took both desserts."

Dewey threw back his graying head and damn near bayed himself out of his uniform.

"I'm glad you find this so amusing."

He took up his notebook and pencil.

"The only thing I find amusing is how your batting average keeps right on climbing."

"I'm not sure I follow you."

"One more at bat," he made another entry in the book, "two more tropes down." He showed me the list. It now included *forced proximity* and *reunion*.

I was demoralized as hell.

Who wanted to bat a damn thousand in this category?

"So now I'm some kind of contender in the loser derby?" I asked him.

"Oh, no, baby," Dewey tucked his notebook back into his pocket, "you're way beyond that. You're a goddamn All-Star."

CHAPTER SEVEN

Forbidden Relationships—and why
they should stay that way.

The Bells of St. Mary's had always been one of my favorite Christmas movies. Growing up, I waited all year for the classic to enter the seasonal rotation at TCM. Since December had tiptoed in on little cat feet, I knew it wouldn't be long until the network added the film to its nightly roster.

Sofie would upbraid me constantly for my insistence that I wait to watch this movie—and other favorites—until they aired on broadcast television. A proclivity that she deemed ridiculous, and every bit as unnecessary and anachronistic as my car.

Sofie was a true creature of her generation. An arrogant millennial who staunchly refused to watch anything that wasn't streamed commercial free.

She also refused to ride in my car.

"I've spent enough time in Parisian taxis," she complained. "They always smell like cheap cologne and regret."

Arguing that she hadn't *been* to Paris since a trip we'd taken together when we graduated from McGill was pointless. She'd made up her mind and she was finished with ruminations on the topic . . . another charming millennial trait.

I liked to think of myself as a misfit. I departed from the

proclivities of my generation in a lot of areas.

Who was I kidding?

I departed in nearly *all* areas. More than once, *maman* had shaken her head and remarked that, unlike my sister, Zoé, I had been born in the wrong century.

So, on the great gift of a Saturday night at home, I proudly made my bowl of popcorn and settled down on the sofa with an oversized throw to watch Ingrid Bergman, luminous in a nun's habit, teach her young student, Eddie, how to box. During commercial breaks for pharmaceuticals that had been developed to treat a slate of health conditions I prayed weren't headed my way, I scrolled through news headlines on my phone—a demonstrable nod to my generation's dependence on social media.

I did make some exceptions.

It was during one such commercial break touting an effective remedy for plaque psoriasis that I gave into curiosity and checked my SheDate app to see who had swiped right on my profile yesterday while I'd been in the laundry room with Harper.

Lisbeth was a self-described twenty-eight-year-old who worked as a help desk analyst for Dietz & Watson in Philadelphia.

Interesting . . . how many kinds of help desk queries about deli meats could there be?

She was pretty cute . . .

But twenty-eight was a nonstarter. No way I was going down that whole age gap highway again.

On the other hand . . . I scrolled through details of her profile. She was into rowing—which was quirky and unique— and was working on a master's degree in the Women and Gender Studies program at Penn. She was also passionate about animals, and said she had two dogs named Velma and Shaggy.

But twenty-eight?

Not a chance.

I closed the app and returned my attention to the movie.

By the time the next commercial break rolled around, I was nearly out of popcorn. And I'd also halfway talked myself into rethinking a connection with Lisbeth. I mean . . . I was pretty much out of options. It wasn't like the environment around me was rife with opportunities to make meaningful connections. And I'd had a full forty-eight hours to distance myself from the epic lapse in judgment I'd committed with Tonya.

I actually felt less incompetent because Sofie, the so-called dating professional, had also been a catastrophic failure when it came to reading the tea leaves of a SheDate profile. So maybe that meant I wasn't a complete washout in this arena. And the one thing I had learned about SheDate was that everyone was lying about something. Jane had geometrically understated her age. Bridget had understated her . . . passion *for* geometry. So it was clear that, when push came to shove, this Lisbeth would be concealing something, too. And probably, it was her age. That meant the odds she really was only twenty-eight were about as great as me still being able to fit into that sports bikini I had on in *my* profile photo.

Why not test the waters and see if this Lisbeth person came across as legit?

At the very least, maybe I'd learn something fascinating about deli meats.

It could be good conversation fodder for cocktail parties . . . which I rarely . . . okay, *never* . . . went to. But you never knew. The holidays were at hand and there were bound to be some gatherings at work or here in the building. And this topic sure beat the hell out of talking about dung beetles.

I resolved to give the idea greater consideration tomorrow.

I watched the rest of the movie without distractions. When it ended, I decided to take my garbage and recycling down to the trash room. As soon as I stepped outside my apartment, I realized the hallway reeked of garlic. Which meant someone— or a dozen someones—had been cooking with it.

I cast my eyes about to take a closer look at the wreaths ornamenting various doors along my path to the trash room. None of them sported the recent adornments added by Aldo and Luz—however, several of them still had some straggly remnants of the green ribbon they had used to tie the fat bulbs to the holiday decorations.

Unless Cujo had a hotplate stashed someplace in the building, odds were the residents had removed the free hunks of garlic and put them to good use.

I was surprised to run into Harper at the entrance to the trash room. She emerged carrying a blue plastic bin—empty now.

"Off-loading your empties?" I quipped.

She nodded enthusiastically. "I find it advisable to do this in the dead of night. It drastically cuts down on the amount of mailroom gossip about my wicked excesses."

"I wouldn't worry about that. Not if you're accustomed to drinking wine as good as that bottle you brought to dinner last week."

"Oh, that old thing? I'd been using it as a doorstop."

I laughed. "I don't have anything near as exotic as your excuse to ditch my empties during low-traffic hours. I'm just never at home long enough to take care of it during the daylight."

"I just figured you were a night owl."

"Only on nights TCM is showing *The Bells of St. Mary's*."

Harper looked amused. "Lemme guess . . . Ingrid Bergman?"

"I hate being so transparent."

"It does beg the question about what your real fascination with old movies is about. I begin to wonder if it's more a function of the eye candy versus the quality of the production."

"Yeah, so . . ." I feigned umbrage, "how many wine bottles did you just dump into the bin? Enquiring minds want to know."

"If you want an answer to such an impertinent question, I fear you'll have to sort through the bin and try to guess which ones belonged to me."

"I suppose we could eliminate any Cold Duck bottles?"

"Dear god," her face contorted into a mask of displeasure. "Do they still make that?"

"I guess your reaction means I should remove a fondness for that from my SheDate profile?"

"Let me think . . . *yes*."

"Damn. No wonder I keep meeting the wrong women."

Harper sighed. "I'd hardly be the one to advise you."

"Why not?

"You have to ask me that after spending an evening with Gina?"

She had a point. "I guess it's good Dewey didn't tag me with that trope, too."

"What trope?"

"'Opposites Attract.' For some strange reason, he charges *your* relationship proclivities to me, too."

"He does?"

"Oh, yeah. I got stuck with 'Toaster Oven' on your behalf."

"Well," she said, "to be fair, we each have one of those."

"True."

We stood there a moment longer. It seemed like neither of us wanted to be the first to move along.

"Guess I'll head back." Harper took the plunge. "I'm up against a deadline."

"What's this one about?"

"It's a retrospective piece about the thirty-nine James Beard restaurant award winners and finalists Philly's had since 2016."

"I bet that research was a blast."

"Sadly, I didn't get to do the research. My job is just to make the article read like it's written in intelligible English."

"Still," I mused, "It would be fun to try them all."

"I'll send you a copy of the article. It might make a great guide."

"For?"

"Thirty-nine first dates." She smiled and gave me a small wave. "Goodnight, Izzy."

"Night Harper." I watched her walk away.

Suddenly, emptying my trash seemed like the loneliest job on the planet.

I determined that as soon as I got back to my apartment, I was going to swipe right on Lisbeth.

On Sunday morning, I spent four hours trying to research the compass cues dung beetles used to travel at night, just by light emanating from the Milky Way.

Scientists already knew that night-migrating birds had learned navigation by reading the constellations surrounding the sky's northern center of rotation—just like sailors had done before the development of modern navigation systems. Constellations in the northern part of the sky consistently remained a reliable reference for north–south journeys. In the same way, dung beetles seemed adept at effective navigation by referencing brightness differentials visible in gradients of the night sky. This ability facilitated their ability to roll their dung balls to locations safe from the preying instincts of competitors, also wanting to feed on the same fresh animal droppings.

It was perverse and counterintuitive that the beetles navigated more effectively in conditions with less ambient light emanating from only the Milky Way—than during a full moon when the night sky was illuminated by light from the brightest stars in our galaxy.

A paradox. And contrary to human experience.

What were the practical applications of this ability for human beings? And how did this facility contribute to the beetle's development of the means to extract clean water from pits and troughs on their backs through fog-basking? Any relationship? No relationship?

And who really gives a flying fuck? My tired mind was brazen enough to ask the important questions.

My thoughts swung back to the question Adam had asked me on Thursday. What *would* I do once I finished this degree?

If I finished it . . . Because it was obvious I'd been dragging my feet for a reason. I couldn't just lay my epic lack of progress at the feet of my sucky work schedule.

So the bigger question loomed.

Did I want to have a career working for the railroad?

And if I did, was settling for being a conductor a cop out? Should I aspire to more than this?

My mother certainly had.

And what about the study of biomimicry had appealed to me in the first place? It had been quirky and fun to think about—looking at nature to find solutions to everyday problems. Who wouldn't want to be the next person to invent something as essential and ubiquitous as Velcro? You'd be famous and get to live high off the patent royalties. Right?

But, shit . . . I seemed wholly inept at finding workable solutions for the simplest problems in my *own* life—much less anyone else's. How the hell could I think I'd ever succeed at crafting universally applicable remedies to everyday challenges when I couldn't even navigate a damn dating app without landing myself in some impossible situation?

I pushed back my papers in disgust.

This was getting me no place.

I reached for my phone to check my messages. Wonder of wonders, Lisbeth had written back.

> Hi. It's great to hear from you. I think we might have a lot in common.

I typed back—more than anything, to see how creepy I felt talking with someone who was nearly fourteen years younger.

> Me, too. I was reluctant at first to reply to you because of our age difference. Does that concern you at all?

No. I seem to always be dating older women. I think it's because my interests are broader than those of most women my age. So it's not a problem for me if you're okay with it. And to be fair, it's not that big a difference.

> I didn't think I would be at first. But you're right. It's not that much of a gap.

Absolutely. And I like meeting new people. and you never know how things will go, right?

> That's true. I don't mind sharing that I haven't had the best experience so far meeting people on this platform.

I'm not surprised. There are a lot of catfishers out there. You really have to be careful.

> I wonder why people find it hard to be honest about who they are?

Probably because they think no one will like them if they tell the truth.

I can promise you that I am being 100% honest about myself.

I thought about my misleading profile photo. How honest was that?

In fact, I'll share with you that my profile photo is about 15 years old.

I suppose that's not a big surprise?

No. The sunglasses were a big giveaway.

Really? Nobody wears those anymore?

Not that big.

I feel like a nerd.

Nerds are cool. That makes you unique.

A lot of things make me unique. What about my profile made you want to meet me?

What about my profile made you want to meet me?

I asked first.

Okay. You sound cool. You have an interesting job. You're Canadian.

What about being Canadian is cool?

For starters, you aren't from Trenton.

That's true. Is being from Trenton a bad thing?

If you have to ask, you've never been to Trenton.

Okay. This Lisbeth was showing some potential.

We exchanged a few more messages before signing off. I asked her about her interest in rowing and she shared that she'd done it as a team activity while an undergrad at Drexel. She really liked the sport and now rowed a couple days a week with an amateur club on Boathouse Row in the city.

I was impressed and heartened that Lisbeth didn't immediately suggest we meet. I didn't either. I was content to just take my time and see how the association developed.

I spent the rest of my Sunday doing some early online shopping for Christmas presents. The only thing I was sure about was that I'd be working over the holidays, so getting together with my family was certain to be a no go. That meant I'd have to order gifts early enough to allow for shipping.

This would be my third year in a row having to spend Christmas riding the rails. I missed being at home in Frelighsburg with *maman* and *papa*—or Montréal, where we sometimes went, depending upon Zoé's schedule. As much as I hated being away from my family and friends, I had to admit there was a certain kind of camaraderie that developed among the crew members who were stuck working the holiday shifts. There was an infectious kind of excitement you took part in when you were instrumental in getting travelers home for the holidays. They'd board the trains, loaded down with packages or, if they were students headed for home on winter break, big duffel bags bulging with dirty laundry. Most people were in great spirits and ecstatic to be en route to wherever they were going. And this one time of year, USRail permitted us to depart from the strict uniform code and add festive seasonal accents to our attire . . . things like scarves or holiday ties. Even jingle bells. And the café always featured special seasonal-themed coffee blends and confections.

After all, nothing said ho, ho, ho like a steaming cup of Joe with sweet herbal and maple notes.

Although it did bum me out that I'd probably miss our building's annual open house this year. We'd already received save-the-date notices about it in our mailboxes.

I wondered if Harper would attend? The event conflicted with Hanukkah this year—I knew because I'd already looked up the dates. But by her own admission, Harper wasn't religious, so I didn't expect it to be a problem.

I went back and forth on whether or not I should get her a gift. Just something small? Dewey and I always exchanged presents. And I now thought of Harper as part of our *klatsch.*

But what?

A box of five hundred dryer sheets?

Or tickets to attend the New York City debut of Charles Busch's latest off-Broadway romp, *Ibsen's Ghost: An Irresponsible Biographical Fantasy.* I figured I could ask Sofie, too, so it didn't seem like a date. I didn't want to send Harper mixed messages or creep her out and make her think I was now sniffing around her after our fake outing.

It was tough to determine what, if anything, was too much.

My shopping adventure was cut short when I got a call from crew scheduling. Another staffer had called in sick, and I'd been tagged. Not only was it flu season, it also was early December, which meant everyone holding a line took time off to travel or be at home with loved ones.

The only good news? I'd be on the Zephyr again.

I hoped JoAnn would be working. *Did I ever have a story for her.*

By the time Monday morning rolled around, scheduling had contacted me again to tell me that I needed to pick up the trip in Baltimore instead of here at 30th Street Station. That was incredibly odd and unusual, especially since the Baltimore leg typically used a crew from another zone. But who was I to question what USRail was prepared to pay me for the extra four stops—two down, and two back up to my usual starting point? I was becoming seasoned enough not to question why the railroad did any of the things it did.

So, I got to the station bright and early and hopped on a MARC train to deliver me to Penn Station in Baltimore. I only had to wait about twenty-five minutes for the northbound Zephyr to roll in. JoAnn was not on the train, but the senior conductor told me she'd be getting on in Springfield—a little more than six hours and twenty-three minutes later.

We were only nine days into December, but already the trains were sporting some holiday flair. A steward had hung twinkling lights around the ceiling of the café car. The tables had printed placards advertising the special seasonal beverages and dessert items. I even saw a sprig of mistletoe hung surreptitiously over the doorway of the vestibule that linked the passenger cars to the engine.

Yep. Santa Claus was comin' to town.

We'd just left New York City and finished scanning passengers in when I felt my cell phone vibrate. Checking personal messages was a big no-no while you were working, so I had to wait until my lunch break after the big locomotive switch at New Haven to sit down and see who'd contacted me.

To my surprise, it was Harper.

> Hi. I hope I'm not committing a
> capital offense by contacting you
> at work. Dewey told me this morning
> you'd been called up for service.

Hi, yourself. Don't worry. They stopped caning us for breaches of protocol soon after we got collective bargaining.

> Good to know. Remind me to light
> a candle on Samuel Gompers' birthday.

It is a vastly overlooked national holiday.

> Where are you headed this time?

Vermont. Eventually.

> Ohhhh. Snow!

Bite your tongue! I don't want a repeat of last week.

> I won't keep you, but I was wondering
> if you knew your schedule for the next
> few weeks?

Sadly, no. The only thing I can be sure of is that I'll be working on Christmas.

Well that's a drag. I was hoping
I could talk you into going with me
to the holiday open house on the 17th.

In our building, you mean? If fate smiles
upon me and I manage to be at
home, I'd love to go with you.

Yes, our building. And bless you. You
can save me from having to go with
Luz. She keeps asking.

Oh, my! I guess she didn't get ALL the
gossip about you in the mailroom. But
to be fair, she'd make a fetching companion
with that buzz cut and all the tats.

Thanks.

Well, worry not. If I can contrive to
be off, consider yourself accounted
for.

Thanks, Izzy! Now you be safe
and don't get caught in any
lurking snow drifts—or right triangles.

Very. Funny.
See you in the rinse cycle!

LOL. That you will.

After we signed off and I went back to work, I caught myself whistling "Have Yourself a Merry Little Christmas" the rest of the way to Springfield.

JoAnn was demonstrably happy to see me after we completed the crew change in Springfield and rolled out for the short hop to Holyoke. She said she'd been blessed to be off last week during the snowstorm that had ground travel in the northeast corridor to a halt.

"You don't know what you missed," I told her.

"Oh, but I do, A.C. I've been doing this job since you were a tyke, drooling over your Lionel train set. I've suffered through more weather events than Jim Cantore."

"The snow is *not* what I was talking about."

"Oh, really? Do tell . . ."

"Maybe later, after our shift," I said. "You have dinner plans?"

"I do now."

"Is there any place walkable in St. Albans that'll still be open when we get there?"

She nodded. "One or two places. We'll figure it out after we get this beast bedded down for the night."

"Sounds great." I turned to head toward the front of the train to alert passengers that we'd be pulling into Holyoke in twenty minutes.

"And, A.C.?"

I stopped and turned back to face her. "Yeah?"

"If you don't quit whistling Christmas tunes I'm going to shove a sprig of holly up your ass and hang you on the front of the engine."

"Heard, boss." I doffed my cap and continued along my way.

The rest of our duty day was blissfully uneventful. The only excitement came when a passenger bound for White River Junction knocked an enormous barrel of cheese puffs off the overhead luggage rack while trying to extract his suitcase. The barrel crashed to the floor, and, because its lid hadn't been fully secured, its contents spread out along the aisle and beneath the seats like a cheesy, orange tidal wave. Of course, the young traveler the puffs belonged to started screaming. Passengers who were impatiently trying to reach the exit doors stomped and crunched their way past the mayhem without apology. One enterprising five-year-old thought it was the perfect opportunity to perform an impromptu flash dance in the aisle, smashing as many of the puffy treats as possible. She built up to a spectacular finish, jumping and twisting in her attempt at perfect triple salchow—while still carrying her cup of hot chocolate.

She did not stick the landing.

Instead, she stuck to the floor.

Her beleaguered mother, who'd been busy trying to wrangle another aspiring Olympian, simply cursed and growled, "For god sakes, Kayley Sue, quit fucking around and get your ass up off the floor."

For the record, when Kayley Sue complied with the . . . gently delivered directive . . . the back of her pink coat was smeared with a bilious-colored, cheesy sludge.

I actually felt sorry for her. When they reached my exit door, I bent down and whispered, "Keep practicing. You nearly nailed that jump."

Her little face beamed up at me.

I wanted to take her home with me . . . just like that snow-covered dog I'd seen south of New Haven.

I thought about Nicholas Cage in *Raising Arizona*. He'd been right: life was hard on the little things.

The best we could do to remediate the cheese magma was try to clear it out of the aisles. The cleaning crew in St. Albans would have to deal with it when they went through the train cars overnight. I saw JoAnn talking with the station attendant after we pulled in. She pointed out the location of the contamination car.

He did not look thrilled to have to share the news with the night shift.

After the train had been moved into the yard and we'd completed our paperwork, we were ready to undertake the short walk up Lake Street to check in to the town's ancient Hampton Inn.

I hoped the ice machine on the fourth floor had continued its meteoric rise in proficiency and was now putting out more than eight cubes an hour.

After all, it was Christmastime. And I still believed in miracles.

Once JoAnn and I were seated at our table inside Nelly's Irish Pub, we didn't waste time tarrying over the menu—or deciding what to drink. We both wanted beer. Lots of it.

JoAnn ordered a Zero Gravity Double IPA and I got a Long Trail Double Bag.

The operative word in our drink orders was *double*. And one of the acknowledged best parts of overnighting in Vermont was access to the amazing slate of craft beers brewed in the tiny state.

Nelly's was a favorite go-to on these overnights because, not only was it one of the only walkable restaurants that stayed open past nine, but it also had a reliably friendly and attentive wait staff and great pub food. It was located in a circa 1850 brick building that had been the customs house back when the railroad first came through St. Albans. Even though the old building had gone through countless iterations, the corner spot still retained some of its original, revivalist charm.

I loved the local flavor the pub dishes sported. My favorite— although I knew it was deadly—was the Canadian-style poutine: hand cut French fries smothered with pulled pork, French onion gravy, and artisan cheese curds. In self-defense, I was quick to point out that JoAnn's maple mayo burger didn't rank much higher on the heart-healthy scale.

"So, when are you gonna regale me with tales of your latest dating exploits?"

I sighed. "Why does this make me feel like some kind of mobile ant farm?"

"Honey," JoAnn laughed, "it's not about voyeurism. It's about chemistry."

"Or in my case, geometry."

"Meaning?"

"Meaning my last foray into SheDate wonderland served up a nymph-like, sixth-grade teacher with a penchant for three-ways."

JoAnn nearly snorted beer out her nose. "Are you kidding?"

"Nope. She thought I'd enjoy joining her and her friend—who she'd conveniently brought along—to play 'find the hypotenuse.'"

"My god. What the hell did you do?"

"Should I be offended by the fact that you have to ask me that?"

"Well . . . when in Rome."

"It was Providence."

"No pun intended."

"I ran like hell."

JoAnn laughed.

"Yeah. Like *you'd* have done something different."

"Maybe. Back in the day."

"What day would that have been?"

JoAnn tossed a coaster at me. It sailed across the table like a frisbee. "Fuck you, A.C."

The server arrived to deposit our food.

"Enjoy, ladies."

"We promise not to keep you here late," I pledged.

"No problem at all. Do you want another round?"

JoAnn and I exchanged glances.

"Hell yes," she said. "We're not driving."

"Coming right up." She collected our empty glasses and headed for the bar.

JoAnn tucked into her burger. "God, as disgusting as these things should be, they're really amazing."

"No comment." I was too busy dipping my fries into French onion gravy.

Life could be fucking good.

"So, Adam told me he asked you about whether or not you planned to stay with the railroad after you finished your doctorate."

I nodded. "Did he also tell you what I said?"

"He did. It surprised me."

"How come?"

"I just had you pegged as an aspiring starlet . . . you know—doing this job between films."

I choked on a cheese curd. "As if."

"So, are you truly ambivalent about leaving the railroad when you finish the dissertation?"

"I think I might be. It's weird. I always thought I'd lay a patch getting away from USRail faster than I fled that Providence restaurant on Thursday night. But now?" JoAnn waited. "Now, I don't really know what I want."

"You know, there is zero dishonor in staying with a job you like."

"I know."

"Do you?"

I nodded. "But it would be a blow to my parents."

"Oh? Do they live your life for you?"

"Of *course* not." I hadn't meant to sound so defensive. "Sorry."

"It's okay. I get it. My mother wanted me to be a flight attendant. She thought it was glamorous and a great way to see the world. My mother, for the record, never got more than

191

ten miles beyond the city limits of Hamburg, New Jersey—not even to visit New York City, which she thought corrupted young girls and consigned them to lead lives of sexual deviance and dissipation. I had a hard time convincing her that was Trenton, and not New York."

"But you did become a flight attendant."

"For a while. Until I realized that I had some kind of altitude-induced narcolepsy. Imagine nodding off while you're handing some business class asshole his Jack and Coke."

"So you had to give up the dream?"

"I had to give up my *mother's* dream. Yes. So I got reassigned to reservations. And guess where I ended up living? Hamburg, New Jersey."

"And there you stayed."

"I did. For twenty-five years. And only then, did I discover my real passion."

"Mayo on burgers?" I quipped.

"Okay. My *second* passion. The first, I think you might share."

I had to admit she was right. "But how do you defend it?"

"We don't have to defend it. It's our *choice*—not some publicly traded stock that holds us accountable to shareholders."

"The heart is a lonely hunter, sometimes." I thought about the parting message from the novel of the same name. *The most fatal mistake is not to have courage enough to dare.* What was I willing to dare? Anything? Everything?

JoAnn had been watching me as I tried to work it out.

"One of the worst things about staying with this job is that I can never get a damn cat."

"That matters to you?"

"Yeah. I had one—or at least, I had access to one, for nearly five years. No matter how bad things got with Tonya—Felix was always happy to see me."

"*Felix?*"

I nodded.

"You named a poor, unsuspecting cat, Felix?"

"No. Tonya did."

"And it still took you five years to figure out this person was nuts?"

I shrugged. "It takes me a while to pick up the clue phone."

"Let me ask you something," JoAnn began. "Do you remember what it took to learn all the signal signs in conductor training?"

"Hell yes." It had been a nightmare—a nearly impossible task. There were hundreds of them—all like different languages because they spanned so many railroads that traveled over common routes. And we had to know them *all*. When we were tested, we had to score a perfect one hundred percent. Anything less was a fail—because anything less could spell catastrophe for two trains sharing the same stretch of rail.

"This decision facing you is no different," she said. "Just learn to slow down and read the signs."

"Spoken like a true veteran."

"If that's supposed to be a cute way of saying I'm old, you can go fuck yourself."

I laughed.

"Thanks, boss."

It was just past ten by the time I got back to my room at the Hampton Inn. I wanted nothing more than to shower and crawl into bed—hopeful that all the fried food I'd ingested wouldn't keep me awake half the night.

I had several voicemail messages. One from Sofie, asking if I wanted to meet her for breakfast on Sunday. Another from *maman*, asking if I knew that TCM would be showing the George Cukor classic, *Holiday*, with Katharine Hepburn and Cary Grant, on Sunday night. A third was from crew scheduling, notifying me that they needed me to stay on the train through to Baltimore on Friday, instead of ending my shift in Philly.

That sucked. It meant I'd have to ride the MARC from Penn Station back to 30th Street Station—which wouldn't get me home until after 8 p.m.

I also realized I had a new SheDate message from Lisbeth. This time, she was suggesting we meet—for drinks on Friday night.

Just my fucking luck.

I wrote back to tell her I'd love to, but my work schedule was jacking me around, and I wouldn't be getting back to Philly until eight that night.

"That's okay," she responded. "I won't be getting to the club before seven thirty. Why don't you just come straight there when you get back? Just for one drink—a nightcap."

She's twenty-eight, I kept reminding myself. *They don't even* think *about going out until you've been in bed for three hours.*

"Are you sure that's not too late?" I asked her.

"Nope! Just come for one drink. It'll get that first meeting out of the way."

I had to admit she had a point. "Okay. What's the name of the club?"

"It's a small place called Monstercade—on Farimount Avenue. There's parking around the block behind the building."

"Okay. Got it. See you then."

She gave me a thumbs-up emoji and signed off.

Monstercade? I looked it up on my phone. It seemed to be some kind of trendy bar appointed with full-sized retro arcade games.

Weird. But then, who was I to judge? I got titillated by the chance to watch a George Cukor movie from the '40s . . . *with my mother.*

To each his own.

For once, the MARC had been running on time, and it was only 8:02 when I hopped off the train at 30th Street Station. I caught a bus that took me to Fairmount Avenue and walked the final three blocks to find the entrance to Monstercade. I felt ridiculous to still be in my uniform and pulling my roller bag behind me. I hoped the joint might have some kind of reception area where I might safely ditch the bag until I left.

No such luck.

The place was jammed with people and blasting earsplitting music loud enough to make my fillings vibrate. It was some kind of Nu-Metal, too. The type of shit Sofie loved—when she was out clubbing and not at home listening to Melody Gardot.

Oh, Jesus. Is that fucking Slipknot?

It was.

I remembered their mantra: *Who needs friends when you have a Slipknot playlist?*

Yeah. Okay.

I literally had to elbow my way past wall-to-wall clubbers who were, I noticed for the first time because the place was so fucking dark, oddly dressed.

Okay. *Oddly dressed was an understatement.* They were *fantastically* dressed. Like in costumes. Like in *tribute* costumes.

Fuck. *This was a cosplay bar* . . . accented with the barely audible, yet unmistakable tones of Ms. Pac-Man bonging away in the background.

As my eyes adjusted to the low light, I began to make out details of some of the costumes. Wednesday Addams nearly tripped over my roller bag. I quickly reached out a hand to steady her. She looked at me with expressionless eyes.

"I'm really sorry," I began.

She was busy taking in my uniform and cap. "Cool. Are

195

you, like, Ringo?"

"Ringo?" I asked with confusion.

"Starr. The train conductor from *Thomas the Tank Engine.*"

"Oh. Um. Yeah."

"Sick." She continued along her way.

Whatthefuckever . . .

I pushed my way past three Zeldas and some chick dressed like a badass Zorro. I didn't see any men, which led me to wonder if there were such a thing as a *lesbian* cosplay bar.

"Dude!" Someone clapped me on the shoulder. "Tom Hanks, right? *Polar Express?*"

I'd never realized there were so many iconic train conductors.

I should get out more often, I mused as I kept fighting my way to the bar to try and find Lisbeth—*like* I'd have any shot at success at that in this crush of glammed-out people.

I accidentally bumped into another reveler with my damn bag.

"I'm so sorry," I blurted.

"Badass costume," the girl, dressed like Poison Ivy, cooed. "Who are you? Ringo?"

"No. I'm . . . Pierre Michel." I decided to go with it.

"Who?"

"You know . . . *Murder on the Orient Express?*" I prompted.

Blank stare.

"The train conductor?"

Blank stare.

"Agatha Christie wrote it?" I prompted.

More blank stare.

"Okay . . . can you tell me where the bar is?"

Ivy pointed just ahead.

"Thanks." I pushed on.

Someone at the bar was waving furiously at me. I peered through the darkness to try and make out who she was. When I got closer, I realized that this had to be she . . . *Lisbeth.*

I mean, she had all the earmarks . . . spiky black hair, nose ring, skintight black jeans, leather jacket, butch collar, and tats. Lots and lots of tats. The most impressive one was the wasp climbing her neck.

She was Lisbeth, all right. Lisbeth *fucking* Salander from *The Girl With the Dragon Tattoo.*

"Izzy?" she practically shouted to be heard over the din.

I nodded stupidly.

"You made it. Sick."

Getting a good look at 'Lisbeth' up close allayed my fears that she'd been lying about being twenty-eight.

It was clear she wasn't a day over eighteen.

"Are you old enough to be in here?" I asked.

She rolled her eyes. "For fuck's sake . . . you sound like my mom."

"Your mom?" I asked. "You mean the one in your profile photo?"

She shrugged. "I'll look like that someday."

Yeah, I thought, *in a couple of decades.*

"Look. It's late so let's just cut to the chase. How *old* are you?"

"Nice way to kill the vibe we had going."

Vibe?

"Well, I tend to not want to spend my second dates in jail."

"Look. I didn't lie about *everything.* I really am into rowing."

"Good for you."

"I'm even trying out for the team at Rosemont."

Rosemont? The Catholic college in Main Line Philly? *The place with all the nuns?*

Oh yeah. Lisbeth Salander would fit *right* in there . . .

"When's the tryout?" I asked.

"Next year, when I apply."

"Next . . ." I felt the blood drain from my face. "You're still in *high school?*"

197

"Lower your fucking voice, man. You wanna get me kicked out of here?"

I held up a hand. "I gotta go."

"You don't even wanna buy me one drink?"

"Not unless it comes with a shooter of hemlock."

She looked at me like I was from another planet.

"Later . . . *Lisbeth*." I backed away from the bar. "Lose my number, okay?"

I hadn't walked very far when I heard her thin voice yell, "Loser!"

For the first time since meeting, we'd found something we could agree on.

But, at least, I was walking out on a first date with something more akin to integrity than panic.

CHAPTER EIGHT

Slow Burns—and other missed opportunities.

All I wanted when I got back to Hopkinson House was a drink. That's not true. *I wanted five drinks.* In rapid succession.

There was no sign of Dewey when I entered the building. It was just after 9:30 p.m., so it had been unreasonable to expect him to still be at his post in the lobby. And I knew Sofie was unavailable too. She had said she'd be out of town until tomorrow, attending a seminar on effective property/casualty loss reserves.

Whatever the fuck that was . . .

I was tired and cranky and just wanted someone to make me feel better about almost ending up with a second career, stamping out license plates in Muncy.

The elevator stopped on seven and when the doors opened, Aldo and Luz got on.

"You two are sure burning the midnight oil," I commented.

"We got to if we want to crack this Cujo case," Aldo explained. "Dewey won't let us follow any leads during regular work hours."

Luz agreed. "He says it makes the residents nervous."

"That might be true," I replied. "But I think most people

appreciated the garlic you handed out."

"They weren't supposed to *cook* it," Aldo stated. "It was supposed to keep Cujo from stealing those wreaths."

"But we've been making notes." Luz handed me a folded sheet of paper. "All the things we know Cujo has stolen or torn up. Take a look."

I scanned the sheet of paper. In block printing, one of the pair had written,

1. GOLF SHOE (RIGHT)
2. CHIRSTMAS WREATH (NONTRADITIONAL BLUE & WHITE RIBBONS)
3. GARLIC (42 BULBS DISAPPEAR)
4. THROW PILLOWS ON 9 AND 12 SWAPPED
5. RED BULBS IN LAMPS ON 16

"What can you make outta that?" Luz asked.

I was tempted to tell her I could make a hat, a brooch or a pterodactyl . . .

"What's this about the throw pillows and red lightbulbs?" I asked instead.

"That's new," Aldo piped up. "Cujo switched up all the throw pillows between nine and twelve."

"Are you sure that wasn't housekeeping?" I asked. Each floor had a mini reception area near the elevators, with a sofa, console table, and lamps.

"Yes, ma'am." Luz oozed confidence. "The sofa on nine is plaid and the one on twelve is *striped*."

"Nobody mixes them patterns up," Aldo said. "I asked Miss Abramowicz in 2604, and she said it would be 'highly irregular.' And she knows about this kind of thing."

"That's right," Luz added. "She writes for that *Philadelphia Magazine* that's in all the hotel rooms."

"What about the red lightbulbs? You guys think Cujo

did that, too?"

"Who else would want to do something like that?"

"I get that, Luz. But don't you agree that swapping out lightbulbs might take a bit more manual dexterity than an oversized rodent would possess?"

"With all due respect Ms. Lebrun, me'n Aldo *never* thought Cujo was a rodent. That's just what Dewey wants people to think so they don't get all upset."

I handed the paper back to her. "I wish you both luck getting to the bottom of this."

Luz refolded the paper and tucked it back inside her pocket.

"Don't you worry," she said with confidence. "We'll catch the little bugger."

The elevator dinged and the pair got off on twenty-two. Lord knew what they were on the way to take care of. I just hoped it wasn't the distribution of another ration of garlic. After several days of enduring the hallways reeking of the persistent odor, I'd have welcomed another bout with Mrs. Dahlby's lutefisk.

The apartment seemed cold and empty when I stepped inside. I ditched my suitcase and hat and walked over to open the balcony door.

Even at this time of night, the city wasn't quiet. The roar of traffic noise was ubiquitous. It was cold and clear, and the sky was ablaze with thousands of stars. It had snowed earlier that day and the field of white that stretched across the park looked like it was internally illuminated. Everything seemed brighter and cleaner. More at peace.

I actually thought I could smell the snow. It, too, seemed . . . fresh and unencumbered. Imbued with possibility.

Bad night to be a dung beetle, I thought. They'd be confused as fuck trying to navigate their way to a safe location to bury or ingest their poop balls.

I stood out on the patio until I got too cold. Back inside, I stood stupidly in the middle of my kitchen thinking over the debacle the evening had turned into.

I really wanted a drink. But I had a policy never to indulge by myself. That had been drilled into me during my eight weeks of conductor training. Too many of my predecessors and colleagues had ended up having to enroll in assistance programs for drug and alcohol abuse.

My cellphone dinged. I closed my eyes and prayed to every god I could summon not to make the call be from crew scheduling—or 'Lisbeth.' It would've been a tossup to determine which would be more unwelcome.

To my surprise, it was a text from Harper.

> I hope, wherever you are, this doesn't wake you up. But I just saw that *Holiday* is going to be airing on TCM Sunday night. I knew if I didn't tell you now, I'd never remember.

I am actually standing in the middle of my kitchen, and you did NOT wake me up. I literally just got in from my trip.

> Oh, good. I mean—not good that you had to work so late. But good that you're finally home, and I didn't wake you.

Thanks for telling me about the movie. My mother was one step ahead of you. She wanted to be sure I got to see it. Oh— and you get extra points for italicizing the title! I didn't even know that was possible in a text message.

> It's the curse of being an editor. Don't

wish it on anyone else. And I wondered if she might've told you. But then, I wasn't sure about Canadian TV schedules for these channels.

Why are you still awake? It can't be because you're addicted to reading TV Guide (note no Italics).

> LOL. You mean apart from the fact that I have no social life? I got a wild idea—an impulse that I didn't bother trying to talk myself out of.

You're in good company. I was just standing here bemoaning that I have no one to share a nightcap with.

> If that's an invitation, I'd be happy to take you up on it.

Really? I was hoping I sounded pathetic enough for you to take pity on me.

> You don't need to be pathetic. You just need to ask. Where do you want to meet?

I guess the trash room would be out?

> I'd hardly call it *de rigueur.* Would you like to pop over here? I think I have another doorstop I can live without.

You don't have to ask me twice. You're in
2604, right? Impressed I know that? The
president of your fan club just told me.

Oh, great. Luz? But, yes. That's
my apartment number.

Ten minutes? I'd like to change out of this
uniform.

See you then.

Harper opened her door immediately after my first soft
knock. I only felt mildly bad about showing up on her doorstep
at this ridiculous hour. But it had been clear that she wasn't ready
for bed either. And I liked her company. She was easygoing,
smart, funny, and generally nice to be around.

And she was a welcome change from the dating hellscape
I'd been inhabiting of late.

Even though this was not a date . . .

Harper waved me inside and closed the door.

"I realize I should've asked you what you wanted to drink
and not made an assumption. Is wine really okay? I have other,
albeit less rarefied, swill."

"Wine is better than okay. At this point, I'd drink Drano—
so you're saving my ass."

"I'm happy to oblige." She walked to the small kitchen that
was like a mirror image of my own—only hers had much nicer
appliances. I especially liked her Wolf cooktop and French-door
wall oven.

Culinary high cotton, so to speak.

"I gather I'm not the only one who likes to cook?"

Harper was busy preparing to open the wine. "What do you mean?"

"I am having a serious attack of avarice over your kitchen appliances."

"Don't. They're what I have in lieu of a social life."

"I'd be inclined to think they'd work in the opposite direction. You could use them as bait to lure unsuspecting future conquests in to sample your wares."

Harper laughed and let my clumsy innuendo slide. "Go make yourself comfortable. I'll bring the wine right along."

"Okay."

I looked around her small living room. It was bright and alive with colors and artwork. She'd shelved one entire wall of the room and filled it with books. The setup included a built-in desk with recessed lighting. Her laptop and a ubiquitous stack of bulging manila folders sat atop it.

I liked her furniture, too. She seemed to embrace color. She had an orange Mansfield-style, retro leather sofa with dramatic, rolled arms—and two inviting club chairs upholstered in a smoky ash color.

Her bevy of throw pillows were all covered with bold, Turkish Kilim patterns—riffing off the large black and tan flatweave rug that anchored the space.

Luz had been right to ask for her opinion about mixing plaids and stripes.

This was the kind of room you wanted to sink into and never emerge. I wanted to pull it on like a warm sweater and settle in for a long winter's nap.

She had music playing at low volume when I arrived. It sounded like Phoebe Snow. "Poetry Man" had always been one of my favorites. It was one of those jazzy and ethereal singer-songwriter tunes that never grew old.

Harper arrived with our glasses of wine.

"I love this place."

"Thank you. I'm flattered."

Harper sat down on the sofa—which left me having to decide where to sit. If I sat beside her, that might seem . . . impertinent. So, instead, I opted for one of the club chairs facing her. I have to admit, she looked pretty good framed by that massive wall of books. There was a cutout in one section of the shelves, and the space was filled with a large Rothko exhibition poster that was alive with blocks of violet, orange, black and red.

I pointed at the poster. "That thing is gorgeous."

Harper turned to look at it. "Thanks. It's just a lithograph from a show at the Guggenheim in the seventies. But I love it."

"It fits this room like a glove."

"I think so, too. Although to be honest, I kind of decorated the room around the poster."

"Luz was right to ask for your opinion about the throw pillows being mixed up."

"Oh, god." Harper picked up her wine glass. "I thought about just confessing to that particular crime so those two could get a good night's sleep."

"Why didn't you?"

"Well . . . I mean . . . mixing stripes and plaids?"

"Too much of a leap for you?"

"I think I developed a facial tic just considering the idea."

"You do seem to like order."

"What makes you say that?"

"Um," I tilted my head toward her kitchen, "I couldn't help but notice that the spice bottles in your rack are alphabetized."

"Aren't everyone's?"

"Yes. Absolutely. Without question." I sipped my wine. It was excellent. *Of course.* I made a happy noise. "What's this one?"

"It's a Barolo. I worried that it might be too big just to drink without food—but what the hell?"

"I love it."

"Good. It was either this or the dregs from that Cold Duck

bottle in the trash room."

"You're quite a comedienne, aren't you?"

"You have to be in my line of work."

I felt myself really beginning to relax from the long week—and the seismic upset that ensued after the night's debacle at Monstercade.

"Is being a magazine editor that stressful?"

"It is when you have to be serious about spending your days reviewing content that is deeply unimportant."

"I wouldn't call your magazine deeply unimportant."

"No?"

I shook my head. "Deeply unimportant is spending every spare second of your life researching the nocturnal habits of dung beetles."

I could tell that one surprised her. "Seriously?"

"Oh, yes. These are the rich and full details of my scholastic pursuits."

"Dung beetles?"

"Believe it or not, they live in the desert, but they possess the ability to transform fog into clean drinking water. Imagine if we could harness this same technology and use it to make Barolo from tap water. Now, wouldn't that improve life for the multitudes?"

"At least five thousand of them, I suppose."

"Ah, that's the thing about biomimicry. Unlike Jesus, we're engineers, and we think on a grander scale. So, not five thousand—but five-*hundred* thousand."

"It's true he moved in smaller circles." She seemed to consider my analogy. "That'd be a shit ton of Barolo."

"Would the world be a better place, or what?"

She laughed. It was that same, silvery sound I'd heard before. "What kind of progress are you actually making?"

"On the dissertation? Not much. I find that even when I have blocks of time to work on it—which is not often—I work harder to find other things to distract myself."

"Why do you think that is?"

"I begin to think maybe it's because I don't really want to do it. Not anymore."

"I don't think that's unusual, do you? Most people get bogged down during this process, don't they? I know I did when I was writing my master's thesis—and it wasn't anything near as dense or complicated as what you're working on."

That tidbit of information interested me. "Where'd you get your degree?"

"I'd rather not say."

"Ohhhh . . . a mystery."

"Not so much."

"Then why keep it a secret?"

"Because you'd think it's just . . . textbook for my ilk."

"Your *ilk?*"

She shrugged but said nothing more.

"Okay. You wanna play hardball? I have an easy remedy for that."

"What's that?"

I pulled my phone out of my pocket. "I'll just Google your ass."

"Oh, come on. That's not fair."

"You'd rather have me guess?"

"I'd rather have you not care at all."

"Too late." I held up the phone. "You choose. Door number one—I Google it. Or door number two—I guess."

She thought it over. "How about I take the big box on the stage?"

"I don't recall offering that as an option."

"It's *always* an option."

"Okay, smartass. What happens with the big box?"

"I just tell you."

I put my phone down on her coffee table. "That works."

"Dartmouth."

"But of course."

"See? I knew you'd be an asshole about it."

"*Non.*"

"That's a matter of opinion," she said dryly.

"Oh, come on. It's not your fault your parents are rich."

"I *still* had to get in," she insisted.

"Pouting really suits you," I teased.

"Well, Ivy League or not, it didn't prepare me for the job I ended up with—that's for sure."

"Hey—neither did mine."

"So, we're both a couple of misfits?"

"Looks like it." I found it hard to believe that Harper couldn't get any kind of writing gig she wanted. So something had to be keeping her where she was. "What would you *rather* be doing?"

She looked surprised. "Rather than working for the magazine, editing bad prose?"

I nodded.

"I'd like the time to finish my book."

"No way? You're writing a book?"

"I am."

"That's so great. What's it about?"

"Hold your applause. It's a novel set in the 1950s."

"It is? That's unique. Why the '50s?"

"The main character is a French-trained chef who barely survives the polio epidemic that killed her lover. When she recovers, she drags what's left of her wounded spirit to a remote island and lives in isolation—crafting elaborate recipes no one will ever try. Only gradually does she come to realize that she's stopped aging."

I was fascinated by the concept. "Damn. This sounds like a real feel-good novel."

Harper laughed. "My publisher thinks so, too. They keep pushing me to add a new love interest for the hopeless chef."

"First—you have a publisher? And second—you'd rather not take their advice?"

"Yes, I have a publisher. And, no. It isn't that I don't want to take their advice. It's that I'm not sure Marguerite—the chef—*wants* to change her life."

"And she has to want to in order for it to work out?"

"Exactly."

"This reminds me of that old, 'How many shrinks does it take to change a lightbulb?' joke."

"I don't think I've heard this one. How many?"

"One, but it has to want to be changed."

"My sentiments, exactly." Harper chuckled. "Marguerite may not *want* her lightbulb changed."

"She's not alone in that."

"No." Harper met my eyes. "I'm beginning to figure that out."

An idea occurred to me. "Can I see it?"

"What?"

"The book. I've never seen one while it's actually being written."

"There's nothing mysterious about it. It's just a stack of pages with tons of notes in the margins."

"I still want to see it."

"Okay," she said somewhat dubiously. "I'll go get it."

She got up, walked to her desk, and retrieved what looked like a printer paper box. When she returned, she set the box on the table between us. "*Et voilà.*"

I cautiously moved over to sit beside her on the sofa. I rested my hands on the lid to the box.

"May I?"

"Of course. There's nothing inside that will hurt you."

"No acerbic prose or biting commentary?"

"I didn't say that . . ."

I lifted the lid and took a gander at the typewritten pages.

There were a lot of them.

"How many pages is this?"

"About two hundred and forty."

"Damn. How many is that in printed book form?"

"Um," she took a minute to do the calculation. "Maybe three hundred and fifty pages? Give or take. But remember, this is unedited. So the final count will change."

"It's still impressive as hell."

I looked over the title page. *Work in Progress*, it read. By Harper M. Abramowicz.

"Catchy title," I quipped. "I would've expected something . . . pithier."

"Since it *is* a work in progress," she explained, "I'm not yet sure what title will fit the ending."

I flipped through a score of pages. Each chapter began with a quote.

"Who is M.F.K. Fisher?"

"She was a famous food writer and cookbook author in the '40s and '50s. Think Julia Child before Julia Child."

"I'd really like to read this." I looked at her.

"I'm sorry . . . you'll have to wait for the movie."

I bumped her shoulder. "That's not fair."

"I know." She topped off our wine glasses. *Again.* "I suck."

I replaced the lid on her manuscript box and dropped back against the sofa. "I didn't realize until now how tired I am." I yawned and stretched out my legs. "This is a great couch."

"I'm sorry for dragging you out. Do you want to go home?"

"On the contrary. I feel very relaxed here. With you," I added, sleepily.

"Good. Now do you want to tell me what you'd rather be doing than researching dung beetles?"

"Oh," I yawned again. "That one's easy."

"What is it, then?"

"I'm already doing it."

"The railroad?" she asked.

I nodded. "Is that too . . . simple?"

"No. What makes you think that?"

I closed my eyes. The warmth of the comfortable room, the soft music, and the big Barolo coursing through my veins was really making me sleepy. "I don't wanna . . ."

"You don't want to . . . what?" Harper's voice sounded like it had traveled a great distance to reach me.

"Disappoint . . ." I muttered.

"I doubt you ever do," I heard Harper say. Or at least, I thought I heard her say it. It could have just been my tired mind whispering what I wanted her to say. Then she stopped talking—or I'd traveled too far a distance to be able to hear her. I felt like I was falling, but I wasn't afraid. I wanted to give up and relax into the sweet feeling of weightlessness. I was only vaguely aware that I'd given up trying to make sense of what or where I was. All I knew was that my weightlessness had subsided and my head had become heavy—so heavy I couldn't continue holding it up. So I let it fall, along with the rest of me, into a place of warmth and contentment.

I had no idea what time it was when I jolted awake. I don't know what caused me to bolt upright the way I did. Maybe a free-floating surge of panic that I'd breached some kind of etiquette. And it took me a full minute to realize where I was—stretched out across Harper's sofa. I had a pillow beneath my head and was covered by a thick fleece throw.

I felt like an idiot. I had a vague recollection of falling asleep—on Harper's shoulder.

What a loser.

"You're awake."

It was Harper's voice—coming from the chair where I'd

been seated earlier.

I rubbed my eyes and looked at her. "What happened?"

"You fell asleep."

I sat up. "God. I'm sorry."

"What on earth for?"

"Crashing on your couch like a drunken teenager."

"Don't be silly. It's fine. I wouldn't have left you there all night."

"What time is it?" I was almost afraid to ask.

"It's just after midnight." She placed the book she'd been reading on the table beside her chair.

"Oh, man. I'm really sorry."

"Please don't be. You were exhausted from your trip. I shouldn't have served such a big wine. It's my fault."

"No, it isn't. It's mine for drinking on an empty stomach. I know better." I clumsily folded the throw and got to my feet. "I think it's past time for me to head home. I hope I didn't . . . do or say anything stupid."

"No." Harper stood up, too. "Your reputation is safe." She followed me to the door. "Although, there is one thing I wanted to ask you about."

What had I said? I closed my eyes in mortification. *Dear god, don't let it be anything embarrassing.*

"What?"

"You kept calling me Felix and trying to . . . pet me."

Oh, shit. Yep. Embarrassing as fuck. *Nice work, Iz.*

"Sorry. Felix was my . . . *Tonya's* . . . cat. I . . . miss her."

Harper nodded sympathetically. "I am guessing a lot?"

I shrugged. "It's hard to always come home to an empty apartment."

Harper seemed like she wanted to say something but didn't. Instead, she nodded and opened the door. "Can you make it home okay?"

"Oh, yeah. This is one walk of shame I know how to make."

I stepped outside. "Night, Harper."

"Goodnight, Izzy. Regardless of what your tired mind is telling you, I enjoyed the evening."

I nodded at her shyly and began the walk back to my apartment.

When I rounded the corner and saw the elevators, I noticed something . . . strange.

Old Mrs. Mariota from eleven had kicked off her shoes and was standing on one end of the sofa. She was busy doing something to one of the lamps on the console table. Beside her shoes on the floor, there was a box full of . . . *lightbulbs.*

Red lightbulbs.

You have to be kidding me?

I hurried forward to prevent her from falling off the couch.

"Mrs. Mariota?" I called out. "Let me help you. I don't want you to fall."

The old woman was barely four feet tall. I had no idea how she'd even managed to climb up there.

I gently took hold of her thin arm. Just to steady her. "What are you doing out here this late?" I asked.

"*Devo sistemare queste cose*," she said. "The lights are wrong."

"Wrong? What's wrong with them?"

"*Rosse. Devono essere rosse. Per Natale.*"

"Red? For . . . for *Christmas?*" I asked.

"*Sì. Per Natale.*"

"*Bueno*," I said. "Come down." I took hold of both arms and slowly urged her to step down from the sofa. Luckily, she complied.

When I reached into her box to extract another red bulb for the second lamp, I noticed that she'd also collected some garlic. A lot of it.

I wondered where she had stashed the golf shoe?

I quickly screwed the red bulb into place.

"*Buon Natale*," I said.

She beamed at me—just like Kayley Sue had after her failed triple salchow.

"Let's take you home now." I pointed at the elevator. "*Casa?*"

"*Sì, sì,*" she said.

We took the elevator to the eleventh floor. When the doors opened, a worried Leo Mariota greeted us, wearing only his pajamas.

"*Nonna! Dove sei stata?*" He looked at me anxiously. "I've been all over the building looking for her. This is the tenth time she's done this in the last month." He took hold of her arm and began to lead her toward their apartment. "I think it must be that new medication they put her on. She keeps doing crazy shit."

"She had these." I handed him the box of lightbulbs and garlic.

He looked shocked. "*Nonna? Hai preso queste cose dalla mia borsa?*" He looked at me. "She must've taken these from my workbag. I'm an electrician."

"*Non l'aglio.*" Mrs. Mariota said firmly. "Not the garlic."

Leo rolled his eyes.

I fought an impulse to laugh. "Don't worry. She didn't hurt anything."

"I hope not. I'm calling her doctor today." He urged the tiny woman forward. "Come on, *Nonna*. It's bedtime."

"One thing," I asked him.

He stopped and looked back at me.

"Did your nonna find . . . a golf shoe . . . by chance?"

He looked distressed. "Do you know who that belongs to? I wanted to post a note about it in the mailroom, but I've been so busy with work, I haven't had time. She keeps picking stuff up and bringing it home."

"Don't worry about it. I'll do it for you."

"I'd really appreciate it. Some of this shit is just random. The other morning, I got up and found a 500-amp ground clamp on the kitchen table beside her box of Muselix—and it *wasn't* mine. Where the hell would she get her hands on something like that?"

"No clue. But I'll add it to the note. What's your apartment number?"

"Eleven-fourteen. I'd be really grateful if you could find the owner—and maybe mention the damn cat, too."

Cat?

"What cat?" I asked.

"Beats the hell outta me. She came home one night with this big yellow cat. I've asked *everybody* who it belongs to. No takers. We gotta find the owner . . . I have allergies."

I was glad Aldo and Luz didn't know about this *heist.*

"I'll see what I can do. Have a good night." I waved at the small woman. "You, too, Mrs. Mariota."

"*Buon Natale!*" she called out to me.

"*Buon Natale*," I replied.

I got back on the elevator and punched the button for twenty-six.

So Cujo ended up being an eighty-five-year-old grandmother with late-night wanderlust.

I decided I'd tell Dewey and let him figure out the best way to tell Aldo & Luz.

After all—it was nearly Christmas. I didn't want to be the one to break their hearts.

When I met Sofie at Morning Glory on Sunday morning, I wasted no time telling her I was finished with SheDate and had decided to uninstall the app. She looked like I'd just said I was shaving my head and moving to South Florida—which, to her, would be tantamount to enlisting in the Marine Corps (where bad haircuts were implied).

216

"*Tu es folle.*"

"I am *not* crazy. This fucking dating app is crazy. It's like . . . the devil's playground."

"Don't be so dramatic. You just had a rash of bad luck."

"*Bad luck?* Sofie . . . I nearly hooked up with a seventeen-year-old. In case you need me to clarify that for you, we're talking about statutory rape."

"You *so* did not nearly hook up with her. You said you could tell immediately that she was underage."

"That's beside the point. It was a nightmare. *My* nightmare . . . the one where I end up doing a seven-to-ten stretch at the crowbar hotel."

"Oh, for god's sake, Izzy. Not in Pennsylvania. The legal age for consent here is sixteen."

"Who do you think I am? Matt Gaetz?" I looked at her with incredulity. "And *why* do you even know what the age of consent is here?" I held up a hand before she could answer. "Never mind. Don't tell me."

"Will you please relax. *Nothing happened.* You're fine."

The server arrived to take our orders. I noticed it was the same loquacious guy we'd had the last time.

At least he hadn't arrived when I'd mentioned statutory rape.

Maybe things were looking up.

As usual, Sofie ordered for us.

"We'll have two orders of the challah French toast with turkey bacon and extra maple syrup."

"Coffees?" he asked.

"In buckets." Sofie batted her eyes at him.

"I'll have that right up." He finished writing on his pad with a flourish.

"Thanks, doll face." Sofie handed him our menus.

He touched me on the shoulder before gliding off. "Are you keeping it between the ditches, honey?"

"Barely," I replied. "It's been one of those decades."

217

"Tits up, girlfriend. Channel your inner cat, and you'll land on your feet." He winked at me and disappeared into the ubiquitous throng that defined this place on Sunday mornings.

"What he said." Sofie leaned across the table to peer more closely at me. "You look like shit. Did you get any sleep last night?"

I shrugged.

"Why not?" she demanded.

"What the hell am I doing with my life?"

"That's *all* that kept you awake?"

"All?" I was incredulous at her reaction. "Forgive me if my night of abject angst doesn't rise to your threshold for warranting sleeplessness."

"Give me a break. It's not angst—it's horniness."

"Excuse me?"

She folded her arms. "You just need to get laid. It's becoming pathological."

"That's not it, believe me. I just *got* laid—and it only made matters worse."

"Whoa, whoa, and whoa." Sofie held up a manicured finger. "Back this train up. What do you mean you just got laid?"

I ran a hand over my face. *Great. Just great.*

"Last week. On the trip. During the snowstorm. We had a full ground stop overnight in New Haven."

"And you picked someone up in a bar? *Finally?* Is my work here through at last?"

"No. It wasn't . . . a stranger." I had no idea why I was stalling. I knew she was going to drag it out of me. It wasn't like I could dump a bucket of chum into the water and *not* expect the shark to ram my rowboat.

"Oh? Call me even more curious. A colleague? An old acquaintance?"

"Both, actually."

Sofie raised a perfectly arched red eyebrow. "Intriguing.

218

Anyone I know? Was it someone from McGill? *Ô mon Dieu!* I bet it was that *petite peste* from Lisbon. You always had a thing for Eurotrash."

I held up a hand. "Please stop."

"She was *relentless*. Remember that weekend we borrowed your father's car and she left her panties in the glovebox?" Sofie laughed merrily. "We thought he was going to cut off your trust fund."

"I don't *have* a trust fund . . . that's *you*. And it wasn't Beatriz."

"*That's* the tart's name . . . *Beatriz*. As if naming *her* after a saint would tame that epic libido. She's the only person I've ever met who could say, 'harder, baby' in nine languages."

Our server arrived with two steaming mugs of coffee. I looked up at him gratefully.

"Could I trouble you for an extra cup of this?" I asked.

"Sure honey." He patted my arm. "No problem. I've had nights like that, too."

"Yeah, but this one I want you to pour over my head."

"You girls crack my tight ass up." He laughed and sailed off.

"So, tell me," Sofie was busy dumping a pint of cream into her coffee, "where'd you do it? In the café car? As I recall, she always got the munchies after sex. Didn't she like cramming Milk Duds up her . . ."

"*Stop*." I interrupted her. "Just . . . *stop*. It wasn't Beatriz. It was . . . Tonya."

"*What?*" Sofie slammed the cream pitcher down on the table. Had she not already drained it, it would've gone everywhere. "Have you lost your mind?"

"It *wasn't* planned. The ground stop stranded us in the same hotel. We went out together to find a place to eat. Then later, she just showed up at my room, and . . ."

"And may I point out that *this* gigantic lapse in judgment had *nothing* to do with SheDate? An 'accidental' dalliance with Vampyra makes all your other dating escapades look like a bad game of Crokinole."

"It wasn't my idea, okay? It was just a . . . situational decision. Not premeditated."

Sofie was nodding sympathetically. "So, all you could do was lie back and let it happen?"

"Will you fucking lighten up? I feel bad enough as it is."

"Okay." She took a deep breath and sat back. "But, Izzy? You cannot let this one mistake set you back irreparably. Don't overreact like you are prone to do. Call this what it was: a lapse in judgment. Then shake it off and move on."

"I am not trying that fucking app again. Give it up."

"Do you remember when we binge-watched that miniseries about Julia Child?"

I nodded. It had been one of the rare occasions I'd been able to get Sofie to sit still for more than four hours. She'd been mesmerized by the story of the famous chef's rise to celebrity.

"And do you recall how long it took to bake the perfect French baguette?"

"Yes. A long time."

"A *very* long time. They went through nearly three hundred pounds of flour. And when they finally got the formula right, Julia said it was like the glorious sun suddenly breaking through shades of gloom."

I sighed.

"You know I'm right."

"Maybe."

"Izzy? If something is worth having, it's worth fighting your way through some adversity to get it right."

I looked at her morosely. "Okay."

"You know I'm right," she repeated.

I nodded. "I'll keep trying."

"Good." She picked up her coffee mug. "Now is there anything else I can do for you today?"

I thought about it. "Maybe one thing."

"*Quoi?*"

"Save me some fucking syrup?"

"*Peut-être,*" she grinned, "if you're lucky."

Dewey laughed his ass off when I told him about Mrs. Mariota.

"Those two idiots are gonna need a new damn hobby."

I agreed. "I figured you should be the one to tell them."

"Is this an early Christmas present for me?" he asked.

"Yep. But do it soon. Otherwise, you'll never get the scent of garlic out of the carpets in this joint."

Dewey took a drag on his cigarette. "You know, some of the residents have said they like those red lightbulbs."

"Seriously?"

He nodded. "They think it adds 'a holiday flair' to the 'otherwise drab' elevator bays."

"They think making a vestibule look like the waiting room in a brothel is *festive?*"

"What can I tell you? Most of them are from Jersey—and let's face it: that décor was already seventy-five percent of the way there."

"Good point."

It was snowing—those big wet flakes that cling to everything but never amount to much accumulation. Dewey and I were huddled beneath a portico to keep it off our clothes and hair.

"When's your next trip?"

"Not sure. Scheduling hasn't contacted me yet. I'm sure it won't be long. The holidays are infamous for people calling in sick."

"That's true in any profession. I'll be pulling my share of double shifts here, too."

"I hope I get lucky and don't get called up before mid-week."

"Why?"

"So I can be here for the open house on Tuesday night. I've missed it three years in a row."

"That's true. Tell you what . . . if you can manage to be here, we'll come up with a special way to reveal the true identity of Cujo to the dynamic duo."

That was a novel idea. "Do you think Leo Mariota will go along with that? He seems pretty protective of his grandmother."

"Oh, he will. Especially when we honor her service by putting her on the committee in charge of holiday decorations."

"Oh, man . . . that's inspired."

"Hey? I earn *my* stripes every day."

"You are a true veteran, Mr. Pepper."

Dewey checked his watch. "Time for me to get back inside. But before I do—how are things progressing in the trope-a-thon?"

"Oh, dear god . . . not you, too?"

"Hey," he withdrew his notebook from his coat pocket, "I am the official chronicler of your maiden voyage through the Sapphic Romper Room."

"What the hell is that?"

"I think you call it 'SheDate.' Now . . . what's the latest?"

"The latest will take more time to describe than we have now. Suffice it to say we met at some Gen-Z cosplay bar and she wasn't a day over seventeen."

His eyes grew wide. "How the hell did that happen?"

"She used her mom's profile photo and lied about everything else—except her passion for rowing, which she hopes to pursue *next year* when she goes to college."

"Girl," he shook his head, "you're gonna end up on *60 Minutes*." He scribbled something in his notebook before tucking it back into his pocket.

"Okay . . . what the fuck did you write down this time?"

He smirked at me. "*Forbidden Relationship*, sister. And you found yourself a doozie."

"That's me," I declared sarcastically, as we headed back inside. "A die-hard overachiever."

CHAPTER NINE

Ice Queens—and other opposites that don't attract.

Fate was on my side, and crew scheduling did not call me into work for Monday—they actually tagged me for a trip on Wednesday. That meant I would be able to attend the holiday open house on Tuesday with Harper—saving her from a potential date with Luz.

All day, I wandered around the apartment feeling guilty about falling asleep on her sofa last night. The worst part was not remembering exactly how I got from her shoulder to lying down with a pillow and throw.

And what about that part where she'd said I kept calling her Felix, and tried to pet her?

Pet her . . . *where*, exactly? She'd said her head—but I wasn't sure she was being truthful.

And how asleep had I *really* been? Why did I remember some parts and not others?

It was one of those situations Sofie always called a "goat fuck." To be fair, I never really understood why a goat fuck was synonymous with something mixed up or misguided, but I appreciated the simile, nonetheless. And it certainly seemed to apply here.

My dissertation research sat untouched on the kitchen table. I had zero enthusiasm for spending the day deep in the throes of dung beetle culture. I resolved to try and read the next book club selection—the one Harper had lent me in the laundry room. But I soon got caught up in an unwitting game of "count the adverbs." Once I'd topped a hundred and twenty-six in just the first three chapters, I gave up and put the book aside.

I wondered if Harper struggled with the same challenges crafting her *Ghost Writer* novel. It had to be difficult to find ways to suggest how characters react and behave without resorting to so many excesses in language. I mean . . . writing *without* adverbs would be a lot harder. How would you tell the reader what the characters were feeling just by the context of their actions or speech?

It's why I was better employed as a train conductor. I could barely divine my own feelings half the time.

The TCM broadcast of *Holiday* was airing at five thirty. I decided that it would be a great excuse to order a pizza from Angelo's. I'd have to fire up my cranky-ass car and go pick it up, but it was *worth* it. My favorite was their "Trenton"—made with whole milk mozzarella, EVOO, oregano, pecorino romano, and finished with fresh ground tomatoes.

In short, orgasmic. And worth the indignity of getting the fucking Peugeot out of the garage to go and retrieve it.

I planned to order it a full forty-five minutes before the start of the movie—mostly to allow for how long it was probably going to take me to get the damn car going—so that gave me about twenty minutes to kill. So I picked up my phone and, reluctantly, launched the SheDate app.

Why had I promised Sofie I'd try this insanity again?

My "Likes You" grid had several new hits. It didn't take me long to work my way through them.

"Deloris" was clearly just looking for a hookup. Her profile photo showed mostly cleavage—a very impressive expanse of it—and she stated that she was married and had her spouse's permission to look for fun with someone who was into role-playing.

Swipe left.

"Razia" said she was a person who "loved to dance like no one was watching" and "had a lot of love to give" and just needed the right person "to give it to."

Swipe left.

"Celine" said she was a native of France, interning at a high-end fashion company on a J-1 exchange visa sponsored by the French-American Chamber of Commerce. She was looking for someone to help her with her "full initiation" into American culture. She was especially eager to explore dating and romantic customs with special emphasis on polyamorous relationships.

Swipe left.

"Lillian" was a forty-year-old bank executive who stated she was on SheDate "for a long time, not just a good time." She was looking for the right person to help her have a reason to "delete this app"—and asked anyone viewing her profile to swipe right if they were interested in getting to know her for longer than one date.

She had a believable profile photo, too. It looked like the kind of professional headshot you'd have taken for a staff directory at work. *She really did look like someone who worked in a bank.*

She did not sound like much of a risk.

And she lived just outside Philadelphia in Lower Merion.

I sat tapping the bottom of the phone while I thought it over.

Why the hell not? At least I wouldn't have to meet her in some off-the-wall city.

I swiped right.

Let the chips fall where they may.

I was on my way into the parking garage when I ran into Harper. *Literally.* She was rounding the corner from her car when I slammed into her because I was too busy fumbling around to find my car keys in the bottom of my backpack than paying attention to where I was walking.

"*Oh, god!*" I grabbed hold of her arms to keep her from falling. "I am *so* sorry. *What a klutz.* I wasn't paying attention."

"It's okay, really." She steadied herself. "No harm done."

"I was looking for my damn car keys and I didn't see you." I released her arms and stepped back. "Are you just coming in?"

"Yeah. I got halfway to my apartment before I realized I'd left my damn laptop in the car."

"Working on a Sunday? Bad girl."

"No choice. I had a meeting with a writer who refuses to use electronic proofs. So we had to go over my edits in person."

"For real? Why on earth would you work with someone who won't use technology?"

"When she's a guest author with three Pulitzers, you make an exception."

"Oh," I said. "That old schtick."

She laughed. "Where are you headed?"

"Angelo's for pizza. I'm celebrating that I don't have to report for work until Wednesday."

"Oh, that's great news. So, you'll be able to make the party tomorrow?"

"Yep. I was gonna text you later to say you were safe from Luz's machinations."

"Thanks. I owe you."

I got an idea. *A great one . . .*

"What are you doing right now?"

"Nothing, really. Why?"

227

"Wanna ride with me to Angelo's? I'll make it worth your while . . . dinner and a movie."

"Oh . . . I don't know. I don't want to crash your evening."

"Crashing my evening would mean showing up uninvited to sell me skin care products. I am asking you to eat pizza and watch Katharine Hepburn use her feminine wiles to save Cary Grant from her undeserving, socialite sister."

"When you put it that way, how can I refuse?"

"I was hoping you wouldn't." I took hold of her elbow. "Come on, you can help me back this beast out."

We walked deeper into the garage.

"When was the last time you drove it?" she asked warily.

"I think Bill Clinton was president?"

Harper grabbed hold of my sleeve and tugged me to a standstill. "Why don't we take my car?"

"Where's your sense of adventure?" I teased. "My car's not *that* bad. Once you get past the first few lungfuls of dust and diesel fumes, it's quite addictive."

"They said the same thing about Cheetos—except for the diesel fumes."

We'd reached my car. "There she blows," I quoted Melville. "A hump like a snow-hill."

Harper was looking the Peugeot over like she expected it to burst into flames if we tried to start it.

"There *is* something whale-like in its countenance," she observed. "How does one say 'Moby Dick' in French?"

I pretended to think about it. "I think it's pronounced, 'Moby Dick.'"

"Very funny."

"The fact remains, the French were famous for this type of robust, full-bodied design and viability on rough terrain—much like the talents of the women who starred in their films during the same years these cars were in production."

"Really?" Harper looked dubious. "I think your

characterization might be a bit. . . . aspirational."

"Well, gird your loins and climb on in."

"Do you carry adequate liability insurance?"

"How rude." I faced her. "I think you're spending too much time with Sofie."

She climbed into the front of the car and dutifully attached her seatbelt.

"Here goes nothing." I pulled out the choke and started the car. It grated, shook, and rattled, but it started—and proceeded to belch blue smoke for a full minute. When the idling settled down to a modest roar, I slipped it into gear and began to back out.

When we reached the exit to the garage, I remembered that the defroster wasn't working on my side.

"Do me a favor," I asked Harper. "Open the glove box and pull out that bandana hankie."

"Why?" she asked. "Are we knocking off a drive-thru?"

"We'll be knocking something off, all right, if you don't hand it to me so I can wipe off the inside of the windshield. The defroster is on the fritz."

Harper was digging around inside the glove box. She held up a small green bottle.

"Perrier? Seriously?"

"It came with the car."

"Here's the hankie." She handed it to me.

I was busy fighting the choke and trying to shift in traffic without lurching into the car ahead of me. "Can you reach over here and wipe it off for me?"

"Not without unfastening my seat belt."

"I promise not to get you killed. And I'll have better odds at holding up my end of that bargain if I can fucking see out of this windshield."

"Okay, okay." She freed herself and scooted over to my side of the car. She wiped the window clear, but it immediately fogged up again as soon as she finished. "This is ridiculous. Why don't you get it fixed?"

"Because I rarely drive it in the winter months."

"Well, why are you driving it today?"

"I didn't want to bring my pizza back on the bus."

"Ever heard of Uber?"

"Are you nuts? That'd cost me about seventy-five bucks on a Sunday."

Harper was still furiously wiping at the windshield. "Well, next time just call me and I'll make you a damn pizza."

"Chill. We're almost there."

"This pizza had better be worth it."

I was stunned. "You've never had Angelo's pizza before?"

"Nope."

"Oh, honey . . . this is gonna change your life."

"Good. I was hoping something would." She refolded the hankie in an attempt to find a dry spot—without success. "I'm going to have to take off my shirt next to keep this damn window clear."

"Don't make vain promises you have no intention of keeping."

"Can you open your window a little bit? That might help clear this up."

"No."

"Why the hell not?"

"It doesn't open."

"Are you sure this thing isn't a submarine?" Harper's ministrations now were just pushing the moisture around in circles.

I glanced at her. "That would explain so much."

When I returned my eyes to the street, I couldn't believe our good fortune.

"Fuck! A parking space." I swerved into it so quickly it sent Harper sprawling. She ended up mostly on my lap, still hanging on to her wiping cloth.

"Shit, I'm sorry!"

She struggled to sit up. "Sure you are."

I ignored the guy behind us who was busy laying on his horn and flipping me off. I was too busy enjoying the sensation of Harper splayed all over me.

"Do you always drive like a maniac?" Harper struggled back up and shifted over into her seat.

"What are you talking about? This is a primo spot."

"It wouldn't have killed us to walk another fifteen feet."

"You know this is the street Rocky ran down."

"I know. *Philadelphia Magazine*. Remember?"

"Yeah. I guess you've done features on that."

"Only about seventy-five of them."

I was still shifting gears, trying to leverage the Peugeot into the tight spot. It fit like a . . . like a French submarine crammed into a space made for a Mini Cooper.

"It's hard to overstate the importance of a good parking space. We want to keep the pizza hot, don't we?"

"Isn't this why god created ovens?"

"Come on. You gotta experience this place."

"Is that a Flyers banner over the door?"

"I don't know what you're talking about." I reached over and covered her eyes with my hand. "Thank god we left the extra muffler in the car."

The interior of Angelo's South Philly was like a walk back in time—and not just because they only took cash. The space was long and narrow and packed to the gills with workers in black T-shirts throwing, topping, baking, cutting, and boxing pizzas. And towers of white boxes so high they nearly scraped the tin ceiling were stacked in every available space. We were lucky and, for once, the line was not out the door.

The aromas inside were intoxicating. Angelo's was equally famous for its authentic steak sandwiches. As many people were leaving with bags full of those as boxes containing what, arguably, was the best pizza in Philadelphia.

It was clear that someone who worked here had gone nuts with a label-maker. There were little strips of notices stuck all over the place. ORDER HERE. PAY HERE. CASH ONLY. CAUTION. SURFACE IS HOT. And yet another CASH ONLY, conveniently stuck to the top of the ATM machine that sat just inside the door.

Danny, the owner and self-described Pizza Stalker saw me walk in.

"Izzy! Lemme guess—you're The Trenton?"

"You know it."

"We got it right up front."

"Danny, this is Harper. She's never had one of your pizzas before."

"Oh." He took her in and shook her hand. "We make memories here, Harper. Food memories. Because that's what memories are, right? Food makes us remember the best things in our lives."

"It's great to meet you, Danny."

"Harper works for *Philadelphia Magazine*," I explained.

"Hey!" Danny hugged her. "You did a story about us when we opened this location back in 2019."

"I hope it was a good one." She smiled at him. "I'm sure it should have been."

"The best," he said. "I'm gonna give you a free steak to say thank you."

"No—you don't need to thank me."

"Forget about it. It's done." He called out to one of the guys in the open kitchen behind him. "Maggio? Gimme another steak with onions and mushrooms." He turned back and clapped me on the shoulder. "You two beauties have a great night."

"That's the plan. Thanks, Danny."

"Remember to follow your dreams, kid. Whatever you got,

follow your dreams."

He stopped to tell one of the cashiers that our steak was on the house. Then he disappeared into the sea of black T-shirts in the kitchen.

"That was Danny," I said.

"He likes you," Harper declared.

"I know. Thank my sister, Zoé. She flirts outrageously with him whenever she visits. A trip to Angelo's is required."

"I see." She nudged me. "Those cash register decorations remind me of our lobby."

There was an abundance of fake greenery and brightly colored glass balls wound around the bottoms of the three registers. I felt sure that *Nonna* Mariota would've enhanced the cheap décor with low-contrast lighting and artfully placed throw pillows.

"Yeah, but just wait," I told Harper. "Dewey has something special in mind to spice up our holiday appointments."

"Oh? That sounds intriguing."

"Lebrun!" a cashier called.

Our order was ready. I paid for it—after repeatedly telling Harper to back off—and we were on our way.

The ride back was less eventful. When we reached my place, Harper set the oven at two hundred degrees and slipped the pizza inside while I got two beers out of the fridge.

"Which do you want?" I asked her. "A double IPA or this," I squinted at the can, "pilsner lager?"

"Do you have a preference?"

"Nope. I pretty much drink anything."

"Then I'll take the IPA."

"I kind of figured you'd go for the rough stuff."

"I beg your pardon . . . a double IPA is not rough."

"Well, then, what the hell *do* you consider rough?"

"You *have* met Gina . . . right?"

"Good point." I got two plates down. "Steak or pizza first?"

233

"Um. Both?"

"I love a woman who cannot commit."

"*Au contraire.* I have the opposite problem. I commit to everything."

I served us each a large slab of pizza and half of the sandwich.

"Then why are you single?"

"Because right now, I'm committed to being by myself."

"I'm beginning to think that's the key to happiness." I handed Harper her plate and a wad of paper towels. "I think I'm ready to ditch the dating app and embrace my life of solitude."

"Why? Shouldn't you at least give it a fair shake before you abandon ship?"

"What's your definition of a fair shake? Ending up in jail for statutory rape?"

Harper's eyes grew wide. "Excuse me?"

"My last date turned out to be seventeen years old. She'd used her mother's photo and probably most of her bio, too."

"My god."

"Yeah. For real." I led the way to the living room. "Come on. We'll sit on the couch. We can put our plates on the coffee table."

I turned on the TV and tuned it to TCM. We had about two minutes until the movie started.

"I still don't understand why you refuse to stream these. Don't the commercials drive you nuts?"

"No," I explained. "They're part of the total experience. Remember how Danny said food is memories? To me, watching these old movies with nine million commercial breaks is memories. And they're my best memories, too—all those nights as a kid, watching them with *maman* and Zoé."

"That does sound pretty special. My mother would rather be flayed alive with knives than forced to sit through a commercial—unless it was for a Turks & Caicos Club Med package."

I laughed. The movie was beginning.

Harper took a cautious bite of her pizza. "Oh, my *god* . . ."

"Told you. Wait'll you dive into that cheese steak."

She was still chewing and making happy sounds. "It had better be great," she said between bites. "I'll probably have to burn this sweater to get the smell out of it."

"It's a holistic experience," I insisted. "Besides, you probably just washed it six hours ago."

"That's ridiculous." She sounded offended. "It's been at least *eighteen*. I know because I only do knits on Saturday nights."

"And I thought I had no social life."

On the screen, Johnny Case (played superbly by Cary Grant) was meeting the quick and erudite Linda Seton (played by Katharine Hepburn), sister of his shallow fiancé, Julia (played by Who Cares?)

The film had a classic setup: good-humored, self-made man of the people meets a stuck-up New York heiress on a skiing trip. They have a whirlwind romance, end up engaged, and she brings him home to the family's Fifth Avenue mansion to meet her domineering banker father. Of course, her sister, Linda, falls in love with Johnny, who she sees as a kindred spirit—but courageously refuses to acknowledge it while he is still engaged to Julia. Johnny shares Linda's feelings but determines to remain true to his promise to Julia. But fate and true love intervene. Julia ends up choosing her creature comforts and high society lifestyle over the simpler existence Johnny wants. Feeling freed to pursue the man she loves, Linda follows Johnny to the ship that will take him away on what was to have been his honeymoon trip. There, the two are free to confess their love for each other and a textbook HEA ensues.

Recast Johnny Case as Joanie Case, and it could have been a sapphic romance.

I supposed Dewey really was on to something with all those damn tropes.

"Think you've had enough of Angelo's pizza to know if you'd

235

like another slice?" I asked Harper.

Harper didn't hesitate and offered me her plate immediately. "I'm a hundred percent sure of that."

"It's as good as I promised, isn't it?"

She looked at me intently. "It really is."

I got us each another serving and turned the oven off. There was easily enough left for another meal.

We were about halfway through the pizza—and the movie—when my phone rang.

It was *maman*.

"Bonjour, *Maman*," I answered. "*Regardes-tu le film?*"

She said she was—and remarked (like she always did) that the acrobatic stunt Cary Grant and Katharine Hepburn performed was amazing.

"Well, he was an acrobat before he became an actor," I reminded her.

She asked me if I knew my holiday schedule yet, and I told her no, but I expected to have to work.

"*C'est vraiment dommage*," she said with disappointment.

She was right. It was a drag.

"If I get lucky and end up working the Zephyr, I'll let you know. We could at least meet for breakfast."

"*Oui. Ce serait bien.*" The movie was coming back on. "*Il est temps de te laisser! Je t'aime.*"

"I love you, too. *Au revoir, Maman.*"

I hung up. "That was my mother," I explained to Harper.

"I kind of figured."

"She's watching the movie, too."

"That's really sweet."

We'd reached the part of the movie where Katharine Hepburn was confessing to her brother that she'd fallen in love with Cary Grant—but was determined never to speak of it as long as he was committed to her sister, played by Who Cares.

"I never understood this part." I whispered the comment

to Harper, as if we were seated in a dark theater surrounded by other moviegoers. "It doesn't make sense."

"It doesn't?"

"No. If she really wants him—and he obviously wants her—why doesn't she just tell him?"

"Maybe because it's not that easy. What if she risks it and finds out he really *doesn't* want her? It would be a disaster."

"But he totally wants her. You can tell."

"How?"

"It's no accident that he keeps seeking out her company. Whenever things go south with snobby Julia, he ends up alone with Linda in the playroom."

"True. But is that enough to hang your hopes on?"

"I think so. Maybe he just needs to be shocked to wake his ass up."

"Possibly," she said.

"You don't sound convinced."

"Maybe I haven't seen the movie enough times to be sure."

"Well, I have," I insisted. "And he totally should've laid one on her in that New Year's Eve scene. It was clear she wanted him to."

"She pushed him away."

"She didn't mean it."

"You're nuts. She totally meant it."

"Only because he was engaged to her sister," I insisted. "Not because she didn't want him to."

"I disagree. She didn't trust his motivation. She thought it was situational—just borne of the moment."

I couldn't tell if Harper was just being a contrarian, or whether she really expected me to prove I was right.

I decided on the latter and chose to accept her unspoken challenge.

"Okay. Let's suppose I'm Cary Grant."

"You aren't tall enough."

"Please try to take this demonstration seriously."

"Okay," she capitulated. "Go ahead with your theory."

"It's New Year's Eve and we've just been dancing. The clock strikes midnight." I put my arm around her shoulders. "And I—remember I'm Cary Grant, here—move in to kiss you." I leaned in close enough to her to feel her breath on my face. "What do you do?"

She opened her mouth to reply, but no sound came out.

"I'm still waiting . . ." I whispered.

Her eyes closed then. And . . . I kissed her.

It was quick. Gentle and soft. I pulled back. Still no resistance. So I did it again. Longer this time. She tasted . . . fragrant— like sweet leaves of basil and the promise of summer. I felt her hand touch the side of my face. We were falling back into the sofa cushions. It was getting out of hand . . . my ridiculous experiment had gone too far. I knew I'd brought this on myself. It was exactly what I feared would happen if I gave in to my attraction to her. I was losing focus.

We needed to stop while we still could.

I was half on top of her now.

I suddenly jerked myself upright like I'd had a damn bungee cord attached to my back.

"God. God, I'm . . . *I'm so sorry*," I said. "I didn't mean to . . . it was only supposed to be a joke."

Harper seemed flustered, too. "It's all right," she said. "No harm done. It's not your fault."

"Geez. Harper, I'm sorry. I didn't mean to act like a jerk."

She looked as embarrassed as I felt. "You're not a jerk."

"I promise this isn't why I asked you to come here." It sounded pathetic, even to me.

"Please," she said. "Stop apologizing. It was just . . . the moment. You don't need to worry." She met my eyes. "It didn't mean anything."

"No," I agreed belatedly. "It didn't. It was just the movie."

"Right. Just the movie."

"Um . . ." I tried to think of something to lighten the mood. "How about another beer?"

"I think that's a good idea."

"Great." I hopped up and headed to the kitchen. I stood with my forehead pressed against the inside of the refrigerator door. *What a fucking loser. I'll be lucky if she ever talks to me again after tonight.*

I returned to the sofa with our two beers.

"What'd I miss?" I asked, as I handed her another bottle of the double IPA.

"Not much. Just Johnny giving in to what Julia wants instead of following his heart."

"I hate when that shit happens." I sat down at a respectful distance from her.

Harper took her time before replying.

"I do, too," she said quietly.

Consistent with every other dating experience I'd had so far on SheDate, Lillian wrote to ask if we could meet for an early cocktail before the holidays got any closer. After the debacle with Harper, I was more anxious than ever to get myself out of harm's way and find someone safe to date—because like it or not, for me, someone safe equated to someone *not* living in my building. I was determined not to repeat the mistake I'd made with Tonya. I could not face the humiliation of another failed relationship that had nearly cost me my found family in Hopkinson House. They mattered to me—the people in this quirky community I'd called home since I'd been a child, staying here with Papa. And I'd nearly lost all of that when Tonya decided to dump me like a bucket of empties in the trash room.

The truth was, I *liked* Harper.

I liked her a lot. She was the first real friend I'd made in years—someone who got me in all my twisted ways. The last thing I wanted was to mess that up. In my experience, mixing friendship with sex—or worse, *romance*—always ended badly. I'd lose a lover and a best friend. Or worse . . . a cat.

And that potentially spelled disaster for Harper, too. I didn't want to risk ruining her life along with my own. She belonged here, too. Although Gina had lived here while they were together, she'd never become a part of the community like Tonya had. Harper said she had never engaged with any of the residents or staff. And that she'd moved out shortly after they broke up. But Harper was like me. Harper embraced her life here.

And there was no way I was going to risk ruining that—for either of us.

So, when Lillian asked if I wanted to meet her for drinks on Monday night, I agreed. She said there was a new (to her) distillery in Ardmore she'd been wanting to try out and asked if I'd like to meet there. The place was supposed to be renowned for its tasting room, showcasing its own label whiskeys and gin—and they also had a menu of excellent craft cocktails.

No food, so that implied that Lillian wasn't planning on more than she advertised: a first meeting and a simple cocktail.

Even though I'd hoped she'd suggest something more centrally located for each of us, I thought her choice of establishment sounded fine, so I agreed to meet her there at five thirty.

It had started to snow when I left Hopkinson House and headed for Ardmore. The cold weather systems from the northwest kept right on rolling through, one after another. Sadly, driving made more sense than navigating the roster of buses I'd had to have taken to get there. So, I got the Peugeot out for the second time that month and braved the elements to travel the thirty-five miles to the Manatawny Still Works and Tasting Room.

My mind was still full of the disastrous end to my evening with Harper. Kissing her had been so . . . spontaneous. Ill-advised. And stupid.

It had also been fucking fantastic.

And that was the part that kept haunting me.

I could've been offered the chance to pick what hid behind any one of twenty doors, each offering a potential shot at happiness—and I'd be certain to select the option that only contained an express ticket to misery.

Think about Lillian, I kept telling myself. Think about how nice she seems. How grown up and balanced. How stable. How great this could be if it worked out . . . after all, she lived half an hour away. There'd be no chance of running into her at the elevators, in the mailroom, or in the laundry room.

She might as well be in another country.

It could be perfect, I told myself.

And it was obvious she liked good hooch . . . a woman like that was hard to come by.

The snow gained in intensity once I crossed the Schuylkill River and started heading north toward Ardmore. At first, I thought Lillian was nuts for suggesting we meet at five thirty. But maybe it was good she wanted to meet so damn early. At least the visibility was better.

Damn, I really needed to get the defroster in my car fixed. Keeping the inside of the windshield cleared off was becoming a serious drag. Of course, Harper had neatly folded the bandana hankie and returned it to the glove box after our trip to Angelo's. And, of course, I couldn't reach the damn glove box. So I had to find a safe place to pull off so I could grab it. I'd been trying to use the sleeve of my jacket, and that was just creating a bigger mess.

I feared this weather was a harbinger of the kind of trip I was going to have later in the week. I started out on the Nor'easter for the first half of the trip. Then scheduling gave me the required eight hours of "rest" in New Haven before hitting me with another four full days of travel. I'd finish up on the Zephyr in St. Albans on Christmas night, then deadhead back to Philadelphia on Boxing Day.

It was a classic, USRail two-step. Two trips out; one trip back—and a measly eight hours of rest in between.

And it sucked scissors.

At least I hoped the extra time away would ease any feelings of awkwardness between Harper and me. She'd said—multiple times—not to worry about it. She'd said it was all fine. She'd said no problem. It was just the moment.

That it didn't mean anything.

That was the part that gnawed at me the most. The truth was—even though I was the one who'd backed away—I wanted to believe it had meant something to her.

At least a little bit.

Okay. Whatever. I supposed we'd get to test her hypothesis when we saw each other tomorrow night at the party.

Maybe she would've been better off going with Luz, I thought. She'd have known better than to try to . . . get horizontal with her.

God, I was such a fool. And I'd had no self-control. It was worse than my performance that night in New Haven with Tonya. Worse because I didn't really care about Tonya—but I did care about Harper. I cared about Harper a lot. Too much to risk ruining our friendship.

My brief stop to pull over and try and clear the windshield had been pointless. I'd just about given up on being able to see well enough to continue on when I realized that I'd finally reached Lancaster Avenue in Ardmore.

And mercifully, there were several convenient parking spaces directly across the street from the entrance to Manatawny Still Works.

I pulled over and turned off the car. I was only eight

minutes late—not bad considering how quickly the weather was deteriorating.

It wasn't too late to call this off and just slink back home, I thought.

But, no. I steeled my resolve and got out.

Here goes nothin'. I ducked my head and made my way across the street, trying to dodge the swirling snow.

Lillian hadn't been hard to find when I got inside. The place wasn't very busy and there were only a few people sitting around in the comfy chairs scattered about, nursing their whiskeys in Glencairn nosing glasses.

Lillian was seated at a small table for two not far from the bar. I recognized her right away because she looked exactly like her profile photo. She hadn't ordered anything yet, which impressed me. I walked over and introduced myself.

"Are you Lillian?" When she nodded, I continued. "I'm Isabelle. Awful weather tonight, isn't it? I wasn't sure I'd make it."

"Perhaps you should've left a bit earlier, Isabelle?" she suggested.

"May I sit down?"

"Of course. Please do."

I pulled out the other chair and tried to shake the snow off my jacket. "I actually did leave in what I thought was plenty of time. I have a rather old car, and the defroster doesn't work all that well. It made driving a bit of a challenge."

"Did you rule out public transportation?"

Okay . . . what was up with this travel inquisition?

I decided to give her the benefit of the doubt. She was probably as nervous as I was.

"In fact, I did. But I would've had to change buses four times to get here. Maybe next time, we could meet someplace closer to the city," I joked.

"We'll see." She did not sound overly enthusiastic about the possibility.

The bartender showed up carrying a glass of . . . something. He sat it down in front of Lillian.

"I hope this one will be more to your liking," he said. "It's one of our most popular blends."

Lillian didn't bother thanking him. "I hope so, myself."

He took a deep breath before looking at me. "May I bring you something from the menu?"

I smiled at him. "Sure. I'll have whatever you think is your best whiskey. Neat."

"That would be our Four Grain American." He nodded. "I'll have that right up."

"Thanks."

Lillian watched my interaction with the server with interest. "I don't know how advisable it was to trust him to recommend a beverage."

"Why not? He works here. He should know what's regarded as their best product."

"I made the same mistake when I arrived. The result was less than satisfying."

"Really?" I picked up the menu. "Which one did you get?"

"The Four Grain American."

"Oh." I was flummoxed. "You didn't like it?"

"Not so much. It tasted like it had been strained through an old sock."

"Some whiskeys can be peaty," I observed. "Scotches, too."

"It wasn't peat."

"Okay . . ." *Geez lady. Lighten up.* I looked around the interior. "I like the vibe here. It's . . ."

"Like a Cracker Barrel?" she suggested.

"No. That wasn't what I had in mind. I was thinking it's

more like a happy intersection of warm wood tones and stainless steel. Kind of a modern industrial flavor."

Lillian looked around the space. "More like a design aesthetic that cannot commit to a single principle."

This woman was one tough customer. I wondered if she was determined to find fault with everything in life, or if I was just catching her on a bad night.

I decided to give it another try. After all, I really did want to try the whiskey.

"So, what made you get a SheDate account? It doesn't really seem like it would be your *métier*."

"Just as punching tickets on a train doesn't seem like yours."

I had to bite back a sarcastic response.

"In fact," I said, "they actually expect us to do more these days. We get to oversee coupling and uncoupling of the engines and we actually have to take breaks from ticket punching to hop off the train and throw the manual switches that control the track direction."

"Is that considered highly skilled?" she asked.

"It is if you're a passenger on another train sharing the same set of tracks."

She didn't make any reply.

The bartender arrived with my whiskey. "Enjoy," he said, before heading back to the bar area.

I picked up the glass and inhaled. It had a great nose—full of vanilla, orange, and malt. I tasted it. The mild heat was a very welcome addition to the cold outside—and in here at my table.

"I think this is delicious."

Lillian looked at me like I'd just blasphemed against the Holy Spirit.

"I suppose I have a softer palate," she declared.

"I suppose you do," I agreed. "May I ask you a question?"

She seemed surprised. "All right."

"Why did you want to meet me? You knew I worked as a

conductor—which you seem to think is tantamount to working at Jiffy Lube. So why bother if you had such low expectations?"

"That's pretty impertinent."

"Is it?"

"I won't deny that I wasn't overly optimistic about your prospects. But if you don't periodically take a chance on something you think won't work, how can you expect to cover all the bases?"

"So it's a law of averages kind of thing?"

"Possibly."

"And what do you think of your grand experiment now?" I took another swallow of my whiskey. I didn't think I'd had enough of it to claim that it had given me false courage, but I wasn't feeling particularly tentative right then, either.

As far as I was concerned, this uptight bitch could gather her skirts and ride right on home on the broomstick I was sure she'd left double-parked outside.

"I think I'm glad you're enjoying your drink."

That seemed halfway magnanimous. I almost thought about revising my opinion of her. Fortunately, she wasn't finished with her summation yet.

"You should at least get something worthwhile out of the evening—especially since you endured so much hardship to get here." She pushed her chair back and stood up. "If you'll excuse me? I have another engagement."

She walked off without looking back.

And she didn't pay for her drink, either.

I felt my face grow hot—and it wasn't just from the whiskey. *What the fuck was that about?*

Short answer: I'd just been dumped by Jane 2.0. Whoever said lightning doesn't strike the same spot twice had obviously never spent time on a dating app.

I had the singed ass to prove it.

The bartender walked back over carrying another drink.

"On the house," he said. He set it down in front of me. "She was one for the record books."

He got no argument from me.

The snow had not lightened up one bit while I'd been inside Manatawny.

My car was now covered. It looked like some kind of bulbous snow hump.

I got the brush and snow scraper out of the back seat and did my best to clear the windows.

At least the fucker started on the first try. But without a defroster to keep the windshield clear, I knew there was no way I'd be able to make the drive home safely. *What had I been thinking when I decided to take the damn car out in this?*

To be fair, the snow had not been predicted to amount to this much. But, still . . .

I deliberated about what to do. I tried Uber—only to find I'd have a four-hour wait. And getting a cab that would take me all the way to center city was about as likely as Lillian having a change of heart, and coming back to pick up the tab.

I could leave the car and walk to the nearest bus stop. That would only take about twenty minutes . . . in shoes that would be soaked in less than four.

Or I could call someone to come and get me. But who?

Sofie was about as reliable as a golden retriever. Odds were she'd get distracted by something shiny on her way, and I'd be stuck here until the spring thaw.

I decided to call Dewey and see if he could bail me out. He wasn't too happy about my whereabouts.

"What in the Sam Hill are you doing up in Ardmore?"

"I had a date."

"*A date?* It's not even seven o'clock. Where'd you meet?

Chuck E. Cheese?"

"Hey," I reminded him, "after my recent nightmare at Monstercade, that's really not very funny."

"Okay, okay. What's going on? You need me to send in the cavalry?"

"Sort of. My car defroster is broken and it's snowing like crazy up here. I can't see to drive back."

"Why the hell did you drive then? Or is your weather app broken, too?"

"Cut me some slack, man." It wasn't like Dewey to be so irascible. "I didn't feel like changing buses four times."

"Sorry." He relented a bit. "We're trying to get the solarium set up for the party tomorrow and Frick and Frack are getting on my last nerve. What do you need? Want me to try to find you a cab or an Uber?"

"I thought about that. But even if we could find one, it'd be midnight before I got back. I thought about calling Sofie, but she's probably already on a date."

"She is—kind of. I saw her leave with Harper about twenty minutes ago."

What the hell? "Where were they going?"

"Out to dinner, I think."

Oh, great. All I needed was for Harper to tell Sofie what had happened last night. Sofie would hand my ass back to me in so many pieces I'd never be able to sit down again.

"Are you still there?" Dewey asked. "I think I have an idea that might work."

"Well, let me hear it. I'm desperate."

"I just thought of someone I might be able to send to pick you up. Tell me the name and address of the place you're at. I'll shoot you a text with an ETA."

"I owe you big time, man. It's the Manatawny Still Works. Forty-nine West Lancaster Avenue in Ardmore. Seriously, dude. Let me know how I can make this up to you."

"I wouldn't say no to a bottle of that Four Grain American. That's some good hooch."

Was there anything this man didn't know about?

"You've been here before?"

"Hell, yeah. My middle kid used to work at the distillery in Pottstown. They chose this gig over going to college. They brought samples home all the time. So I ended up getting all the joy and none of the tuition payments. And lemme tell you . . . that shit's smooth as a baby's ass."

"I'll take care of it. At least something good can come out of this evening."

"Date another bust?"

I laughed bitterly. "This time, she actually walked out on me."

"Do I wanna know why?"

"Apparently, I wasn't rarefied enough to suit her. I think she's a narcissist. Her head was stuck so far up her own ass, she disdained anything that didn't look exactly like her."

"Ice, ice, baby." Dewey laughed. "Good job, Izzy. You hooked yourself a genuine Ice Queen."

"Yeah? Well for me, this lottery is over."

"Don't be hasty. Just sit tight and let me find you a ride. You can amuse yourself shopping while you wait . . . I think you just got my Christmas list."

"Right. Thanks, man."

I hung up and trudged back across the street to the distillery. This time, I took a seat at the bar.

I was halfway through my flight of whiskeys when Dewey texted to tell me that my ride was already on the way. He said the ETA was twenty minutes.

I texted back.

249

Is there some secret about who's coming
to get me?

I want you to be surprised.

That sounds ominous.

It isn't.

I just got a flight of whiskeys. Hope I
have time to finish it.

Anything good?

So far, I really like this peated single malt.

I'll take one of those, too.

Remind me to take the bus next time.

I'd just finished paying for my purchases when the street door
opened, and Luz walked in. Dewey had said I'd be surprised, but
I'd actually half expected it to be one or both of the maintenance
duo.

"Am I ever happy to see you."

Luz was busy looking around the place. "Do they have real
stills in here?"

I nodded. "Good ones, too. Tell you what—how about we
make a date to come back here and I'll treat you. It's the least I
can do to pay you back for coming all this way to get me—and
in such crappy weather."

"That'd be great. Can Aldo come, too? He's out in the truck."

Of course he was . . . I wondered if Dewey had broken the news to them about Cujo's real identity.

"Sure," I said. "We'll make a night of it."

I thanked the bartender for taking such great care of me, and Luz and I headed out into the snow.

Her ride was a massive Chevy Silverado 1500 ZR2. It was clear she didn't have to worry about getting stuck in the snow— or in anything else, for that matter. The thing looked like it had enough ground clearance to ford the Schuylkill without getting the running boards wet.

She'd left it running and steam swirled around it like it was a bull pawing at a winter pasture.

When we reached the truck, Luz instructed me to sit up front.

"Aldo'n Cujo are in the back," she explained.

Cujo?

I climbed in and immediately heard a chorus of "*Buon Natale!*"

Mrs. Mariota and Aldo were snugly strapped into their seats in the back of Luz's chariot.

"Mrs. Mariota?" I asked. I looked at Aldo. "How did . . ."

"Her grandson told us to bring her along," he said. "She loves the snow. Don't you *Nonna?*"

"*Sì. Amo la neve.*" She beamed. "I love the snow."

"We promised her we'd take her to Popeye's after we picked you up," Aldo said.

"She loves that spicy flounder," Luz clarified. "Ain't that true, *Nonna?*"

"*Il pesce è buono,*" Mrs. Mariota beamed. "*Buon Natale!*"

I fastened my seatbelt, and Luz roared out of the parking space in a hail of snow.

"So, I guess this means Dewey told you guys about Mrs. Mariota being our mysterious cat burglar?"

"He sure did." Luz chuckled. "We felt stupid about it at first, but then Aldo said it didn't mean any of our clues about Cujo were wrong."

"That's right," Aldo added. "We told him from the get-go that Cujo wasn't a rat."

He had a point. Mrs. Mariota was definitely not a rodent.

"And Leo asked us to help find out who that golf shoe belongs to."

"And the cat," Luz added. "He really wants to get rid of that thing."

"We're all on the decorating committee, now, too." Aldo sounded smug. "*Nonna* is helping us with ideas about where to hang Christmas lights."

"*Buon Natale!*" rang out from the back seat. "*Che nevichi!* Let it snow!"

Yeah. I had to hand it to Dewey. *He had figured out a good way to leverage this.*

Luz made great time getting us back to Philly. Before I knew it, we had pulled into the snow-covered parking lot that flanked the Popeye's on Chestnut Street.

"We're lucky this joint's still open." Luz opened the driver's door and called out to Aldo. "Come on. You can help me carry the food. I don't wanna fall and bust my ass."

"Right behind you." Aldo got out of the truck, and they disappeared behind a wall of snow.

"*Perché sei così triste?*"

I turned around in my seat. Mrs. Mariota was staring at me with her clear, round eyes.

"I don't . . . I don't know what that means," I said, apologetically.

She pointed at my face. "*You.* Why are you sad?"

"I . . ." I was surprised by the directness—and perception—of her question. Sitting alone with her in the seclusion of Luz's monster truck—in the middle of a fast-food parking lot during a blizzard—already felt strangely . . . confessional. It was surreal enough that telling her the simple truth was easy. "I'm . . . I keep messing up."

She continued to stare at me.

"Dimmi di più a riguardo." She made a rapid gesture with her small hand. "More."

In for a penny, in for a pound. I took a deep breath. "I keep meeting the wrong women, hoping that one of them will end up being the right woman. But none of them are. And I think that's my fault because I'm the one who's wrong—*for them.* The truth is, I know what I really want, but I won't let myself have it. And I think I took too long to figure it out."

"Vedi la neve? Copre tutto. Ma si scioglierà, e il mondo si rivelerà di nuovo."

I stared at her, trying to divine her meaning. Something about snow . . . and the world being . . . *new.*

"See the snow?" She spread her arms to encompass the storm closing in around us. "It will melt away. The world will be . . ." she searched for the word, *"revealed* . . . again."

I wasn't sure how to reply.

"Lei ti aspetterà." Mrs. Mariota smiled and reached forward to pat my shoulder. "She will wait for you."

We both heard the stamping of feet and looked toward the sound to see Luz and Aldo, trying to shake the snow from their jackets and hats. They were both laden with bags and cardboard trays containing soft drink cups.

In ten minutes, we were back at Hopkinson House.

I offered to escort Mrs. Mariota back to the apartment she shared with her grandson on eleven.

He met us at the door and expressed gratitude for the night off.

"She really enjoys getting out," he said. "And I never have the time to take her. So this, tonight, was really great."

"I think Aldo and Luz enjoyed it, too." I patted Mrs. Mariota on the back. "I think your *nonna* has made a couple of good new friends."

253

Nonna beamed up at me. She looked adorable standing there with her white Popeye's bag clutched in her hand. She reached into the pocket of her red cloth coat and withdrew something that she pressed into my hand.

"*Buon Natale!*" she said.

I smiled when I realized it was a bulb of garlic.

"*Buon Natale, Nonna,*" I replied.

CHAPTER TEN

Friends to Lovers—and other alms for the tattered soul.

The Christmas open house was in full swing. Dewey declared that it had record turnout, too—an occurrence he attributed to the rotten weather. Most other holiday gatherings that might've tempted residents to venture out had been canceled or rescheduled because of Winter Storm Jorge. The first wave of the system had rolled in yesterday and decided to park its ass and sit a spell on top of Philadelphia.

Dewey had Christmas music playing at just the right level. I wasn't sure, but he must've programmed some Eartha Kitt playlist. I swear I heard "Santa Baby" three times in the first half hour.

As near as I could tell, everyone was here. I recognized several members of Dewey's sapphic book club, as well as a few of the regulars from the laundry room. There also were some notable appearances by people who didn't live in the building. Dewey's wife, Avis, was there—resplendent in a shimmering red cocktail dress. And Sofie had consented to drop by long enough to have a glass of cheer before heading out for another evening amusement.

Inclement weather was never an impediment for Sofie. I

recalled how once at McGill, we'd been under shelter-in-place orders when an unprecedented late spring storm had spawned tornadoes that ripped a mile-wide path across the city. Sofie'd had plans to attend a party at a loft in the Ville Mont-Royal borough, and nothing would deter her from venturing out.

"It's just drizzling," she insisted when I tried to talk some sense into her.

"Yeah, but you're taking my *father's* car."

She blew me off. "That thing is impervious to acts of nature. No self-respecting tree would ever choose to fall on it. The indignity would be beyond endurance."

In the end, I lost every argument I could cobble together, and she sallied forth for the evening. In typical fashion, she came to no harm and partied until after 3 a.m.

Her successful navigation of that crisis made her less willing to make concessions to others.

Hence her appearance here tonight.

She was off in a corner, talking with Harper . . . *of course*. They both looked terrific. As was her custom, Sofie was glammed-out in some skimpy creation that should've included NC-17 warnings on its label. Harper was a knockout, too, wearing a simple black dress that, on her, looked anything but simple. From this vantage point, I had my first real opportunity to admire her charms from a distance. She truly was, as Luz had pointed out, one fine-looking woman.

I was dying to know what they were in such earnest conversation about.

Aldo and Luz were there, too—laughing and joking around with Leo Mariota and his beloved *Nonna*. They both looked very dapper in their shiny suits with festive holiday ties, which Leo shared had been conscripted by *Nonna* from . . . someplace. I noticed that Luz didn't seem too heartbroken about not getting to attend the party with Harper. We actually had arrived together, as arranged. Our elevator ride up to the solarium had been awkward as fuck. That had been mostly my fault, since Harper made several attempts at light conversation. I still felt shy and embarrassed. It had taken every ounce of restraint I possessed not to grill Harper about what she and Sofie had discussed during their dinner date the night before. After all, why would I even know they'd gone out together?

I'd already acted like a cad. I didn't want to add stalker to my résumé.

Sofie had made a beeline for Harper as soon as she'd arrived and whisked her off to the corner where they now stood, sipping on their glasses of wine and conversing in what, to me, looked like hushed and confidential tones.

I just knew they were talking about me.

Dewey approached me as I stood glumly beside the platters of cheeses and crudités.

"Why do you look like somebody just pissed in your corn flakes?"

"I think I messed things up with Harper."

"Oh, yeah?" He looked intrigued. "What things?"

"Friendship things. I think I crossed a line."

"Most lines are meant to be crossed."

"Not this one."

He reached for a slice of red bell pepper and dragged it through a vat of ranch dressing.

"Aren't you supposed to get your own serving of that before you dip?"

"Who made you the appetizer police?" He picked up a carrot stick and repeated the same action.

"Okay. Don't blame me if you contract some horrible, infectious disease."

"I'll assume the risk." He gestured at Harper. "Why won't you?"

"Why won't I what?"

"Take a chance on Harper. It's about time for you to climb

257

aboard and ride that gravy train. Don't you think?"

I looked at him with surprise. It wasn't like Dewey to be so . . . suggestive.

"I cannot believe you said that."

"Why?" he asked. "Did my analogy impugn the reputation of a train?"

"You know what I meant."

"I do. And the fact that *you* know it means you've thought about it yourself."

"Come on, Dewey. You know my rule."

"You mean that dumb-ass idea you have that dating someone else who lives in the building will end in the destruction of life on the planet or some other bullshit?"

Dewey and I had been friends for a long time, but I'd never known him to be so direct—or derisive.

I pointed at his glass. "How many of those have you had?"

"Enough to know that your so-called 'rule' is nothing more than a chickenshit defense mechanism to protect you from getting hurt. And guess what? We *all* get hurt—whether we want to or not. That's what being alive and human is all about. *Taking chances.* And I don't mean those half-assed chances you've been taking with all those walking tropes on SheDate. You knew when you walked into every one of those situations that not one of them had a shot at working out. But, Harper?" He drained his wine glass. "Harper scares the shit out of you because you know she *might*."

I didn't bother to try and argue with him.

I knew he was right. And he knew I knew it.

More than anything, I wanted to crawl beneath the buffet table and hibernate until spring.

"I acted like a jerk with her, Dewey. We kissed the other night, and I freaked out."

"No shit, Sherlock? I'm guessing you ran like a rabbit."

"More or less."

"Well," he said with resignation. "'Tis the season. Try to figure out how to make it right before it's too late."

"I don't know if I can."

"Here's what I *do* know. If you want something bad enough, you won't be afraid to work for it."

"I leave tomorrow—then I'm gone for the next two weeks," I told him. "I won't be back until the day after Christmas."

"That gives you plenty of time to figure something out."

"I don't even know how to start."

"You can quit being such a fucking Eeyore—that'll get you started. And then you can pray she doesn't get a better offer in the meantime."

I hadn't even considered that possibility. "You think she might?"

He cast his eyes heavenward and shook his head.

"You see that over there?" He gestured toward Sofie and Harper. "That tidy little bundle of hotness in the tight black dress? You tell me . . . how long do *you* think that'll stay single, pining for attention from you?"

I didn't reply. I didn't have to.

Not long, was the answer. But I was still scared shitless. Maybe Dewey was right. Maybe it was good that I'd have two weeks on the road to try and figure this mess out.

"Get your head out of your ass, Izzy. While there's still time." It was like he'd been reading my mind.

"Now," he grinned at me, "where's my whiskey?"

I told him he'd get it later, after the party. He went back to join his wife, and I wandered over to join Sofie and Harper. I was determined to act like less of a douche for the remainder of the evening.

"Can I get you two beauties another glass of wine?" I asked.

Sofie looked like I'd offered to fetch her a shooter of cyanide.

"No, thank you." She thrust her half-filled wine glass at me. "As charming as this soirée has been, I need to make my excuses and depart. I have a pressing prior commitment to attend to."

"Oh?" I asked. "Did you manage to find an all-night nail salon that is undaunted by blizzard warnings?"

"*Vas te faire foutre.*" Sofie kissed Harper on both cheeks. "You, I shall see on the morrow. You?" She regarded me with exaggerated indifference, "I shall see when you've learned some manners."

"I love you, too," I said, as she swept off to retrieve her overcoat from the valet Dewey had on hand to manage the outerwear of the nonresidents in attendance.

"She loves me, too . . . right?" I whispered to Harper as Sofie departed.

"I think we can assume she does," she whispered back.

"Good. Otherwise I massively overpaid for her Christmas gift."

"What'd you get her?" Harper asked.

"A five-year subscription to *TV Guide*—and an infrared neck and décolleté collar, guaranteed to reduce aging and fade blemishes."

"I can see why she values your friendship."

"I know, right?"

I think I succeeded at not acting like a dweeb for the better part of an hour. As a consequence, Harper seemed more relaxed and we happily engaged in our customary repartee until the event was winding down and people were starting to leave. It was while we were in the queue heading for the exit that Mrs. Mariota, who was behind us in line with Leo, tugged at my sleeve to stop us.

"*Guarda! È per te!*" She pointed above our heads.

"She says, 'Look—it's for you,'" Leo translated.

Harper and I both looked up. Someone had fastened a sprig of mistletoe above the door.

"*Fallo. Fallo.*" She pushed me toward Harper. "*Buon Natale!*"

Leo looked at me apologetically. "She has old-fashioned ideas."

I glanced at Harper. "I'm game if you are."

"Why not?" she answered.

I bent forward and kissed her gently. Then did it a second time—a little less gently—just to be sure.

"*Bellissima!*" Mrs. Mariota clapped her small hands together. "*Buon Natale!*"

"*Buon Natale,*" I repeated to Harper.

"*Buon Natale,*" she echoed.

I felt a tiny surge of something unfamiliar.

I wasn't sure, but I thought it might have been hope.

The first few days of my trip were a nightmare. Weather delays caused by storm system Jorge stretched from the Ohio Valley, across Pennsylvania, and well into upstate New York. By the end of the week, we'd be traveling with it right up through the New England states.

I hoped it wouldn't be déjà vu all over again.

On Wednesday, we'd had plenty of slowdowns and a couple of brief ground stops—but nothing like that mess in New Haven. At least, not yet.

Most of the crew on the first trip were extra board hostages like me. It was unusual for me to be the crew member with the most seniority. But I felt good about how I managed to step up and oversee the routes. I had to give credit for that to the exceptional people I'd trained with—conductors like JoAnn and Adam, who never skimped on anything and always went the extra mile to give passengers the best possible rail experience. The work was exhausting, but when I checked into my hotel room at night, I felt satisfied about the performance I'd delivered.

I also realized the work had been much more fulfilling than spending four days immersed in the cultural proclivities of dung beetles.

In fact, I'd just about had it with dung beetles. *Entirely.*
Maybe I was beginning to gain some clarity in that area of my life, too?

And I felt at peace with my decision to uninstall the SheDate app. The relief there was palpable. And I had absolutely resolved not to allow Sofie to talk me back into taking another foray into the land of lost content. I was finished with that—even if it meant I might end up consigned to face the rest of my life alone.

The good thing for me was that work was so chaotic I had little time to worry about the carnage of my personal life. Working the Capitol Line was an intense experience. The train ran from Washington, D.C. to Pittsburgh, Cleveland, Toledo, South Bend, and Chicago. And in the week before Christmas, every one of these cities was in the crosshairs for winter storm warnings forecasting high winds and heavy, accumulating snow.

Thursday was worse because we were heading west into the storm. The passenger loads were higher than normal because we were so close to Christmas. The bad weather and constant delays were making everyone cranky and less amenable to changes in itineraries. The train steps and station platforms were icy and we all had to fight to keep passengers from slipping or falling. More and more travelers were venting their frustration and some became downright belligerent. We all did our best to remain upbeat and positive about the slowdowns, explaining to customers that it was better for everyone if we traveled at safer speeds. We'd been lucky that there had only been a few missed connections when the deteriorating conditions dictated that there should've been dozens.

By the time the Limited finally pulled into Cleveland— nearly three hours late—we were all exhausted. The shuttle dropped us off at the DoubleTree and we all had exactly nine hours before we had to report back to the station to depart for Chicago. Overtime pay meant next to nothing when you were running on adrenaline and bad coffee.

When we reached Chicago on Friday afternoon, the worst of the storm system had already blown through and moved east. The bad news was that first thing Saturday morning, we'd be turning around and chasing it as it took aim at cities stretching from Pittsburgh to Boston.

And at the end of it all, I'd get a measly eight hours off in Boston on Monday—before deadheading overnight to meet up with my next line, starting in New Haven. This holiday double-header, compounded by the added headache of adverse weather, was what veterans called a ball-buster. And, although I didn't own a pair, I was pretty sure they'd be well-and-truly busted if I did.

The only good spot of news was the surprise that greeted me when I discovered that JoAnn was working the northern extension of the Zephyr—my gig until the day after Christmas.

At least I'd have a friendly face to spend the holiday with. We'd finish up our trip in St. Albans on Wednesday, and, after bedding the train down for the night, make our way through the snow to Nelly's for a quiet—and probably solitary—Christmas dinner.

JoAnn said the owners of Nelly's Pub had a special fondness for railroad workers, and they always stayed open on Christmas night, just to feed us. She said they were the equivalent of a St. Albans Waffle House—with alcohol and better food.

I couldn't wait to get there. The sooner this trip was over, the sooner I could get back home and begin to figure out how to fix my relationship with Harper—if it were even salvageable. I was determined to call Sofie and ask for her advice—even though I knew I'd have to listen to a ration of shit about how stupid I'd been to drag my feet for so long.

On the other hand, she had been the one pushing me to keep dipping my toe into the SheDate pool—so, in my opinion, she didn't get to have it both ways.

I called her shortly after I checked into my hotel room in

Boston. It was just past 5 p.m. and I hoped it was still early enough to catch her at the office. My odds of connecting with her decreased exponentially once the official holiday commenced. As I recalled, she had the week between Christmas and New Year's off and had planned to go skiing . . . someplace.

"*Bonjour, Izzy.*" She answered the phone on the second ring.

"Where are you?"

"Boston tonight. St. Albans tomorrow."

"*Es-tu au Vermont pour la Noël?*"

"Good memory," I said. "Yes, we'll be in St. Albans on Christmas night. Sadly, not for long enough to see my parents. I deadhead back to Philly on Boxing Day."

"*Merde.* This job is a pain in the ass."

"It is sometimes."

"It is *all* of the time." I could hear her shuffling papers.

"Did I catch you at a bad time?

"*Non.* I have some work to finish up before I leave. I'm glad you called. I have a favor to ask of you."

"You do?" That was odd. Sofie rarely asked for favors. It was more her style to bark out demands and expect immediate capitulation.

"*Oui.* Do you remember my friend, Joséphine Côté, from Rivière-du-Loup?"

"The one with the overbite?"

"Don't be an asshole. Joséphine works for CGI and will be traveling next week. She's going to be staying less than ten miles from your Saint Whatever place. I thought you could meet her for dinner. That way, neither of you will be alone on Christmas."

"Oh, come on, Sofie. I don't want to have dinner with some stranger."

"Joséphine is not a stranger. You dated her."

"I went out with her *once*—and only because you stood us both up."

"*Non.* I had a pressing engagement, and it ran long."

264

"You were getting a bikini wax."

"Try to stay on topic. Joséphine is going through a difficult time right now and shouldn't be alone on Christmas. Come to think of it—neither should you. It won't kill you to make polite conversation with an old friend for an hour. You'd be doing me, and yourself, a favor. So," she was shuffling papers again, "where shall I tell her to meet you, and at what time?"

"Listen. It's not like this town has a hundred restaurants open on Christmas night."

"Meaning?"

"Meaning there is *one* place, and it's hardly *haute* enough to appeal to one of your friends."

"That's irrelevant."

"Really? Does she like fried mac and cheese?"

"Eight o'clock? Nine?"

I gave up. Sofie would never let this drop. And like she said, it was just an hour of my life.

"*Fine.* Eight or eight-fifteen. That'll give us time to get the train into the yard for overnight."

"Name of restaurant?"

"Nelly's Pub. It's on Federal Street."

I could hear Sofie writing down the information. "Good."

"This had better not be a clumsy attempt at another blind date. I'm done with that shit."

"*Excuses-moi?*"

"You heard me. No more, Sofie. I am finished with all of that. I never should've listened to you in the first place."

"Hold your horses. It's not my fault that you've proved yourself monstrously incapable of navigating a few first dates. This has always been your curse. You've never been good at playing the long game, Izzy."

Long game?

"That's just it," I insisted. "This entire online dating scheme is nothing *but* a game. Nobody is up there looking for anything that lasts longer than the average hookup . . . which has apparently grown a lot shorter during the years I've been out of commission. Besides, I think I want something different now."

To my surprise, Sofie didn't challenge my assessment.

"Define 'different,'" she said.

"Maybe I just want to meet someone the old-fashioned way."

"Really? Got anyone particular in mind?"

"You know I do."

"*Oui.*"

"I want the chance to try and salvage it before it's too late." I hesitated. "Do you think it's too late?"

"I don't know. You've acted like an ass."

I closed my eyes in mortification. *It was clear they had talked about me.*

"I at least want the chance to try to fix it." I noticed that Sofie didn't offer any advice, so I decided just to ask her. "Do you have any ideas?"

"Not at the moment. Give me some time to think about it. When are you back?"

"Thursday night," I reminded her. "Boxing Day."

"*Oui.* We'll talk then."

I sighed. "Okay."

"And, Izzy?"

"*Oui?*"

"Be nice to Joséphine. It's not her fault you're miserable."

"I will."

"*Joyeux Noël. Je t'aime.*"

"*Je t'aime.* Merry Christmas, my friend."

The call ended. I don't know what I'd expected, but I felt disappointed by Sofie's lack of inspiration when it came to ideas for jump-starting a deeper relationship with Harper. It wasn't like her to be without a dozen alternative strategies to address any happenstance that might occur. That was her stock-in-trade, after all. Actuaries were never at a loss for the odds on what might or might not happen. They were the bookies of the insurance industry.

Still . . . she'd said we could confer when I got home and figure something out.

For now, that was the sliver of lifeline I was left to cling to.

I cursed my life and the damn schedule I was consigned to. Being on the road for Christmas just meant any shot I had at trying to change direction with Harper would have to wait. To be fair, I'd never been any good with delayed gratification. Once I'd decided on a course, I wanted to set out on it immediately. My problem had never been summoning up the motivation to act once I knew what I wanted. My problem had always been getting past the roadblocks that prevented me from figuring out what the hell "it" was.

But now, finally, I knew what I wanted. And it wasn't continuing to play the relationship lottery by looking for love on a dating app that I was manifestly unsuited for—and demonstrably terrible at navigating.

No.

It was being willing to take another kind of gamble: the one that passed before me nearly every day in the hallways and haunts of the damn building I lived in. Harper had everything but a big, flashing light strung around her shapely neck. The universe had given me more than enough clues to solve this mystery.

It had always been Miss Scarlet. In the laundry room.

And I didn't need to get clobbered by any more of her weapons to wake up and smell the fabric softener.

Now I just needed time and opportunity to figure out what the hell to do about it.

We had a mini-reunion when I met up with the Zephyr on Tuesday morning. Both JoAnn and Anthony had drawn the short straws and were crewing the Christmas week run, too. I'd been pegged to fill in for one of the regular crew who'd requested family leave for the rest of the week.

"How the hell did you get tagged to work the holiday run?" I asked JoAnn during our briefing.

"Who knows? I probably pissed someone off in a past life."

Anthony said he'd volunteered for the run. "I wanted the extra pay," he explained. In typical fashion, he was saving money to make a down payment on a new car for his parents.

The café car was fully decked out this week. Strands of twinkling lights now circled the entire interior of the car. Christmas music played at low volume over the PA system. We even had permission from corporate to replace our regulation caps with Santa hats—but just on Christmas day.

The worst of Winter Storm Jorge was now taking aim at Maine and Nova Scotia. But we were still traveling in its wake. Snow kept right on falling, but it wasn't with the angry vengeance it had demonstrated when I'd been pushing north to Boston. Now it was just . . . pretty. It was more like that fluffy, Hollywood snow that fell during the final scenes of movies like *White Christmas.*

I could deal with that. If we had to work on Christmas, why not make it like a movie set where everyone got a happy ending?

We did our best to facilitate that, too. In general, passengers were now mostly jovial and upbeat about their holiday travel. It was like the train was gliding along inside a snow globe— passing little winter towns that looked pristine and quaint— then continuing along past storybook farms with clusters of fat cows, blowing out puffs of steam while they munched on ribbons of hay that had been unfurled for their breakfast. Each scene was idyllic enough to be featured on a postage stamp.

I knew it would be a different story as soon as the snow stopped and the temperatures began to climb above freezing—which was predicted for our return trip on Boxing Day. I was glad I'd be deadheading instead of crewing the southbound leg. Even though I knew I'd probably step up and help out, anyway. It made the time pass a lot faster if you were busy versus watching the clock, waiting to get home.

I had a running dialogue with myself about whether or not to call Harper on Christmas. As far as I knew, she wasn't spending the day with her family. She'd said something about connecting with them during Hanukkah—which, according to The Google, had ended last night. I figured I'd make a game day decision about calling her once I was safely closeted back inside my room at the anything-but-deluxe Hampton Inn on Lake Street.

I just hoped the dinner with Sofie's morose college pal, Joséphine didn't drag on. When I shared those details with JoAnn, she was dubious about the innocence of the encounter.

"Are you sure it isn't a setup? Meeting someone who just happens to be stuck in St. Albans overnight on Christmas sounds . . . implausible. Don't you think? It's not exactly a commercial crossroads. You know?"

"I know. I thought the same thing at first. But there's no reason for her to pull some shenanigan like that now—especially not up there."

"I hope you plan to fill me in on everything I've missed since our last trip."

"Please don't make me relive any of it."

"That bad?"

"It depends on whether or not you think the threat of statutory rape is bad . . ."

JoAnn had been drinking a cup of the café's festive Holiday

Blend coffee, and about sprayed half of it across the table.

"*What?*" she demanded, while she blotted the worst of it off her uniform.

"Yeah." I quoted the loquacious waiter from Morning Glory, "in the latest installments of *Days of Our Sorry-Ass Lives*, our gal, Izzy got hooked up with a seventeen-year-old cosplay nymph who was bummed her SheDate prospect was too cheap to buy her a drink before running like hell."

"I thought the age of consent in Pennsylvania was sixteen?" JoAnn asked.

I looked at her with disbelief. "Why the fuck does everybody know this?"

"Never mind. You said 'installments'—like there were more dates?"

"Just one more. A left-brained virago with an abject disdain for anything remotely blue collar. She must've been in denial about my job—either that, or she only focused on my graduate work. Either way, she made Miranda Priestly look like Shirley Temple."

"I dunno, Izzy. I think you may have reached diminishing returns with this dating app."

"You think? What tipped you off?" I laughed bitterly. "I'm resorting to the old ways."

"Bars? Clubbing?"

"No."

"What, then?" she asked.

"Adopting twenty cats and spending my declining years screaming at parking meters."

JoAnn thought about it. "That could work, actually."

The engineer alerted us that we were twenty minutes out from Springfield. It was snowing steadily, and I knew that JoAnn's knee was still acting up. So I told her I'd hop off and throw the switch this time.

She saw right through me. "Normally, I'd argue with you.

But today, this thing is killing me."

"I could tell by the way you flung that last L22 roller bag. It was like you had a personal vendetta."

"I hate being so transparent."

"Come on." I got up. "Let's go rouse the multitudes."

As passengers were queuing up at the exit doors, I waited for the train to slow enough so I could safely jump off and run ahead to manually engage the track switch. The thing was covered with snow, so it took longer than usual to clear it off, pull the set pin, and coax the lever forward. I had to throw most of my weight into it, but finally felt it give way and heard the satisfying sound of the tracks shifting. I replaced the pin and backed away while the train glided over the transition point cleanly. It was still incredible to me that with all the advancements in technology, this process hadn't changed since the railroad first pushed through here in 1839.

I supposed if something simple worked, there was no good reason to change it.

A mechanical switch required no electrical power. No backup generator. No computer chips. No AI to manage its activation. All it took was one lowly person to hop off a slow-moving train and push a lever into its opposite position. It was engaged, or it wasn't. That was it.

A switch was dumb. And it was simple.

I thought over the transitions in my past and how those had occurred whether I'd been actively engaged with them or not. In the journey known as life, we moved forward, or we moved backward. If we weren't going in one direction, then we were going in the other. But no matter which way we went, one thing was clear: we never stopped moving. And the odds of ending up at the correct destination had everything to do with being smart enough to throw the switch when it was time to change course.

Standing there in the snow, watching the Zephyr glide past me, I finally understood that it all really was that simple.

JoAnn teased me unmercifully about my non-date with Joséphine.

It was clear she thought Sofie had pulled another fast one, and I was going to be sailing into a gift-wrapped Christmas surprise.

"You're nuts," I told her. "I've met this woman before and, believe me, there's not a snowball's chance in hell Sofie would think I'd hook up with her."

"Why not?"

"For starters, she's married and has four kids. And I'm sure about that because I looked up her Facebook profile as soon as Sofie told me about the rendezvous. She really does work for CGI, and she manages teams all over Québec and the northeast U.S. Joséphine isn't on a fishing expedition, and neither am I."

"Well, either way, I plan to sit at a table near yours so I can observe the entire interaction. If things go south, you can drop a cheese curd and I'll know it's time to swoop in and save you from a potential hostage situation."

"Thanks, but I don't think that'll be necessary. My plan is to be out of there and safely tucked into bed by nine thirty."

"That reminds me . . . I'll leave six or seven ice cubes in a cup outside your door."

"What a pal you are."

"Buck up, A.C. One day you'll get a room on the fourth floor, too."

It was just a few minutes before eight when we reached the end of the line in St. Albans. After successfully off-loading the smattering of stragglers who were still aboard, we stood by until the train was successfully settled off the main tracks in the station yard for the night. The snow had stopped—briefly—but more was predicted overnight. It was damn cold and the wind blowing up Lake Street was biting and relentless.

JoAnn asked if I planned to check into the hotel before heading to Nelly's to meet my "date."

"No, I think I'll head straight there. The sooner I get there, the sooner I can call it a night."

She and Anthony offered to take my bag to the hotel and leave it at the front desk so I wouldn't have to drag it behind me. I thanked them profusely and walked the short two blocks up Federal Street to Nelly's Pub.

There weren't many customers—hardly surprising for eight o'clock on Christmas night. But the hostess recognized me right away and called out, "Merry Christmas" when I entered.

"And to you," I replied. "It's beyond great that you stay open this late—and on a holiday, too."

"It's no biggie. We all trade off." She picked up a menu. "Your friend is already here. Let me take you to the table."

I followed her, wondering vaguely if I'd still recognize Joséphine. It had been more than twenty-five years since I'd last seen her. I did a double-take when the hostess stopped at a table, neatly tucked into the back corner beneath a massive Jameson sign—and I think my heart skipped a beat or two as well.

It wasn't Joséphine sitting there. *It was Harper.*

It took my tired brain most of a minute to figure out what I was seeing.

"Are you going to sit down?" Harper finally asked. I thought she sounded amused.

"How did you . . ." I began. "Why are you . . ."

"Here?" she answered.

I nodded stupidly.

"There are about a hundred explanations. But the only one that matters is that I knew one of us had to make the first move—and I figured if I waited on you, I'd probably be too old to get out of my chair without assistance."

I was still overcome with surprise and disbelief. But I

followed orders and sat down across from her.

Harper was here? In St. Albans? On Christmas night?

"Why did Sofie . . ."

"Lie to you?" she finished my sentence.

"Well . . . yeah."

"She thought you'd appreciate the gesture. In fact, she asked me to give you this." She slipped a small envelope across the table.

I took it from her and opened it. It contained a note, handwritten in Sofie's characteristic, no nonsense block print.

DEAR BELOVED IDIOT,

I HOPE YOU APPRECIATE MY CHRISTMAS
GIFT. IT CAN BE DIFFICULT TO FIND
THE RIGHT THING FOR SOMEONE WHO
HAS EVERYTHING, BUT IS TOO STUPID
TO REALIZE IT. THANKFULLY, HARPER IS
SMARTER THAN YOU ARE, AND SHE WAS
WILLING TO RISK MAKING THIS TRIP. I HOPE
YOU DON'T DISAPPOINT HER. WOMEN
LIKE THIS DON'T COME ALONG OFTEN.
BUT IF YOU DO MANAGE TO FUCK THIS UP,
I CAN ALWAYS TRY TO RECONNECT YOU
WITH THAT COSPLAY INGENUE.

BY THE WAY, YOU OWE ME BIG TIME FOR
THE UPGRADE TO BUSINESS CLASS ON
HER FLIGHT—I FELT SHE DESERVED THE
EXTRA LEG ROOM AND FREE COCKTAIL
SINCE SHE WAS TRAVELING AT THE LAST
MINUTE ON A HOLIDAY.

YOU CAN THANK ME LATER FOR THE CAT,

A GIFT FROM YOUR KLEPTO NEIGHBOR,
MRS. MARIOTA. HARPER SAID YOU'D
PROBABLY WANT TO NAME HER CUJO.
I TOLD HER IT WAS SOPHOMORIC AND
UNORIGINAL ENOUGH TO APPEAL TO
YOU.

SHE DID NOT DISAGREE.

BE NICE TO HARPER. AND FOR ONCE, BE
KINDER TO YOURSELF.

YOU DESERVE TO BE HAPPY, SO QUIT
FIGHTING IT.

TOUT EST BIEN QUI FINIT BIEN.

ENDLESS LOVE FROM,

YOUR SOFIE

I couldn't fight the tears that spontaneously appeared and threatened to overwhelm me.

"Are you okay?" Harper asked with concern.

"Did you read this?" I held out the note.

"No. But I don't think I need to."

"I've been such an idiot."

"I'm not inclined to disagree with you."

"But you came all the way up here . . . on Christmas."

"I'm Jewish, remember?" She smiled. "But I simply asked myself, what would Katharine Hepburn do?"

I reached across the table to take hold of her hand. "I don't deserve you."

"Oh, but you do."

Harper laced her fingers with mine. Her hand felt warm and soft and it was just the right size.

"I do?"

She nodded again. "Someone's got to straighten out your shitty load sense."

I laughed and wiped at my eyes. "I actually might . . . I think . . . I mean, I'm pretty sure that . . . I might . . . love you."

Harper looked happy at my admission—and relieved, too.

"I sure as hell hope you do. If you don't, it's going to be awkward as fuck spending twelve hours together on the train tomorrow."

"You're riding *back* with us?"

"That's the plan, yes. Unless you'd rather I not."

I shook my head. I was still in a daze and struggling to make sense of everything.

"No. I can't think of anything I'd rather do than ride home with you."

"Good." She smiled. "I confess I did pack *Anna Karenina*, just in case."

"You won't be needing it."

"No?" she asked.

"No. Not when we can live out our own train story—with a happier ending."

"Is it happier?"

"It is for me."

"Then I'm glad I splurged and got a room on the fourth floor. Word on the street is the ice machine works better up there."

I heard a burst of strangled laughter and looked over to see JoAnn watching us from the bar. She held up a frosty mug of beer.

"Cheers, A.C. Looks like your non-date is working out just fine."

276

I looked at her with disbelief. "Were you in on this, too?"

"No comment." JoAnn winked at Harper. "I think you can take it from here." She wandered off to join Adam and Anthony at their table.

"My god. How *many* conspirators does it take to change a damn lightbulb?"

"Just one," Harper answered. "But it has to want to be changed."

"Oh . . ."

I gazed at her through the dim, amber light, overwhelmed by my great, good fortune. It flooded over me like the sweet promise of paradise found. Here we were, *together*—at Nelly's Pub in St. Albans, Vermont. On Christmas night. I was on the cusp of getting everything I'd ever wanted. Right now. *Tonight.* Here in this *unlikeliest* of places, with the *likeliest* of all possible women. *With Harper*—who'd been absolutely, perfectly, unabashedly made for me since the moment she'd first educated me about Norwegian lutefisk. And for once, I understood that I was—finally and determinedly—smart enough, strong enough, and self-aware enough to know that it was time to throw the damn switch and change direction.

"It does," I assured her. "It *wants* to be changed."

"Good." I thought I saw something glisten in her eyes, too. "And just in case you hadn't figured it out yet, I love you, too."

I smiled at her like the happy idiot I was.

"Now," she said. "How about we order something to eat, so these good people can go home before it gets too late."

I did not disagree with her.

"Then what?" I asked.

"Then," she picked up her menu, "you take me to bed for a long winter's nap."

After we'd eaten, we left Nelly's and slowly walked, arm in arm, back along Federal Street toward the hotel. Harper stopped me when we reached the old St. Albans depot.

"Is that your train?" She pointed at the Zephyr, sitting nobly in the station yard.

"It is," I said proudly. "That's my home away from home."

For the first time, I didn't feel the need to apologize for it, or explain that it was just something I was doing until my real career started. No. It *was* my career—and I loved it. It fit me just right—in all the same ways Harper did.

"It's beautiful," she said.

I looked at her in the soft light cast by the streetlamps.

"You're beautiful," I told her.

We kissed. And this time, there was no surge of panic. No fear that I was making a mistake or undertaking something I'd live to regret. I pulled her closer and held on to her as the heat of her body surrounded me with warmth.

When we finally separated, Harper blinked up at the sky.

"It's snowing."

That seemed right, too.

"*Buon Natale*, Izzy," she whispered.

"*Buon Natale*, Harper."

I took her hand in mine and led her through the falling snow toward our hotel on Lake Street.

ACKNOWLEDGMENTS

I owe a huge debt of gratitude to the crew of Amtrak's Vermonter, which runs between Washington, DC and St. Albans, Vermont. My multiple research trips on the train were limited to the northern route, between Springfield, MA and St. Albans. As a consequence, I got to know the regular crew working that leg quite well. They were tireless answering my questions about life on the rails. If any aspect of Izzy's work experience gliding in and out of towns along the route rings true, you can thank conductors JoAnn and Adam. I took copious liberties depicting their characters in this book, and nothing is intended by that except admiration, good humor, and the co-opting of their names.

I have always loved train travel, and now plan to make annual trips on the Vermonter a regular part of my experience. If you've never done it—treat yourself. You won't be sorry. And, P.S.—the hot dogs in the café car are amazing!

Sandy Lowe deserves a ton of thanks and credit for her encouragement and the keen insights and suggestions that helped bring this story to life.

Salem West and Christel Cogneau read early versions of the manuscript and made valuable suggestions that improved the story. And Christel corrected all my bad French . . . again.

Carole Cloud was instrumental in helping me accurately depict life in Philadelphia's Hopkinson House.

Carleen Spry and Nancy Squires both made the book better through their careful proofreads and content edits of the manuscript.

Thanks and sincere appreciation, as always, go to my publisher, Bywater Books, and our entire community of authors and readers. Bywater Books and Amble Press are publishing some of the best LGBT+ literature in print, and I am very proud to be part of this extended family.

I could never have written this—or any of my books— without the love and enduring patience of my family. You graciously tolerate my prolonged absences so I have the freedom to retreat and write these stories. They would not be possible otherwise, and I will always be grateful for your indulgence.

I wrote this book during a very cold and snowy March in Vermont—watching the ferries travel back and forth across the icy water of Lake Champlain, between Plattsburgh, NY and Grand Isle, VT. The constancy and rhythm of those crossings, twenty-four hours a day, seven days a week, matched my own determination to craft this story in the short time allotted to me. I lived this story—every aspect of it—in twelve-hour days across four weeks. For the great gift of working in such wonderful surroundings, I am indebted to my wonderful and generous hosts, Ellen and Jeff Long-Middleton.

My fervent hope is that your experience reading this story matches the joy I had writing it.

–Ann McMan

ABOUT THE AUTHOR

Ann McMan is the author of fourteen novels and two collections of short stories. She is a two-time Lambda Literary Award winner, an eleven-time winner of Golden Crown Literary Society Awards, a five-time IPPY medalist, a Foreword Reviews INDIES medalist, and a recipient of the Alice B. Medal for her body of work. She divides her time between Winston-Salem, NC, and Grand Isle, Vermont.

She can be found at:
www.annmcman.com
www.bywaterbooks.com/ann-mcman/
https://www.facebook.com/ann.mcman/

A NOTE ON THE TYPE

The body of this book is set in Adobe Caslon Pro. William Caslon was an English gunsmith and designer of typefaces. In 1722 he created an extended set of serif typefaces that were based on seventeenth-century Dutch old style designs. Because of their remarkable practicality, Caslon's typefaces met with instant success. These, as well as all of their consecutive revivals, are referred to as Caslon. Among those revivals are two Adobe versions, called Adobe Caslon (1990) and Adobe Caslon Pro, which includes an extended character set.

Bywater
BOOKS

Bywater Books believes that all people have the right to read or not read what they want—and that we are all entitled to make those choices ourselves. But to ensure these freedoms, books and information must remain accessible. Any effort to eliminate or restrict these rights stands in opposition to freedom of choice.

At Bywater Books, we are all stories.

Please join with us by opposing book bans and censorship of the LGBTQ+ and BIPOC communities.

For more information about Bywater Books, our authors, and our titles, please visit our website.

https.bywaterbooks.com